THEFT BETWEEN
THE RAINS

Luba Lesychyn

COPYRIGHT INFORMATION

ISBN (print): 978–0–9936054–5–1
ISBN (epub): 978–0–9936054–4–4
ISBN (mobi): 978–0–9936054–3–7

First published by Luba Lesychyn, 2019

Cover artwork and design by Laurie Barnett

City of Toronto landscape photo enhanced from a photo by Cédric Blondeau

Headshot by Images by Andy K – Fine Art Photography

DEDICATION

With deepest love and gratitude to my parents, Paulina and Bohdan Kulchyckyj, who gave me a solid foundation for my magnificent life, and to my biggest supporters and inspirations, my beloved brothers Zenon Kulchisky and Andy Kulchyckyj.

Theft Between the Rains has been funded in part by a grant from the Shevchenko Foundation

CHAPTER ONE

Lying slumped back in a chair, my body felt as though a truck had dumped a load of concrete over me. I mustered enough energy to crank my head upwards, but my brain was foggy, punch-drunk, as if I'd overdosed on gluten. In a mirror on the opposite wall, I caught a glimpse of my reflection. What was that dark mark on my throat, small and round? My head drooped downwards, and I noticed the door swelling open, incrementally, a sliver of light growing by millimeters. And then...a leg came into view. And, another. Where was I? Who was this coming in? Was I asleep, having one of those 3:00 am witching hour anxiety dreams? Should I get up? I couldn't get up. Neurons were misfiring. I knew that person at the door. He was saying something to me...but the words seemed out of sync with what I was hearing.

Why did this guy sound like Johnny Cash...singing "Hurt"? Oh my god, it was Marco Zeffirelli, and now he seemed to be screaming at me, but it sounded as though he was underwater.

"Huh, what's going on?" I said. Was I on some kind of drug trip? I didn't do drugs. Did someone drug me?

Marco's hands came towards the sides of my face, tugged at something, and the music stopped. Oh, right. It was all coming back to me. I had been listening to my iPod while working at my desk and I must have drifted off with the buds thoroughly burrowed into my ears. Johnny Cash's cover of the Nine Inch Nails' song was playing on the device. Ooow – my neck was stiff, and I elongated it upwards, ostrich-like.

"Holy shit, are you hurt, Kalena?" said Marco.

"Why? What are you talking about?" I looked at my hands, patted my chest, scanned my body.

"The wound on your neck." Marco scrambled to dislodge the two-way radio holstered at his waist.

The mark I had seen in the mirror. Chin raised, I slid a finger across the moist splotch on my throat and rubbed the residue between my fingertips...and smiled. I licked my fingertip. "Chocolate...with a hint of salt." Although the combination of chocolate and salt was one of my favorite pairings, I hoped it wasn't my own body's salt that had mixed with the minimally sweetened dark chocolate.

"Are you kidding me, Boyko?" Marco returned the walkie-talkie to its place. "Did you get someone from the Art Department to do that for you? It looks like a real bullet wound."

"Just a fluke, I guess. Not quite sure how I managed to get it there."

"You really need to get a grip on this chocolate addiction of yours. It's totally out of hand."

"I can't argue with that. But it's easier said than done. And why would you even think it was a bullet wound? Who the hell would shoot me?" I snatched a tissue from a box on my desk and erased the remainder of the chocolaty smudge.

"We do work in a joint stocked to the rafters with things worth trillions of dollars." Marco's eyebrows were furrowed. The blackish-blue security guard uniform added to his gravitas. But nothing could take away from his boyish good looks and irresistible charm.

4

"True, but none of it's in my office, other than a few pieces of Stewart's personal African art, and my Turkish rug – nothing that would warrant me getting shot in the throat." But Marco was right about the Royal Ontario Museum's collections which were composed of about six million objects. We had countless priceless pieces and who knew what the total value of the building's contents were, not to mention all the artifacts in storage at the Museum's off-site warehouse.

Drawing closer to me, Marco perched himself on the corner of my desk. Damn, he smelled like cotton candy or sponge toffee, something sugary that reminded me of my youth. My personal aroma, on the other hand, I suspected was more like mildew, wet cat, maybe even seaweed. I tilted my nose downwards, took a discreet whiff, in hopes that the Earth-friendly deodorant I wore was as effective as promised.

"It's kind of none of my business..." Marco shifted his weight from one foot to the other. "But weren't you wearing that same outfit yesterday?"

Lowering my head once again, I took an even deeper inhale. Did I really smell that unrefined? "Mmmaybe." I tugged at the bottom edge of my aubergine jersey top, smoothing out the wrinkles.

Marco's gaze darted over to a small mountain of multicolored Mexican blankets stuffed randomly into the corner behind my desk. Busted.

"Are you serious?" Like a cork suddenly released from a champagne bottle, Marco popped off the desk and snatched up one of the loosely woven coverlets. "You slept here again, didn't you?"

Still fidgeting with my clothing, I reluctantly made eye contact with Marco. Their green hue reminded me of glacier water I'd once seen in the valleys of Austria. Before allowing a blush to rise, I broke our visual connection, turned my stare to the carpet, and spotted a dark crumb beside my foot. I dipped down and touched the speck only to have it melt upon contact – more chocolate. What kind of feeding frenzy took place here last night that had led to so much chocolate splatter? I had no recollection.

Marco tossed the blanket back into the pile. "You promised me AND your boss you'd never sleep here again."

"Pleeeeeeeeeease don't tell Stewart. He'll have a fit." I was more fearful Stewart might start to think I was too incompetent to get my job done during regular working hours. Maybe I was in over my head, but I didn't want Stewart to know it.

"You're going to blow your adrenals if you keep this up. You're not a zombie, you know. You need to get a decent amount of sleep. I was just reading Arianna Huffington's *Thrive*–"

"Huh, what? *You're* reading Huffington?" How would she even get on Marco's radar?

"Uh, yeah. A friend recommended the book. Anyway, she talks about how people don't get anywhere near enough sleep, as a culture and all."

"I don't have a choice," I spat back like a defensive teenager caught in a lie. "Brenda's in the UK doing her foreign office placement, and I have a guy in Saudi who's been missing for two days. Meanwhile, Stewart's in California, long-term, practically running another museum." I drew my index finger to the middle of my forehead and massaged my third eye in a circular motion. A slight sense of calm swept over my body, but I felt tears forming. Hopefully, Marco wouldn't notice. We'd been through a lot together, but I didn't want him to see me cry.

"Hey, hey, are you okay?" Marco said tenderly. I thought my melting heart would spill out onto my desk.

"I'm fighting a migraine," I grumbled ungratefully. "You're right, though. I'm not getting enough sleep."

Stewart Anderson, Brenda Lockhart, and I comprised a small, cohesive team managing massive projects, and I'd been helming the Toronto office of the Royal Ontario Museum's consulting branch *tutto solo* for almost a month. The pressures had become staggering and sleep had become a luxury.

"Okay, hold on there. Didn't you just about force Brenda to be the first one to vamoose when Stewart gave you guys the chance to work in the London office?"

"That was because I wanted my work practice to coincide with London's Chocolate Week and with the *Salon du Chocolat* in Paris." I was also reticent about working so soon again with the head of our London office, Geoffrey Ogden. No one in the universe, especially not Marco, knew that when I was last abroad, in a moment of utter lunacy and in desperate need of some semblance of romance, I'd had the only one-night stand of my life with Geoffrey – who also happened to be Stewart's best friend. Although women seemed to pull these kinds of moves in books and movies all the time, it turned out to be a moronic thing to do in real life.

"And, by the way, when I sent Brenda packing," I continued, "it was before I knew Stewart was going to take up residence in the States. He was only supposed to be gone for a couple of weeks and now he has me searching for a rental home...and Stewart's wife Patsy is getting ready to join him. They're settling in for the long haul. I didn't sign up for this!"

"That's not good. I know you count on him to keep the

Director and the Museum's board out of your day-to-day business."

"You mean like losing a Museum staff member in the Middle East." I threw my head back in despair. "Just another day in Museum Consulting Services."

"If you need some help, I know people who can track down an MIA at lightning speed."

"I have no doubt." I thought back to a shady character to whom Marco had introduced me – Bob – when I was in a pickle of a different sort almost a year ago. "But I'm going to give it another day or so before I admit to anyone we have a team member missing in action."

"Okay, okay," said Marco. "But can I at least get you to take a nap in the first aid room? I'll make sure it's clear. You really look like you could use forty winks."

Marco's suggestion actually made sense, but as I was slow at sputtering out an affirmative, Marco chimed in again. "And there's something I wanted to talk to you about, but I want to wait until you're wide awake."

The hairs on my arms stood up. Business or pleasure, I wondered.

CHAPTER TWO

The cat nap I took in the first aid room wasn't quite enough to swipe the weariness from my body or spirit, so I headed to the sink in the corner and splashed my face with frigidly cold water. I was catapulted back into alert mode, and a soft glow returned to my cheeks, but the dark circles under my eyes called for more drastic measures. On days like this, my usual flesh-toned concealer was inadequate, so I withdrew a tube of ghoulish green cover-up from my makeup bag. The Physician's Formula product could work miracles on zits, scars, and raccoon eyes, like the ones I was currently sporting.

My hair...that was another matter. There was no quick fix for the exposed dark brown and grey roots, and nothing but a good shampoo could revive the hair's luster and body. One of these days, I swore, I would chop it all off. As I pulled the blonde mane back, I imagined a short cut. That was what I needed. Pert, sassy, easy peasy. I let the drab, lifeless hair fall back over my shoulders.

I inched open the first aid room door to ensure the coast was clear. No one needed to know about my siesta. This room was intended for members of the public who might encounter a medical emergency while visiting the Museum. It wasn't meant to be a crash pad for sleep-deprived staff. However, it wasn't the first time I had escaped into the sanctuary. Many months ago, Marco and I had landed there to strategize on how we might uncover the identity of the international art thief, *Il Gattopardo*, also known as The Leopard, who we suspected was stalking the Museum. Our ploys had been unsuccessful, and the thief was still on the loose, eluding a host of international law enforcement agencies. Could this be the matter Marco wanted to discuss? Or was the lad planning on asking me out again?

As I edged into public gallery space, I was relieved to find the area devoid of beings. With the Museum's main entrance relocated after renovations, traffic in the area was generally minimal. But camera presence was everywhere, so I hoped no one in the control room noticed or cared about my movements. Within a few steps, I found myself at the base of the Museum's most renowned and recognizable artifact, a 285-foot First Nations cedar crest pole. It had been shipped eons ago to the Museum from Canada's west coast, and being so monumentally tall, it had been lowered into the building from an opening in the roof.

Just before Brenda had left for the UK, our office was moved to the other side of the Museum. No longer were we situated near the minerals and gems galleries. Now we were housed beside a gallery space dedicated to special exhibitions. The area was currently occupied by a collection celebrating Canadian film director David Cronenberg. As a cinemaniac, I was originally ecstatic when I heard about the imminent arrival of drawings, objects, and set pieces from the director's films. But no one had warned us there would be a human-sized Mugwump stationed right outside the entrance to Museum Consulting Services. With cigarette in hand and seated in an over-sized director's chair, the iconic alien-like creature from Cronenberg's film *Naked Lunch* was a freakish construct of William S. Burrough's tortured mind and of

Cronenberg's twisted imagination. It scared the hell out of me each time I passed by.

More unsettling, however, was the thought of calling Harry Cavanagh's wife to inform her that her husband had disappeared in Saudi Arabia. Harry was one of a tiny contingent we had sent there to help open a new transportation museum in Riyadh. He was the Museum's best preparator and was extremely skilled at mounting objects in cases, on walls, from ceilings, and his handiwork was as dexterous as a surgeon's. Known for his ingenuity, the amiable Irishman had earned himself the nickname 'Harry Rigger' as he was a master jerry rigger.

He was also a musician, by passion, and was infamous for spending over-nighters jamming and drinking with the boys. Harry had pulled his share of vanishing acts in the past, but when I learned a couple of days ago that he had failed to show up for work, I hated to think of the possibilities.

I bolted past the disquieting Mugwump and as I crossed the threshold into the Museum Consulting Services office, a faint bell chimed. An email had just dropped into my mailbox, perhaps from Harry? But once I was positioned in front of my computer monitor, the only new message was from Stewart with the subject heading, "Skype meeting with Geoff @ 11 am. EOM." End of message? No explanation? What the frig? That was just minutes away. OH, NO! What if they've learned of Harry's mysterious disappearance? Maybe Stewart and Geoffrey have already been notified that Harry's body had been discovered in a sand dune with only his iconic Mark's Work Warehouse boots sticking out. I was so F.I.R.E.D.

Snatching the handle of my lower desk drawer with an unconscious amount of strength, I ripped it off its hinges, and it thudded to the floor like a thirty-pound kettlebell. But as the contents lay exposed, I rejoiced because tucked in the back of the drawer was a Green & Blacks Butterscotch organic chocolate bar, my most recent obsession of choice. There was just enough time to pop a couple of the precious little squares into my mouth before the video call.

With nerves ever so slightly settled, I quickly scanned our new office time-keeping system hoisted high on the north wall of the office. Following our departmental move, the row of four newsroom clocks had been replaced by a digital version – a long, narrow, black pixel board with four time zones programmed in. Lit up in tiny, green lights were Riyadh, London, Toronto, and San Jose. The times all switched to the hour, and I knew both Stewart and Geoffrey would be annoyingly prompt on the call. Quietly, I repeatedly chanted "*Om Gam Gana Pataye Namaha,*" an invocation to the Hindu god Ganesh, the destroyer of impediments and obstacles. Couldn't hurt, I thought.

One last thing before I logged onto the video conference. I tore a strip of opaque Scotch Tape from its dispenser and covered the pinhole camera lens at the top of my monitor. Geoffrey didn't need to see me looking like a demented cat lady or witness me break into tears when they fired me.

When I launched Skype, Stewart and Geoffrey were already engaged, of course. It seemed I was the only punctually dysfunctional one of the crew. I shifted my mouse and clicked as timidly as someone pressing a button that might launch a world nuclear assault. "*Om Gam Gana Pataye Namaha,*" I chanted at a slightly higher volume this time.

Stewart and Geoffrey's faces popped up on the screen. Although they were only a year or two apart in age, Stewart's prematurely white hair and beard made him look the elder of the pair. In contrast, Geoffrey's thick head of chestnut hair showed no sign of thinning or greying and combined with clearly positive results from his metrosexual grooming habits, he was aging ridiculously well, à la George Clooney.

"Kalena, is that you? I thought I heard you mumbling something. We don't have a clear visual."

"Yes, Stewart, it's me."

"It looks as though our London fog has spread to Toronto," chirped in Geoffrey. "Your face is rather a hazy mass."

"Really? How odd." I swiped my hand across the lens as though giving it a cleaning. "Did that make any difference? Can you see me now?"

"Just some vague movement," said Stewart.

"No difference," said Geoffrey.

"Sorry about that, gentlemen. I'll have someone from IT check out my computer camera after we've finished."

"It's a shame we won't see your radiant smile," said Geoffrey.

I was relieved that my beet-red face was invisible to the two men. But what was going on here? There was no sense of urgency in either of the men's voices. And Geoffrey wouldn't be flirting with me if they had intentions of discharging me. They did not know about Harry yet. There was a higher power after all. I broke off another square of the Green & Black's chocolate, flung it into the air, and caught it in my mouth.

"Well, let's proceed, shall we?" said Stewart. "We have some exciting news."

Translation: We have a boat-load more work for you. Forget about ever sleeping again.

"You do?" I said with a chocolate-melting-in-mouth slur.

"Geoffrey, why don't you brief Kalena? I know how thrilled you are."

"My absolute pleasure." Why was it that anything said with a British accent sounded so Daniel-Craig sexy? "As you know," Geoffrey continued, "the transportation museum in Riyadh is nearing completion."

And Harry might be buried in the building's foundation.

"And the opening ceremony is going to be quite the spectacle," Geoffrey continued.

"A spectacle," Stewart echoed with adolescent glee.

"Uh, huh." Are they sending me to Riyadh for the opening? That would be way too extraordinary. Unless, of course, Harry was still misplaced. That would be inappropriate.

"The Prince has decided he would like to produce a commemorative medal that will be given to each and every attendee at the opening ceremony," said Stewart.

"Uh, huh." I seemed incapable of vocalizing anything other than mono-syllabic grunts.

"And our persuasive man in London, namely Geoffrey, convinced our Saudi cohorts to give the commission to us."

"Uh, huh." I paused a bit too long. "Uh, way to go, Geoffrey." Hurrah.

"The margins on this kind of job can be quite substantial, especially since we managed to persuade them to order a thousand medals," said Geoffrey.

"Great."

"We can earn ourselves a nice, little profit," added Stewart. "A nice, little profit."

You mean, because we weren't earning enough from your second income as an acting director in the museum in California?

"And it really should not be too complicated," declared Geoffrey.

I'd heard that one before. "I have to admit, I'm not really

sure where to begin on this one." Were Stewart and Geoffrey truly unaware that the production of commemorative medals was not a skill listed on my resume? I was a history major – Italian Renaissance. Mind you, a lot of commemorative medals were produced in the Renaissance. But medal production processes were not part of my university syllabus.

"I would suggest," said Stewart, "you start with The Royal Canadian Mint. Commemorative coins and commemorative medals are just a notion apart."

Oh, Stewart was beyond brill! Maybe I could turn the entire job over to the Mint – from design through to delivery – a turnkey operation. With cardiac arrest arrested, I leaned back in my chair and rested my head in interlaced hands. But the triumphant moment was soon interrupted when a new face popped into view behind Geoffrey, and a shrill laugh poured out of my computer's speaker.

"Kalena, is that supposed to be you in there somewhere?" asked Brenda Lockhart, our senior consultant. There was no mistaking her perky red-bob of hair and her acerbic tone.

"Yeah. Hi, Bren."

"Are you kidding me?" Another round of laughter followed. "I can't believe you're pulling that 'Scotch Tape over the camera lens' trick...again."

I wished I could have reached my hands through the screen and stifled Brenda with a neck-choke. "What are you talking about?"

"She must be having a bad hair day...or maybe a late night, huh, Kalena?" Brenda exaggerated a wink that totally disfigured her non-lipsticked mouth.

The corners of Geoffrey's lips started to curve into a smile, but Stewart looked puzzled.

"I have no clue what you're talking about. We're having some IT issues on the Toronto end."

"Whatever you say." Behind Geoffrey's back, Brenda pointed at me and then twirled her index fingers around her ears in a crazy/loco gesture.

"Is there anything else we need to discuss right now? I do have to scoot to another meeting," I said, hoping I sounded convincing after Brenda had completely discredited me. "Perhaps we can connect again in a couple of days." Perhaps in a couple of days I will have tracked down Harry.

CHAPTER THREE

Part way through the day, my door burst open and Marco's head appeared, as if hovering, bodiless, like a magician's trick. "What time are you going home?" he asked, his emerald green eyes gleaming.

"Um, not sure." Was he trying to ensure I wasn't going to sleep at the Museum again?

"Can you grab a bite with me then?"

"Oookay."

"Great! I'll meet you at RoCoCo."

"Super choice!" Like a Pavlovian dog, my mouth began to water just pondering the Parisian-like eatery in nearby Yorkville.

Marco's head joined his body as he stepped fully into the office, now back to his usual six-foot stature. "I want to make sure you have something in your system besides chocolate, for once."

I smirked.

* * * * *

At the entrance of RoCoCo's, the aroma of luxurious Valrhona chocolate enveloped me like a sweet fog, coating the delicate hairs inside my nostrils with a nectarous film. For a moment, I felt myself weightless, floating, defying gravity.

The establishment's boutique served as a retail ante-chamber to the dining area, and it would take every single molecule of self-control to bypass the exquisite jewelry-case-like displays that were making all of my senses dance. Rather than gems, however, the delicate glass cabinets were appointed with rows of truffle delicacies infused with Bombay chai and Tahitian vanilla, Seville orange and sweet curry. The chocolaty delights sported deliciously creative names like Thai Me Up, Curry in a Hurry, Hot Mess, and Belle du Jour. From there my eyes wandered to wall displays strategically populated with pastel-hued macarons flavored with lavender and cassis, figs and red wine, passion fruit and pistachios. The white floors and walls formed a perfect backdrop highlighting the vibrant wares. I dug in my heels and cantered forward like a horse with blinders on.

As I passed towards the next room, the ethereal airiness of the shop area transitioned. What awaited further inside was best described as a den. Here the tones deepened to a palette of masculine browns, with deep saturations of tan and taupe, hazel and mahogany. The sense of formality was heightened with wainscoting galore and weighty furniture. It felt as though I had invaded the inner sanctum of an exclusive men's club from another time. As the décor was not a Rococo style at all, I suspected the owners decided to maintain the previously existing aesthetic and not invest in a massive reno.

A buzzing crowd already occupied the room, but Marco was nowhere among the chatty throng. Before I drew my next breath, the restaurant's host beelined towards me. Like a traditional Parisian waiter, he sported a large moustache, slicked-back hair and joker-like grin.

"Hello," said the man in a fathomless baritone. "Do you have a reservation?"

"I don't think so. I hope you can fit two more in." I spied a small empty table. "What about that one over there?"

"I'm afraid it is reserved. I don't suppose your moniker is Kalena, is it?"

"Why, yes?"

"My most humble of apologies. Marco is awaiting you in our private Fireplace Room. You will have no disturbances there."

Did he just give me a sly wink? What the hell was going on? Why would we need such a degree of privacy?

"Please, follow me. And again, my apologies for not pairing name to face. Might I be so bold as to say that Marco's description of 'really, really cute' is rather an understatement."

A flush swept over me as I was escorted towards a set of brocaded, chocolate-colored draperies hanging at the end of the room. With a gentle push, he separated the heavy folds of fabric allowing me to pass through first. A single log in the fireplace glowed as if a swarm of fireflies had settled on one end of the wood. My eyes adjusted and Marco's silhouette grew clearer. The situation felt surreally odd. The room was more suitable for clandestine lovers than for colleagues.

"I will leave the two of you to peruse the menu. Simply pull that cord behind you when you're ready to place your dinner order," said the host, nodding towards an enormous tasseled golden rope straight out of a Bedouin tent in the middle of a desert. I was beginning to feel as if I was in a David Lynch film, where everything was a bit askew. All we needed was a smoke machine to heighten the atmosphere to the next level of eeriness.

"Thanks," said Marco.

"So, what do you think of this room? Kind of cool, eh?"

"Uh, yeah." The oversized wingback chair almost swallowed me up when I sank into it.

Marco slid the menus to the side of the table. "We'll look at those in a bit. First, there's something I want to show you." Marco leaned to one side and began to reach for something under the table while keeping his eyes peeled on me. From a knapsack, he withdrew an electronic tablet and tapped the screen. "Hold on, this'll fire up in two secs." He rested the tablet on the table. "Have you ever been out to Eastern Road?"

"To the Museum's off-site storage facility? No. I've never had an official reason to trek out there." The colossal warehouse was in an industrial part of the city, nestled among nondescript buildings and surrounded by main thoroughfares.

"But you know about the kind of stuff they keep there, right?"

I rolled my eyeballs upwards at the thirty-something. "I've worked at the Museum about ten times longer than you, remember?"

Most museums with large collections, like ours, house a good portion of their inventory in covert outposts. It's mostly a matter of cost. Museums located in downtown cores of sizable cities like Toronto, New York, and Chicago simply couldn't afford the real estate required to store all of their monumental collections at their main centrally located public building. And keeping a goodly proportion of their stockpile off site is also seen as a sort of insurance policy for a museum. If there's any kind of natural disaster or major security breach, a museum's entire cache is not jeopardized.

"All of the Museum's overstock is out there. Duplicate

20

specimens and artifacts, and all the jumbo-sized objects," I continued.

"Exactly. I haven't been out there yet, but there's supposed to be tons of dino skeletons, a bunch of old stuffed animals, even ancient Egyptian boats and Chinese carriages. They could probably make a killing if they sold some of that stuff off."

"You know, the Museum can't randomly sell its artifacts or specimens. As a government designated guardian of the collections, ethically, and legally it can't just start dumping its treasures. Deaccessioning is pretty tricky, and there's a complicated protocol involved."

"I was just kidding."

I paused. "What's up? Why are we even talking about this?" The menus caught my sight line and my stomach growled on cue.

"Well, the Eastern Road warehouse is not as busy you might think. A few curators go out there to do some research, but really, it's a ghost town most of the time, especially in the evenings."

I looked down at my black and white hounds-tooth tights. They were way too cute, especially paired with my eggplant Fly London shoes. My outfit that day may have been a bit too Alice-in-Wonderland, but it was still rather adorable.

"Are you listening to me?"

I straightened up my spine. "Go on."

"For the most part, the place is an easy monitor. And there's actually a lot less security than you might think."

"Really?" I needed food.

"A lot less than we have in the main building. But I was working a nighter a couple of weeks ago; remember when we had that crazy thunderstorm, the one where lightning touched down in a few spots around the city?"

"How can I forget? Traffic was a disaster. They're predicting a season of major storms this year, whoever 'they' are."

"Well, the power went out at Eastern Road, just for a short bit that night."

"But generators kick in right away, like they do in the main building, I presume."

"Well, usually in a nanosecond. But this time, it took about ten minutes. No one here seemed too concerned about it."

"Marco, for crying out loud. Is there a point to this story? I'd really like to get home before the sun comes up."

Marco grinned, touched the tablet in front of him and launched a video. The quality of the nighttime recording was substandard due to the lack of lighting, but there was no mistaking a man carrying an umbrella in one hand and a large, flat package wrapped in what appeared to be plastic tarp under his other arm.

"If you had to guess, what do you think this guy is carrying?" asked Marco.

I stared directly into Marco's pupils. "A painting."

"This footage was taken the night of the storm, within a block of Eastern Road."

My heart started racing.

"...and it was pretty close to the time the power went out in the area that night."

CHAPTER FOUR

Feeling faint, like my blood pressure was particularly low, I flicked my arm forward, curving it around Marco's head, and tugged on the tasseled cord.

"Hey, what the?" Marco ducked instinctively and smacked his forehead on the table.

I burst out laughing to the point of losing my breath. "What did you think I was trying to do?" I said attempting to refill my lungs with air…"knock you out with a right hook?"

"I don't know. You've been acting really weird since you got here."

"Me?" I said. "I came here to eat. I'm starving and am about to pass out."

Before uttering another word, our waiter appeared like a supernatural apparition, and the two of us attempted to compose ourselves. Marco rubbed his forehead, making it impossible for me to erase the jumbo grin off my face.

"Ready to order, are you?" the waiter said.

"Not quite —"

"Yes," I interjected. "I'll have the warm lentil salad and some sweet potato fries." I turned to Marco. He looked a bit stunned. "He'll have the steak sandwich and a green salad," I said.

"Sweet potato fries. I'll have the fries too, instead of the salad."

"Excellent substitution. I do believe our sweet frites are

the best in town." The waiter scooped up the menus with grace. "I'll check with you about dessert after you have savored your mains." He retreated almost as quickly as he had materialized.

"Thanks for ordering for me, I guess. Man, life with you is never dull, I'll grant you that."

"Me? You're one to talk? Where did you get that video? Don't tell me it's on YouTube?" There was a small goose egg forming on Marco's forehead, but I was not about to share that with him.

"Nooooo. I got it from a friend of mine, a girl I've kind of been seeing."

WHAT? Was I no longer his reason for living, the older woman of his dreams, the—

"It was a total fluke she shared it with me. She was going to erase it, and then we started talking about the storm and she showed me the clip."

"What was she doing near Eastern Road? Why would this guy have caught her attention?" Who was this woman? She was surely a lot younger than I was…as she should be.

"It's not too far from where she lives. And she's a drainer. She goes out in storms."

"A trainer," I harrumphed. She probably ran boot camps, in extreme rain, no less.

"No, a drainer. She's a river keeper for invisible rivers."

"Interesting. Does she ride an invisible boat to do her job?"

"I know it sounds strange, but rivers are buried underneath cities all around the world. Benny's better at explaining all this than I am."

"Benny?"

"Short for Benedetta. She never goes by that, though."

24

Benedetta, eh. Probably Italian. The last young woman that had her sights set on Marco had been Italian as well, but she'd had a *Fatal Attraction* kind of thing going on. She left the Museum abruptly after having been caught breaking into staff email boxes, including mine. I hoped this new prospect wasn't a sociopath as well.

"Sooooo, what's an Italian drainer doing in your life?"

"She's pretty cool, actually. She came here to do environmental studies at the University of Toronto. Benny's originally from Brescia, in Italy, but she fell in love with a Canadian, stayed here...then fell out of love."

Hmm.

"Cities like Toronto, built near water, have turned their rivers into sewers. Toronto's tops at that. Actually, there's a documentary about this stuff," continued Marco. "I'm surprised you haven't seen it. It's called *Lost Rivers*."

"Nope, missed that one" I said, nodding my head. "But okay, okay, I get it. What I don't get is how she got this particular footage."

Marco's lips parted, but the waiter reentered the room with our food and placed it before us.

"Wow, this looks amazing," I piped in. The plates held generous portions.

The waiter subtly bowed his head and once again disappeared behind the curtain with the stealth of a jungle cat.

I picked up my fork. "Well, spill."

"I think the next step is to meet up with Benny and let her explain first-hand. I just wanted to see if this was, well...something you wanted to look into with me. It's kind of risky for both of us..."

After having caused a huge furor at an important Museum gala while attempting to put a halt to what I thought

25

was an attempted museum heist – only to find out I was far off base – I had sworn to Stewart and the Director that my days of sleuthing for art thieves were over.

"I just have a really weird feeling about this," said Marco.

As Marco spoke, I observed a most gentle flutter of the curtain separating our room from the main dining area, and my gaze drifted towards the floor. Barely visible was the soft curve of a shoe's toe. Another minimally perceptible undulation of the velvet drape followed and suddenly the toe stub was gone.

CHAPTER FIVE

Following dinner, Marco had offered me a lift, but I declined, citing it was too far out of his way. My trek home from the restaurant involved a short leg on the subway followed by an uninspiring streetcar ride down Bathurst Street towards Lake Ontario. I found myself roiling over the fact that Marco had left me hanging. However, just before we went our separate ways, Marco had called Benny, and we set up a time to meet.

Once in the lobby of my building, I entered an elevator cab with several residents. Too tired to strike up a conversation about the weather, I pulled out my phone to check my messages. Four missed phone calls put me on high alert. What the frig? I had forgotten I had muted my device while I was with Marco. All four calls were from the same overseas number. HARRY RIGGER!

Oh no, no, NO! What time was it there now? Seven hours behind. I looked at my watch. Middle of the night, very early morning. I didn't care.

The elevator doors opened in what seemed like slow motion, but as soon as I could squeeze through them, I ran through. Within seconds I was in front of the doorway of my condo and speed dialing to Harry. Straight to voice mail. Fuuuuuuuuuuuuuuuuuuuuuck! Why the hell hadn't he texted me to let me know he was okay? He must have known from

27

my messages I was desperate to contact him. Stupidly, I decided to Google why people disappear in Saudi Arabia. Who knew there would be 1,380,000 responses to that search? I went to bed wondering if Harry Rigger might soon be Rigger Mortis.

* * * * *

Sitting upright in bed, I tapped the shortcut on my phone's home screen to Harry's number in Riyadh. Pause...pause. Nothing to panic about yet. Engaged.

"Hello," said the voice on the other end.

"Ooooooooh, myyyyyyy, goooood! Harry, is that you?"

"Ah, now. This must be Kalena." He sounded rather chipper and disturbingly nonchalant.

"Where've you been? I've lost a decade off my life fretting about you."

"Dearie, I thought you told me you were doing that meditating thing to keep a cap on those nerves of yours," he said with his charming Irish accent.

"Yeah, well when one of your employees vanishes in the Middle East, there's only so much fifteen minutes with Deepak Chopra in the sweet spot of the universe can do."

"What do you mean vanishes?"

"Are you kidding me? I haven't heard from you in days, and no one on the site at the museum knew your whereabouts."

"Well, it seems to me like there must have been a bit of miscommunication here. I was doing some personal work for the Prince, and Stewart knew all about it. So did Geoffrey for that matter."

"They what?"

28

"You know Stewart. He's what you would call a professional schemer, always finagling things. When he heard the Prince wanted some master carpentry done on his palace, he volunteered my services to him for a few days, on the hush, you know, so that Stewart could convince His Highness to give us that medal job. I heard it worked."

I slumped back with a soft thud. "Why didn't you return my calls?"

"They took my phone away. Stewart and the Prince didn't want it leaked I was doing private work on company time. I know it's done all the time, but your boss didn't want anyone finding out, especially since we're getting so close to the opening, and we're running behind schedule. Stewart thought it might not reflect well on the project, so you have to promise me you won't tell him I told you. And best not to tell the wife. She's a saint, that one, for putting up with me all these years, but she's not one to keep a secret under her breath."

"Okay, okay. I get it. I should be grateful you're safe and sound."

"Safe and sound, and I had a grand time. The Prince let me take out his Rolls for a spin and they fed me like royalty. And after working on the cabinetry each day, I had full access to what they call 'the amenities.' It was like living in a five-star hotel."

I thought back to my nights sleeping on a pile of Mexican blankets on the floor of my office.

"But the Prince is unashamedly a persnickety man, he is. I don't envy you working with him on those medals. You'll have to keep listening to that fella in the sweet spot of the universe a wee bit more."

A deafening boom sounded that rattled my windows

and almost shook the flesh off my bones.

"KALENA! What the hell is going on there?"

CHAPTER SIX

The thunder that Harry had heard while we were talking signaled the beginning of a spectacular lightning storm. Toronto hosts more than its fair share of these tempests, but as I observed slashes of light dancing across the breadth of my Lake Ontario view while on the phone with Harry, I knew I was witnessing some kind of unusual disruption in our weather patterns. Somewhat later in the morning, my perceptions were echoed by a plethora of weather reporters commenting on the unusual phenomenon of such a ferocious lightning storm taking place in the morning hours rather than in the evening, when they normally occur.

But I couldn't afford to delay starting my new project any further. On my computer, I Googled Royal Canadian Mint and speedily located a contact name and number for someone in their production office. I took up my phone receiver, dialed, bypassed the automatic operator system, and keyed in the extension.

"Hello, is that Monsieur Pelletier?" I said.

"*Oui.* May I help you?" said M. Pelletier, with a barely detectable French-Canadian accent.

"My name's Kalena Boyko, and I'm calling from the Royal Ontario Museum in Toronto."

"Yes..."

"I found your name on the Mint's web site and, we're,

uh, assisting an international museum with an order of commemorative medals, and I was wondering if the Mint took on such commissions."

"Did one of my colleagues put you up to this?" M. Pelletier sounded as if he were stifling a laugh on the other end of the line.

"Um...No."

"Excuse me. I didn't mean...It's just that we are so very, very busy. And I work with some practical jokers."

"I see."

"I'm afraid our only client is the Canadian government. We would not be able to do your commission even if it were not a mad house around here."

"Are you aware of any companies that do this kind of work?" I said hoping for a miracle.

"Not off hand. But I can give you the name of a well-respected Toronto artist who has designed some of our coins. She may be able to help you out. Just one minute." There was a brief pause. "Vera Zelinka. She is semi-retired, but very experienced. And she has won many awards for her coin designs. She is one of the best in Canada."

"Fantastic." I scribbled down the name

"She's a bit unusual."

I doodled a head with hair sticking up.

"How many medals do you need to produce?" asked M. Pelletier.

"One thousand."

"And how much time do you have to produce these medals?"

"About six weeks. Is that enough time for this kind of project?"

There was an unsettling silence on the line before M.

Pelletier started again. "Even for an experienced artist, it may be very...difficult. It's such specialized work. Not only does one have to be an excellent metal artist, but you must know the foundry process inside and out. I'm not sure if Dr. Zelinka has this additional expertise."

I whipped my pen across the room where it struck a metal filing cabinet and ricocheted. "Dr.?" I inquired.

"Yes, she taught at the University of Toronto. I believe the 'Dr.' might be an emeritus title."

"I see."

"You may e-mail me at the address on our web site, and I'll reply with the contact information for Dr. Zelinka."

"*Merci, mille fois*," I said.

"You're welcome. *Bon courage.*"

"I think I'll need more than courage. But, thank you. *Au revoir.*" I slumped forward like a marionette whose strings had been suddenly cut when I heard a faint bell signaling incoming email. I peeked up at the computer screen. A message from Marco, 'Call me pronto if you can.'

Marco and I had learned from our recent adventure as partners in crime-solving at the Museum that you couldn't be certain if your emails were private. It wasn't so much Big Brother monitoring that concerned us. I had long surrendered to government and corporate surveillance via the likes of Microsoft, Facebook, and Google. We were more paranoid about our own internal observers, whether the higher-ups or individuals with access to the Museum's network who might have nothing better to do than spy on their own colleagues, as had previously happened to Marco and me. So, we'd vowed that any business that was no one's business would be relayed through a land line whenever possible.

I grabbed the phone receiver and dialed the extension

to the Staff Entrance, Marco's usual station.

"Royal Ontario Museum, Staff Entrance," chimed Marco.

"What's up?" I said.

"Change of plan – we're going to meet up with Benny tonight...after work. Can you make it?"

"I...I guess so. But why tonight?"

"She came across something else she wants us to see right away. Apparently, this crazy rain might affect it somehow. So, can you make it? You're not working late on a Friday night, are you?"

"Well, I might have a date...or something." I muttered under my breath.

"So, do you?"

"Well, no."

Date. I didn't even remember the definition of the word. Dearth was a word I understood more expertly.

"Okay, wait for me at the bus layby across from the Museum, just north of Charles Street. I'll pick you up."

"Good plan." Neither of us wanted to be spotted leaving the building together. "What are you driving these days, by the way?"

"I'll surprise you. Do! Gotta go."

God only knew what kind of vehicle he was restoring and in what he might turn up.

* * * * *

While I waited at an intersection in the thick of the University of Toronto campus, the rain gushed down as if some portal to a parallel water world had been cracked wide open.

Luckily, I was protected by my impermeables, but most people on the street were clamoring for any kind of shelter to avoid the dousing. It wasn't long before I heard an ominous rumble, and through the streaming rain, I identified what appeared to be a blue submarine floating up Queen's Park Crescent towards Bloor Street. The horror, the horror.

Before I could draw a calming breath, a large monstrosity of a vehicle roared into the short lane dedicated to the Avenue Road bus stop. A group of students waiting for the bus broke into raucous laughter and one of them screamed, "Hey, is that thing legal in this country?"

Inside the car, I observed the driver lean over to the passenger side and roll down the window in a stuttering motion. "Kalena, is that you under all those polka dots?"

I was sporting my polka-dotted hat, boots, and rain slicker. The hat I had purchased in a pet shop after having seen it in their window display. It matched my coat perfectly, but no one needed to know they had been purchased as separates. "I think you have mistaken me for someone else I said," feigning a Ukrainian accent.

"Just get in the car, Boyko. A bus is about to pull up my ass."

I lowered the rim of my hat down my forehead and then jerked open the weighty sea-blue door.

"Hey, nice ride," yelled someone in the crowd on the sidewalk behind me. "Say hello to Elvis for me."

I leapt so quickly into the car that my soaked rain slicker acted as a slide on the vinyl bucket seat. The only thing that prevented me from ending up in Marco's lap was the large gear box separating the passenger from the driver's side. A resituation of my butt into the center of my seat was required.

"Really, Zeffirelli? Really? What happened to the De-Lorean?"

"I had a buyer before I even started to pimp that ride. Have you got something against my 1970 Dodge Charger?"

"Seriously, who drives a muscle car like this besides you these days?"

Marco gunned the gas, and we zipped ahead defying the gravitational tug on a mass of such proportions.

"You may be an expert on the Italian Renaissance, but it seems you know nada about collectible cars. This is one of 337 ever made of this model. It's one of the sweetest deals I've ever scored."

"It seems every car you get is the sweetest deal you've ever scored," I said shaking my head side to side.

Marco turned my way and did a quick body scan. "Did you corner the market on polka dots?"

"I happen to be very fond of polka dots, and they're more timeless than this gas guzzler." I released a sigh pondering how everything about this car was so wrong. My personal carbon footprint was as small as possible, including driving a Smart Car that probably consumed a tenth of the gasoline of the Charger. But there was no point lecturing Marco on the world's shrinking energy resources. I slumped back in full surrender. "Where are we heading?"

"The scene of the crime."

"What crime would that be?"

"Not sure. That's what we're going to try to figure out."

Whatever it was, I'm sure Marco would solve it. He had skills that impressed me more than I let on and his instincts about people and situations never failed to astound me. It was a shame he had dropped out of the police academy because he probably would have evolved into an adept detective.

The lights at Bloor turned, and we forged ahead like an ocean liner making its way through a narrow canal in Ontario's Trent-Severn Waterway. We chattered about all the eccentrics we encountered in our daily lives at the Museum. There was certainly no shortage of characters to keep us amused at work, and with Marco being a security guard, he was privy to astonishing information about the Museum's underbelly.

We zig-zagged through the city cutting north, then east, then north, then east some more. Suddenly, Marco took a wide swing, from a right lane to make a left turn, and I wrenched my neck as I swung my head around to see if a T-bone impact was imminent. The car hydroplaned through an expansive puddle and miraculously ended on a part of the road with better traction. Memories flooded back to me of a ride Marco had given me to the airport not that long ago, when I was headed to London, and I was sure we were going to become a traffic statistic then as well. But Marco was either a racing car driver in a previous life, or he just had nine lives – fortunately for me.

Marco tossed me a glance and grinned. "Couldn't see the street sign for this damn rain. But I didn't want to miss that turn. It's a long back-track, and we're already late."

"Uh, huh," I said, massaging the back of my neck.

"You okay?"

"Uh, huh."

"I wouldn't have pulled that trick if there were any cars around. I knew we'd come out of it."

I became aware that we were in quite a desolate spot. In fact, we hadn't passed any cars for some time, which seemed rather bizarre for the city at this time of day, even if we were in an industrial area during a ridiculous downpour.

"There she is. There's Benny."

The wall of rain had abated minimally, and the headlights from the monster car created an eerie aura of light around a slight figure that appeared to be dressed for fly fishing – hip waders, a loose-fitting rain jacket, and a brimmed hat all in the same neutral, light-bluish/green palette. She scuttled towards the car, and I pushed the door open for her. "I can crawl in the back," I said.

"There is no need. Please stay. I will climb behind," said Benny with an accent that eluded me. It didn't have a straightforward Italian ring to it.

She removed a small knapsack, then bounced in. Marco cut the engine and turned on the interior dome light. As our new passenger removed her head gear, I had a few moments to scrutinize her. A single, chunky fish-tail braid rested over one shoulder, and small strands that had loosened from the plait were gently waved. Benny's dirty blonde hair was very similar in color to Marco's, whose heritage was Northern Italian. But her skin was a darker tone – in the dimness, I couldn't tell if she was sun-kissed or perhaps had Sicilian blood flowing in her veins. Benny's dark eyes emanated a salt-of-the-earth honesty and a gleam of youth I had long lost. No wonder Marco was dating this vision. If I were him, I would swear eternal love to her at first sight.

"I am Benny," she said.

"Kalena."

"I will give you a proper Italian greeting next time, when we are not in a car." The deep, throaty giggle that followed was so delightful that all walls normally erected between strangers tumbled down. She leaned over and gently tapped

Marco on the shoulder. "So, *come stai*?"

"Good," said Marco having turned around to face the both of us.

"Wow, this is some car. We do not have these in Italy."

"For good reason," I chirped in. "You'd be scraping buildings on both sides of the street over there."

We all laughed, a fog of warmth surrounded us, and I relaxed with relief. What a change from Marco's last cuckoo-for-Cocoa-Puffs admirer.

"So, shall we get down to business?" Marco's demeanor shifted. "You said you had something time-sensitive to show us."

Benny reached into her knapsack and pulled out an iPad. This scenario seemed all-too-familiar. "Marco showed you the video, yes?"

I nodded.

"But I only sent him part of my recording because the file was too large. I watched it again before downloading it, and I realized, well...I had not captured the significance of the situation."

"What is it?" puzzled Marco.

"I came back to the area on another visit and checked against landmarks. This person..." Benny launched the clip for us to watch again, "they are not moving away from your *deposito*."

"What?" Marco and I chimed simultaneously.

"This person is walking towards your warehouse with this package."

CHAPTER SEVEN

The three of us sat in silence for a moment, and I was the first to speak up. "Well, then there's nothing suspicious going on at all."

"I can't believe I got it wrong, too," added Marco.

"But why did you ask us to drive all the way up here, Benny? You could have shared this with us over the phone, and we could be sitting in a nice, dry, cozy spot cocooning this evening." A shiver waved through my body.

"*Aspetta.* I did not have a chance to finish. There is more. Even stranger...When I came for the next visit, I found some markings in a gutter that I do not believe were there before the last storm." Benny fished her hand into her knapsack and pulled out a digital camera. She depressed a button, and when the LED screen lit up, Benny moved the device towards us. "Have you ever seen anything like this before?"

I made out some sort of marking graffitied on the edge of a street. The end of it was elongated, as if being washed down into an actual rain grate.

"I am sorry for the imperfect picture. But this is why I invited you here. I think it is best if you see them for yourself."

"Them?" I quizzed.

"There are a few of them," said Benny.

Benny and I both put our rain hats on, and the three of us bounded out of the car.

"I'm going to grab us some lighting," said Marco as he scrambled around to the trunk, opened it up, and pulled out a massive device of illumination.

"What the heck?" I said.

"A film production company left this behind at the Museum after a shoot. They seem to keep forgetting to come back for it." Marco flipped a switch and blinded me as he shone a light that would have illuminated a Tyrannosaurus Rex.

"For crying out loud, Marco," I yelled, throwing my hands up to block the light.

Benny started to laugh. "You look like one of those escaped prisoners you see in American movies, except you are fashionably dressed in polka dots instead of stripes."

"I didn't know I was going to be going on a scavenger hunt in the pouring rain after work or I would have dressed more like..."

"Me?" Benny looked down at herself. "I know, not very sexy. But when you see where my work takes me, you will understand."

Marco cut the light.

"This way, please," Benny motioned.

We walked less than half a block when Benny accelerated her stride. When she reached a grate in the ground, she crouched down.

"Here...it is still here. But the rain is doing some damage."

Marco raced to Benny's side and turned on the cyclopic lighting device. With the reflective effect from the soaked surface of the roadway, the impact of the glow seemed multiplied a millionfold. And then a blinding flash streaked the sky. I counted...one–two. BOOM!

"Wow, that lightning struck somewhere pretty close by," Marco said with an unusual note of alarm in his voice. "We should speed this up."

We all stooped towards the earth to study the unusual symbol that lay before us. I smoothed my fingers over the painted mark that, as Benny had warned us, was already weathering from the autumn elements. In the center was a cross, and overlaid was a stylized square with rounded corners, ribbon-like. The symbol was surrounded by a triple border, also square in shape, but with rounded corners, and at the four tips of the cross, the framing jutted out into a point, kind of like a bracket. But as we had seen on Benny's camera, the bottom part of the symbol was stretched as if being washed into the drain.

"It looks Byzantine," I said, "but I'm not sure. I don't know this period as well as the Renaissance."

"*Si, si*, Kalena. I thought the same thing, too. This mark reminds me of something I may have seen in one of our older Italian churches."

Another celestial flash cracked the sky open – this time there was no time to count for the thunder. The three of us huddled.

"That was way too close for comfort." Marco grabbed his mega spotlight. "Let's move it. We're not safe here."

"One more second," cried Benny. "Shine the light back down to the ground. I will take one more picture."

"We need to go, NOW. Getting fried by lightning is not a pleasant experience."

"Benny's right, Marco. That paint might not last out this rain storm if this deluge keeps up."

"*Per favore*."

"Oh for..." Marco switched the light back on.

42

Benny ripped out her camera and dropped to her knees like a dancer with no fear of injuring her body. The camera's shutter clicked rapidly, mimicking muffled machine gunfire. Marco extinguished the light and one-handedly pulled Benny back up onto her feet.

"Fantastic. I have it good this time." With super human speed, Benny deposited the camera back into her knapsack. "Follow me," cried Benny. "I know an interesting spot where we can take shelter until the gods stop crying."

"But the car's—"

"This way, Kalena," cried Benny already leaps and bounds ahead.

I pulled my rain hat down until it felt like it was cutting off the circulation to my brain, and I tried to pull my skirt lower. But it was too late. Water dribbled down my legs, and my pantyhose grew more clammy and cold with each second, making the lower half of my body feel like a cadaver. Benny started to sprint and Marco and I joined the rhythm. But while Benny managed to resemble a gazelle, even in her hip waders, I trudged along in my frivolous rain boots with the weightiness of an elephant.

"*Ecco*," bellowed Benny, pointing at something on the ground.

"What?" I said.

"Another symbol."

Marco stopped, did a 360-degree rotation like a fast-motion 3D scanner, and returned to a running pace, barely having lost any distance.

"We turn here," said Benny.

I glanced up at a street sign. Earlscourt, it read. And then Benny veered off the street onto a grassy trail. "Where are you taking us?" I cried out.

"Very near. Please trust me."

A discomfort seeped through my body, and I felt like a hapless lemming being led hypnotically to the edge of a cliff. It was one of those moments where I felt I was silencing my instincts, blocking my third eye. My head began to ache.

After passing through a larger arc, Benny made a sharp turn, with Marco and I swinging behind her. The next thing I knew, we were tripping along a man-made ditch lined with bricks, a narrow channel of water surging through it with the force of the river below Niagara Falls. Shortly we approached a chain link fence surrounding a towering concrete structure enclosed within. She had to be kidding! If Benny thought I could climb that fence in a skirt and clumsy rubber boots...and in this rain. I couldn't scale that barricade even if I was wearing mountain climbing gear. And was this fence grounded? It was potentially a lightning rod of monumental proportions.

In a flash, Benny bent around to the right, glanced back to check on us, and zipped along the perimeter of the fence until she came upon some shrubbery. "This way, you two. *Pronto*."

Benny pulled back some branches of a now leafless shrub exposing a hole in the fencing, and she squeezed through. "*Dammi la luce*," she said to Marco, who passed the light to her, then motioned for me to go next.

"You go ahead," I said.

Marco slipped through, bolted a few steps forward, and I entered right behind him. With my body on the other side of the fence, my mini-tent of a rain slicker caught on a loose piece of the chain-link wiring. Lightning flashed, and I closed my eyes and held my breath.

"C'mon!" screamed Marco.

My eyes opened. I wasn't fried. "I'M STUCK."

Marco plunged towards me, gripped the plastic polka-dotted shell, and jerked it. I watched in horror as the coat tore.

"I'll buy you a new one," he said.

"I got this in Berlin," I muttered under my breath as I forged forward.

The three of us double-backed along the fence to the opening in the structure, dove under a monumental arch-way, and into a concrete portico, as if crossing the finish line of a sprint.

"This storm is insane. I'm really sorry, guys. If I'd known it was going to be this bad, I would've recommended we do this another night," said Marco, breathing heavily.

"How could you know it would turn out like this?" I said half-heartedly, glancing down at my tattered coat.

"I can fix that for you," said Benny. "I must repair my rain wear all the time, and I have become an expert, I think. You will never even know it was broken."

"Ripped," said Marco. "You usually use the word ripped for material."

"Oh, no," I said splitting the coat open. "This is broken." The three of us howled, our shrieks reverberating in the cavernous, blackened space. All tension dissipated. As we pulled ourselves together and settled down, I became cognizant of the sound of rushing water and unease gripped me again.

"Where are we?" I asked.

"Turn on your uber light, Marco...this way" said Benny, pointing downwards.

With obedient compliance, Marco swung the light around and flipped the switch. Initially, the sudden change in light levels found me squinting, but as soon as my eyes adjusted, I was mesmerized by the scene of unparalleled and unconventional beauty illuminated before me.

"Incredible," exclaimed Benny. "I have never seen it this way before."

I tip-toed forward and peered down at an artificial waterfall lined with the same bricks that covered the channel whose path along which we had run. The surface of the brick work was polished smooth from the constant flow of water over it. My focus was then drawn further ahead into a man-made cavern, whose salt-streaked poured-concrete walls vanished into ebony darkness in the distance. The view resembled a vista from a *Lord of the Rings* film adaptation, and it made me feel as though someone had pushed my mute button. When finally able to muster a verbal reaction, all I could utter was, "wow...wow...wow."

"It is something, yes? This is the Earlscourt Sewer, just at Glenlake Avenue. This water falls westward down into the old Spring Creek Ravine at Keele Street." Benny stepped closer to the falling water, and my stomach somersaulted. My fear of heights was so extreme I got nervous even when someone else approached a ledge.

"There are a number of steep slides like this one, three or four of them," she continued. They each have these concrete sidewalks along the sides with the stream running down the middle. Marco...if you point the light over here a bit, you can see the heavy metal railings which I use to go down further. But with this water flow and a bad kind of footwear, it can be dangerous."

"What? You think I wouldn't fare well with these precious polka-dotted boots?"

Benny giggled and continued. "There are smaller tributaries at the South Junction and Indian Grove sewers, but it is almost impossible to climb through them. They do not have any railings. You must wear ropes, like mountaineers."

"Please, don't tell me you've done that," I said.

"It is part of what I do. But this is a tremendous opportunity for me to take some magnificent pictures. Please keep shining the light downwards."

As Benny spoke, she grabbed hold of one of the rails, and my digestive organs went into flip flops again. "I don't think it's a good idea to go down there," I said.

"Kalena's right. Come on back up."

"I do this all the time." With determination Benny descended to a small landing, dropped her knapsack, and pulled out her camera. Before either of us could say anymore, Benny was snapping shots at every angle. "Keep moving the light...let it reflect on different parts of the walls... this is super *fantastico*."

Benny kept changing her position and posture, slipping a few times, but with each misstep instantaneously finding her footing with the nimbleness of a jungle cat. I rotated nervously towards Marco, and my heart ceased. There was not one shadow behind the light, but two.

"MARCO! There's someone behind you!" I yelled.

Marco zipped around and the figure hightailed it. "Hey, hey!" Marco yelled. He turned back towards us. "Benny, get back up here."

Marco set down the light and vanished, but as I rotated towards Benny, she was disappearing, too. The battery on the light was dying – fast.

CHAPTER EIGHT

As the light grew dimmer and dimmer, I detected a blur of a figure pulling itself up the rail aligning the waterfall. Benny was inching her way back to ground level.

"What is it? Where did Marco go?"

"There was someone watching us. Marco took off after them." My gaze darted back and forth between Benny and the direction into which Marco had faded. Promptly, we heard footsteps hastening towards us.

"Hey, you guys okay?" asked Marco.

"Yeah," I said. "What happened?"

"I started to catch up to the guy," Marco said, "but, then I thought there could be a second person who might go after you two."

"Look, the rain's finally letting up," I said. The three of us redirected our gaze to the heavens and, sure enough, the clouds were breaking up. It was as though the gods had turned off a colossal tap.

"We should get back to the car." Marco stooped down to pick up the now fully drained light, and Benny once again set the pace scrambling ahead of us.

"Who do you think that was, Marco? A street person looking for shelter?" I said running along.

"This area's a little isolated for a homeless person's retreat. They like to be out of the way, but also want to be somewhere closer to civilization so they can forage for food

48

and panhandle."

"Good point."

Benny was still steps ahead of us, and as she approached the car, she raised her arm and gestured to us to come.

"What is it?" said Marco.

"Look," said Benny indicating towards the driver's door panel. There was a light splatter of grey paint on the surface.

Marco stroked his finger across the paint speckles, smearing it. "Oh, give me a break."

"How could any kind of paint stick to the car after this frigging rain?" I asked.

"It's probably some kind of epoxy," said Marco as he marched back to the trunk of the land boat. He heaved the lid open, pulled out a rag, and came back to the door, where he started to wipe off as much of the splatter as he could.

"Good thing this car's going to be painted, or someone would have lost their head."

"Look over here," shouted Benny, startling the two of us. "More paint."

Sure enough, there was a small patch of grey paint spray that, had it not been for Benny's acute eye, would have gone unnoticed, probably even in the daytime.

"What the?" Marco was peering further ahead. "I think someone's left us a trail of breadcrumbs."

"Let us see where this guides us," said Benny.

"Marco, what if we ARE being led to some kind of ambush?" I said.

Marco hesitated, then slipped back to the trunk of the car and pulled out a baseball bat. "Never leave home without this. You two can stay here if you want."

My gaze met Benny's. "Nope."

Marco disappeared behind the opened trunk lid once again, then after opening and closing some kind of container and slamming the trunk closed, he strutted towards us — baseball bat under his armpit, a hammer in one hand, and a giant wrench in the other. I went to snatch the hammer from Marco's hand with the bravado of a Viking warrior goddess, but he held onto it.

"You wouldn't even kill a garden slug with this, would you?"

I scrunched up my mouth to one side. "Nope."

"Do not worry, Kalena, I have combat training," said Benny.

I glanced at Marco and muttered, "An Italian McGyver." He released the hammer, and I held on to it firmly.

The three of us moved in unison as we followed the trail of paint splatters, the splotches spaced out about every thirty feet or so. We lost the marks a few times, but combat-trained Benny seemed to have the skills of a bloodhound, and she consistently got us back on the path.

After fifteen minutes of tracking, Marco suddenly halted, and I plowed into him like a bumbling birdbrain in a slapstick comedy. "Geez, Marco. Can you put on the brake lights the next time you're coming to a stop?"

Benny chuckled but Marco ignored us as he performed one of his reconnaissance scans. "I know exactly where we're headed."

"You do? Where?"

"We're just about there." Marco broke into a canter with Benny and me on his tail. Marco wasn't checking the ground any further for markings, but I occasionally tilted my gaze, and I spotted a few more paint spatters as we progressed along our marked route. We approached a large building, and Marco guided us to what appeared to be the shipping and receiving doors of a warehouse. There I saw the last of our trail signs – the portals themselves had almost imperceptible specks of the light grey paint we had been pursuing.

"What is this place? There's no business name..." I walked from side to side of the doors and peeked around a corner looking for some kind of identification.

"It's intentional," said Marco. "The building's meant to blend in, be anonymous."

"This is the Museum's warehouse," said Benny.

"What the hell does this mean?" I asked.

"I'll tell you what it means," replied Marco. "Someone wants us to go inside. But it's not happening tonight."

* * * * *

En route to the car, we tossed out a host of questions and speculations. Who left the trail? Who knew we would be out here tonight? Was it the person who had been spying on us at the sewer? What was the final destination to which we were being led? What we did know for sure was that we would have to find a way to enter the facility at some point. Even as a security guard Marco couldn't just go there without raising eyebrows. But perhaps I could devise an excuse for a visit and have Marco tag along.

When I finally sat down in the bucket seat of the Charger, having redeposited our weapons in the trunk, I realized how weary, cold, and hungry I was. We had covered some serious territory by foot, often at a quick clip, and I had not eaten anything for hours. My hand clawed through my bag until it sensed a familiar texture, like that of a brown paper bag. It could be only one thing – the unmistakable compostable wrapper of ChocoSol Traders chocolate. I discreetly sized the contents, my fingers skimming along the grooves that demarcate individual servings. YES! Four pieces.

Admittedly, I could inhale four squares of chocolate more speedily than a cocaine addict snorting a line. But ChocoSol Traders, known as Toronto's slow food chocolate makers, create chocolate that doesn't fall into the realm of common candy bars – it is hearty, whole food, and just a morsel or two are enough to give one the sensation of having a full stomach.

"Anyone else starving besides me?"

"Oh, yes. I did not think our journey would be such a long one," piped in Benny.

"Yeah, I think we all got an unexpected workout," Marco said glancing at me momentarily and returning his eyes to the road.

I used both hands to snap the chocolate bar into pieces, handed one to Benny, "here you go," and another towards Marco.

"Oh my god, Benny. You are witnessing an unprecedented moment. Kalena is sharing her chocolate."

"Oh, be quiet!" I snapped.

Benny giggled and took a little nibble of the chocolate. "*Spettacolare*! There is something very unusual in this chocolate."

"Hot pepper," I said nodding. "This chocolate's made by a company called ChocoSol Traders, and they use production methods that are about as authentically Mayan as one can find in this day and age."

"Whoa, this chocolate does have a bite," said Marco.

"It's the Five Chili Bullet chocolate," I said.

"It is very warming," added Benny. "*Perfetto* for an evening like tonight."

With my lids softly closed, I felt the heat circulate through my system. "That's for sure."

CHAPTER NINE

"Harry, are you there? Harry...Harry." These sketchy telephone connections drove me around the bend at times. I disconnected and my phone rang. "Harry?"

"That'll be right. Sorry about that. Another bad link."

"So, what's the scoop?" I asked

"Pretty simple, really. A portrait of the Prince with an eagle flying in the sky on one side. And, a palm tree, too. And on the reverse, an image of one of the planes on display in the museum. With the date of the museum's opening."

"Anything more? Like perhaps an illustrated history of Saudi Arabia since the beginning of time?"

Harry chuckled on the other end of the line, then gathered himself. "I don't think they understand the concept of clean design."

"Ya' think?"

"One of the Prince's assistants is pulling together some images for your designer. You do have one on board, don't you?"

I paused. "That I can't answer. When can we get the images?"

"That, I can't answer. They have a different concept of time in this part of the world, as you know."

"That I do. But pleeeeeeease, if you could light a fire under their feet, I would be so grateful."

54

"As always, I will do me best," said Harry.

"Thanks." I leaned my head back.

"I'll talk to ye' soon." The line went dead.

I really didn't need the reminder about not yet having hired someone to design and produce the medal. The person recommended by the Royal Canadian Mint, Vera Zelinka, had yet to return any of my calls and wasn't accessible by email.

I had checked out Dr. Zelinka on Wikipedia and had been impressed. She had immigrated to Canada during the Prague Spring and had established quite a career for herself. From memberships in organizations such as the Ontario Society of Artists and the Canadian Portrait Academy to the Sculptors Society of Canada, she had also taught sculpture at the University of Toronto. But she was best known for some of her effigies of key figures in Canadian history that had been used on Canadian coins and stamps. Her pedigree more than hinted at expensive, but with no other leads, my only alternative was to pursue her and hope I could coax her out of retirement for a minor commission.

Once more, I dialed her number with no expectations, and after just a few rings I was startled when someone picked up.

"Vera, here," she said with what sounded like a strong Czech accent. "Who is calling?"

"My name is Kalena Boyko," I said sheepishly. "From the Royal Ontario Museum. I've left you quite a number of telephone messages."

"Oh, you. Yes. The girl with the Ukrainian name. You have called me so many times that my answering machine was almost full."

"I'm sorry about that."

"I try not to use my phone very much as it is the only

way my husband communicates with me anymore. He no longer lives in this world."

"I see…Did you have a chance to think about my proposal…about the commemorative medals?"

"I find myself intrigued with your project, the notion of creating a portrait of a Saudi prince. It is something I have not encountered in my long career. Although I have done the Queen of England, you know."

"Yes, I read about that. And you are aware that we have a rather modest budget?"

"I have been a member of your Museum for most of my life in Canada, and it has given me much pleasure. But I must go now. We have tied up this phone for much too long. My husband might be trying to connect with me. Goodbye." Click.

I didn't know whether to dance a happy jig or put a bullet through my brain for securing yet another fruit loop to work on one of my time-sensitive projects. Dr. Zelinka and I still needed to discuss terms and deadlines, and that would involve swallowing up phone time reserved for her dead husband. It would be prudent, I decided, to draw up a draft contract and have it prepared when I had some graphics to pass on to her.

With the intention of brewing myself a tall cup of David`s Chocolate Tea, I nudged myself away from the desk when the office door sprang open. I was caught off guard when Walter Pembroke traipsed in.

"GREETINGS, KALENA" he shouted.

"You have my permission to use your indoor voice."

"Oh…um. My humblest apologies. I am so accustomed to verbalizing in a whispered tone in the library that I have made a conscious effort to exercise my vocal cords outside the confines of my work space."

What a tool, but he was an adorable one, I had to admit. He had secretly crushed on Brenda for eons, and when I discovered his fondness for my colleague, I had assisted in transforming him from full-on nerd to chic'ish geek. I thought a romance might soften Brenda. It did – a little. And then, after just having paired up, Brenda had left for the UK.

"What can I do for you?" I stared at Walter quizzically. I couldn't figure out how he had managed to get his hair standing up in so many different directions. Was it intentional or unattended bed-head? His eyes were tiny for the size of his head, and he always seemed to be sniffling. And although his wardrobe had improved since first pursuing Brenda, it barely disguised his boney frame.

The Museum's head librarian plunked himself into Brenda's chair, and I heard the muffled crunch of paper. "Oh, dear." Walter tilted to one side of the chair, removed a small newspaper from his pants pocket and handed it over. "Just delivering this to you. I saw it in your mailbox, and I took it upon myself to bring it to you in person...knowing how much you look forward to your read of *The Art Paper*." As Walter sat back in Brenda's chair, the way he caressed the arms creeped me out.

I noticed a few salmon splotches forming on Walter's otherwise pasty neck. "I have had an opportunity to peruse this issue, and I am relieved, for your sake, to report there are no stories about *Il Gattopardo*...or on any major art thefts. It seems the international police have had a good grip on art crime this past month."

"I'm sure." I snickered. "I was just going to brew myself some chocolate tea. Would you like some?"

"I think not," Walter screwed up his face. "But thank

you, nonetheless, for the offer."

"On another matter...do you ever visit the Museum's off-site storage?"

"Eastern Road? I do. We keep some library archives there."

"Are you due for a trip soon?"

"Well, as a matter of fact, I was going to schedule a half day out there. It can be a refreshing diversion. My job is much more demanding than most would suspect. Those hordes of teenagers, university students texting non-stop, temperamental curators–"

"You have my deepest sympathy. When are you going next?"

"The day after tomorrow."

"May I join you?"

Walter turned his head and narrowed his eyes. "What is this about? What business would you have out there?"

"Well, uh, Stewart wants to me to take some photos. We're responding to a British museum's RFP for off-site storage facilities. It could be quite a lucrative consulting project for us."

"I see, I see. Security would have to sanction your visit, seeing as photography is involved."

"No problem. I'll send a request. And I'll even ask for a security escort and it'll all be on the up and up."

"Well..." Walter leaned forward in the chair.

"Excellent, done deal then."

Walter slowly lifted from Brenda's chair with a noticeable sense of unease.

"This will be an exciting field trip," I said, grinning like a possum.

"As Brenda would say, something smells fishy in the

state of Kalena."

"Oh, Walter. You and Brenda are so paranoid." I hopped out of my chair and herded Walter towards the door. "I have things to do, places to see."

As soon as Walter departed, I raced back to my computer. I speedily shot off an email to Stewart suggesting to him that I journey to the off-site storage to take some shots for the department's photographic database, relatively certain he would think the idea was inspired. Next, I sent one off to our head of security, Malik, with whom I had a solid working relationship. Well, it had been solid up until about a year ago, when my investigative shenanigans got me into a spot of trouble. But I think I was forgiven after having uncovered a dastardly plot to depose our reigning Director.

In the email I suggested that Marco accompany Walter and myself. I wasn't quite sure if it would fly with Malik, but I kept my fingers crossed. And finally, I called Marco on his cell and left him a voice mail message letting him know he was going to be drafted to accompany me to the warehouse. If everything fell into place, we might soon discover why someone was leading us to the storage site.

CHAPTER TEN

"Hi Mom, I said in Ukrainian in as positive a tone as I could muster. I always joked that my family put the fun in dysfunction, but checking in with my parents required me to steel myself for comments about my 'questionable' metropolitan lifestyle.

"Kalynechka," my mother said with honey sweetness, "you don't usually call us at this time."

"I know, Mom, but..."

"Why is she calling us tonight?" my father bellowed in the background, also in Ukrainian. "Doesn't she know OUR program is on?"

"Oh, sorry, Mom." I had forgotten my parents would be spending their Saturday evening watching a couple of Ukrainian programs on the multicultural television channel.

"It is okay, Daughter," my mother said using the diminutive form that I found so endearing. "You can call us anytime you want. But WHY are you calling us tonight?"

I dropped my chin to my chest like a dead weight. "I was having a quiet evening at home and just thought I would say hello."

"Is she coming for Ukrainian Christmas?" echoed my father. I could envision the scene on the other end of the line clearly. My father was sitting in the living room in his worn but cherished La-Z-Boy® chair, refusing to budge his eyes from the television screen while my mother peeked around the divide between the kitchen and living room, waving her arm trying to get my father to hush up.

"Tell Dad I will be there. But it's still a couple of months away."

"Yes, good, dear. But why are you home on a Saturday night? What happened to that young man who took you to the ballet?"

"Mom, that was ages ago, and he was just a friend," I said in reference to Marco.

"Women on television always say 'he's just a friend–' but the men are always more than just a friend."

"You need to stop watching soap operas. Anyway, I'm out late every week night, and I just wanted a nice quiet evening at home."

"When you get old like us, you can stay at home. You should enjoy your younger years while you can."

"I think I am long past 'my younger years.' So how are you two? How is Dad feeling?"

"Oh, good...good. We are both good."

"Ask her if she's still vegetabletarian. It will be fine for Ukrainian Christmas because the dishes don't have meat in them. But this year she has to eat some *kutya*."

I gagged just at the thought of the wheat berry pudding. "Is he watching his diet?" I said to my mother. "You're not still serving him fried T-bones every day, are you?"

"Oh, no. On Fridays we have Filet o' Fish."

"Oh, Mom! You know Dad should not be eating fried food anymore. And why aren't you at least broiling the steak in the oven, like I showed you?"

"I tried one day." My mother had lowered her voice to a whisper. "But your father would not eat it. He said it was too dry."

Well, yeah, because it didn't have butter dripping off it. "I'll let you get back to your program."

"Oh, okay, good. Sleep well and wake up healthy tomorrow."

"You too, Mom."

I pulled a super soft, fuzzy fake fur throw blanket on myself, grabbed the remote, selected the BritBox icon on my phone, and prepared to binge on a good British mystery series.

CHAPTER ELEVEN

As I waited under the stone portico that harbors the Royal Ontario Museum's Staff Entrance, I looked in disbelief at the force of the rain pummeling the asphalt in front of me. What was it with the aqueous weather this year? The damp was so annoying that I was almost looking forward to colder weather. Snow seemed a better alternative to the relentless deluge of water in its liquid state.

I swung the black pleather backpack purse off my back, unzipped the pouch, and reached in to retrieve a Giddy Yoyo chocolate bar. I started to unwrap the dark brown packaging when I heard the sound of an odd car horn. I looked down the driveway that ran between the Museum and the former planetarium building and saw a beige Volvo. That had to be Walter. It couldn't be anyone else...other than Marco, perhaps, with a new fixer-upper.

I tossed the bar back into my bag and moseyed towards the car. The driver's side window rolled down and an arm popped out waving towards me. "Kalena...Kalena," blared Walter, his voice echoing off the walls of the buildings that formed an above-ground tunnel between the Museum and the University of Toronto campus.

"I'm coming, I'm coming," I said scurrying a little faster towards the non-descript box-shaped car. As I neared the vehicle, Walter threw open the driver's door, lunged out, ran to the passenger side, and opened the door for me. "Always the gentleman, Walter." He was truly an elderly man in a younger man's body.

Walter dashed back to the driver's side, seated himself, and turned the ignition.

"Whoa, hold on," I shrieked.

"What is it?"

I glanced down the driveway. "Here he comes."

"Who?"

With ninja-like stealth, Marco was suddenly sitting in the back seat. "Nice ride, Walter. Should have known you'd have the safest ride on the road."

"I am truly confounded." Walter looked more startled than confused. "What are you doing here, Marco?"

"Didn't I tell you he's our security escort? I'm sure I mentioned it."

"Something is not right. I know it. There is something you have failed to disclose to me."

I maintained a neutral expression.

"You lost your job once and regained it by the skin of your teeth. And you may very well be willing to risk your position again, but I cannot be involved. I'm planning on asking Brenda to marry me, and if I am not gainfully employed, I am certain she will not consider the proposal."

With whiplash force, I swung my head towards the back seat, and my eyes locked on Marco's. "Marry Brenda?"

Walter's unbridled energy seemed suddenly harnessed, but I noticed a rosy pallor rising from his neck and flushing his face. "Well...yes. Yes! If I may speak for Brenda, I think we are both captivated by each other, and it has been a rather splendid courtship."

"Are you sure, bud? I mean, you guys are really cute to-gether, but you haven't been going out that long," Marco said, matter-of-factly.

"Although our romantic entwinement has been less than a year, we have worked together for a considerable period of time. And I do believe Brenda feels as I do, that we are soul mates."

Prior to Brenda going out with Walter, it would have been impossible for me to conceive of her having a kindred spirit of any sort on this planet, but I had seen positive changes in her since the two started dating. The pair were an odd coupling, but they seemed to be surprisingly well matched. "Well, good for you. I really, really hope she accepts." I swiveled towards Marco. "Can you imagine a mini-Walter or mini-Brenda running around the Museum?"

"Now, now. Let us not get ahead of ourselves. Brenda must first agree to the engagement. And do not fool yourselves into thinking that I have not noticed that you have redirected the original discussion. If you and Marco are up to old tricks, I cannot be a part of the agenda."

"Honestly," I said, "I really do need to take some photos of the off-site storage site, but there's something unusual we wanted to check on, and I truly don't think it's anything that would be considered inappropriate by Stewart, or the Director, or anyone in authority at the Museum."

Walter's shoulders dropped, and his whole body became less rigid. "I am warning you now, if you are luring me into some questionable antics, I will depart immediately and you can make alternative arrangements to return to the Museum."

"Fair 'nuff," chirped in Marco. "We can live with that."

"Shall we go?" I said.

With a steadfast demeanor, Walter put the car in reverse and ground the gears so intensely, I closed my eyes and bit my lip.

"Deepest apologies. I...I do not ever do that...You two have clearly upset me."

In my peripheral vision, I noticed Marco leaning in. I knew he was going to offer to drive. "Just focus," I blurted out. Walter began to back up smoothly, and Marco retreated.

We kept the conversation light en route to the warehouse. I didn't want to agitate Walter any further. But the conversation soon lulled and the hypnotic drone of the swishing windshield wipers sent my head into bobbing mode. It didn't take much for me to nod off in a moving vehicle. But the rain finally began to ease off, and, mid-way to our destination, Walter turned off the wipers.

As we approached the Museum's off-site storage facility, it seemed far less ominous than it had at night. Walter pulled into a parking space, and we emptied ourselves out of the car. While perusing the mundane building, Walter walked up to the façade and gently stroked it. "She is a beauty, is she not?"

Marco and I both donned quizzical expressions.

"The building is intended to be innocuous, as you know, but it is far more extraordinary than one might imagine."

I felt a history lesson coming on.

"Its brickwork is composed of Toronto clay, which bakes up to a beautiful cherry red."

I peered intensely at the dullish brown wall. "Well it's not so cherry or cheery anymore."

"Regretfully, not," continued Walter. "Not even this clay can stand up to the city's pollution. The brick was made at the Don Valley Pressed Brick Works, which has now been closed for decades. But over its lifetime, it produced 43 million red bricks that built so many of Toronto's houses and iconic buildings, including Massey Hall, Casa Loma, the Ontario Legislature building, Toronto General Hospital, and Convocation Hall."

"And they used the same kind of bricks for a warehouse like this?" I asked.

"Local materials and production made it an affordable option even though it was considered a luxurious one, from an aesthetic point of view. And, although discolored, the brick is quite durable."

"Really fascinating," said Marco. "But can we first walk to a spot just over there?" said Marco, pointing away from the building. "The thing we wanted you to look at is there. Maybe you can shed some historical light on that."

"You have somehow managed to pique my interest," said Walter gleefully. We both followed after Marco.

"One of our curators has a particular interest in the massive pit that resulted from the excavation of all that clay for the bricks," Walter said while stumbling on. "They uncovered layers of shale, revealing a geological record stretching back two million years."

"Here we are," said Marco. "But..."

I looked down at the gutter lining the sidewalk and was astonished by the sight. The symbol we had seen when here with Benny no longer looked washed out at all. In fact, it had clearly been repainted, and the colors had a beautiful luminescence to them.

"This is most interesting," said Walter. "Did one of you create this?"

Marco and I exchanged glances. "Why would you say that?" I said.

"Well it had to have been someone from the Museum. Or someone who knows the Museum well."

"I don't get it." Marco crossed his arms.

"Surely our most perceptive security guard has noticed this on his rounds multitudes of times."

Marco shrugged.

"Oh really, must I give it away so easily?" Walter glanced at me and then at Marco and then back towards me again. "It is one of the symbols from the Rotunda's mosaic ceiling."

"Oh my god, I can't believe I missed that." Marco exhaled heavily.

"The answer was right under our noses the whole time," I said.

"Rather above your heads." Walter winked.

"I don't go into the Museum's Rotunda much these days," I said, "not since it became the ceremonial entrance for the building and we shifted the main entry to Bloor Street."

"But I do. I still go on rounds there ALL the time. I just flunked Security 101."

"The Museum's first director conceived the design of the ceiling with the construction of the 1933 addition. It is intended to reflect the breadth of the collections. The various patterns and symbols represent cultures throughout the ages and around the globe."

"That, I do know," I said.

"The ceiling is made from thousands of sheets of imported Venetian glass, which were cut into more than a million square pieces. It took more than eight months to install with a team of very skilled workers, whom I suspect were imports themselves."

"You couldn't recreate that in this day and age. Well you

could, but the Museum certainly couldn't afford it," added Marco.

"Do you know the meaning of this symbol on the sidewalk?" I asked.

"Iconography can be most complex," said Walter.

"I'll say," I sighed. "I barely made it through some of my art history courses. You have to know the bible inside out to interpret medieval and Renaissance art."

"The Rotunda dome mosaics actually hark back to the magnificent mosaics of the Byzantine world and Eastern Europe."

"Hey, that's what you and Benny said, right?" said Marco.

"Who is Benny?" asked Walter.

"Just a friend," said Marco. "It's kind of a long story, but she was the one who first spotted this."

"What about the symbol?" I prompted.

"In this case, the motif is primarily decorative, save for the symbol of the cross. It is baffling why it's distorted it...making it look like it is being washed into the sewer?"

"That's all you can give us?" asked Marco.

"Actually, there is something represented on the ceiling that is not depicted here. Perhaps it was too intricate for our mysterious artist to paint on concrete. Or perhaps it is the missing element to which they are attempting to draw our attention. But for what purpose?"

Suddenly the details of this section of the ceiling became vivid in my mind. "It's the words that are missing. 'That all men may know his work.'" I recited.

"What's going on here?" said Marco. "Is this some kind of a Da Vinci Code thing?"

Chapter Twelve

"I am most impressed, Kalena," said Walter.

I grinned. "My neurons do fire some days."

"But do you know from what source those words are drawn?"

"Not a clue."

"It's a passage from Job in the Old Testament – a reflection of a time when our Canadian population had a much stronger religious foundation."

"That all men may know his work, hmm." I paused for a few seconds. "Is that a reference to the Museum's role as a keeper of the world's cultural treasures? That by keeping them safely housed, 'all men' will have the opportunity to 'know his works'?"

Walter cranked his head towards me. "You are full of surprises. That interpretation has never occurred to me, perhaps because I have always focused on the literal meaning." Walter continued. "He seals the hand of every man; that all men may know his work."

"Well that clears everything up – NOT," said Marco.

"I agree with your assessment. There is no single understanding. Brenda and I have had heated discussions on this matter."

Marco and I shared a what-the-frig glance.

"Brenda was a student of classic studies, and I have done my share of reading ancient texts, the bible being among them. It makes for stimulating conversation."

"I bet," I said.

"It is actually quite intriguing, now that I have pondered it, as the passage is a contemplation on weather with a regard to God, that we must notice the glory of God not just in thunder and lightning, but in the more common elements of weather."

"Like rain?" I extended my hand out to check for rain drops.

"Precisely! And in the rain and snow of winter, God sealeth up the hand of every man...that is, God has confined all beings to their dwellings. And in this confinement, 'that all men may know his work' refers to the notion that we are intended to be aware of our dependence on God, that we are to remember that God is controlling everything, not just mankind...by way of the elements. It is meant to be humbling."

"That's rather prophetic, when you think about it," I said, "with everything that's happening on the planet as a result of climate change, our disrespect for nature, and man's hubris. We haven't been slowing down to listen to the messages about taking care of Mother Earth, and now she's yelling at us the only way she knows how."

"Well there's a message we should definitely listen to." Marco was staring upwards.

I tilted my head to the heavens and saw that the sky had turned an unusual greyish green color. "That's not normal."

"Run!" roared Walter. "We're about to be pummeled by hail. Either that or the stage is being set for a tornado."

"Oh, for crying out loud. You guys dash ahead. I won't be far behind." I knew I shouldn't have worn these Fly London sling-backs. The sculpted heels made me totter when I was standing, let along running. But before I knew it, Marco was at my side. He slid one arm under my knees and the other around my upper back. I was raised into the air as though I was a weightless blow-up doll.

"Put me down, you nutbar!" I barked.

Walter stood to the side of us, eyes enlarged, while Marco released me, gently allowing my feet to grace the ground once again. "You are insane sometimes!" I yelled.

But before we could draw our next breaths, with the ferocity of squash balls in play, we were being pounded by hail and merciless rain, our opportunity for a safe escape vanquished.

"Just jump on my damned back, will you!" Marco one-eightied and stooped down. I wrapped my arms around his neck, hopped up, straddled my legs around his waist, and he straightened up.

"Ow, ow!" Walter yelped while running, simultaneously trying to deflect the ice spheres from hitting his head.

"Ow, ow!" I yelped. Marco was a bit wider in the girth than I had thought and clenching onto his waist with my thighs had triggered spasms.

The robust security guard scrambled to the building entrance, leaving Walter in his wake. My feet bounced up and down as though loosely attached to my ankles, and one of my shoes flew off. I released one arm from around Marco's neck and pointed down behind us.

"Leave it to me!" Walter scooped up my shoe. "I have it, I have it!" he whooped with delight.

"What's going on back there?" cried Marco, his breath labored.

"Don't worry about it. Just keep running," I said flailing my free arm trying to swat away some of the hailstones.

It was just moments before we came to the main door of the off-site storage building, but there was nothing to shelter us from the elements. Walter handed me my shoe, pulled out a large ring of keys, fumbled, and settled on a distinct Medeco key. After inserting and turning it, he entered a number into a coded door lock beneath the keyhole, and I heard the movement of a deadbolt sliding back into its housing mechanism. "Get in, quickly," cried Walter.

I slid down Marco's back, and as my shoeless foot hit earth, it became saturated with water from the melting hail. I limped through the doorway, and then one leg collapsed as my psoas muscle contracted uncontrollably.

Walter jerked towards me. "Oh, my goodness, are you injured?"

"Huh, what?" said Marco turning his head, but before he had fully rotated, I pressed firmly into my leg and recouped my stance.

"Nothing," I said, looking innocently at him.

Marco grinned, looked ahead again, then suddenly spun his gaze back to me.

I smiled slyly. "What?"

Walter flipped a switch, turning on a small bank of fluorescent lights. Meanwhile, I reinserted my drenched appendage into my shoe. This was going to be a most unpleasant walk-about.

"Awfully dark in here," I said.

"The banks of lights are specifically programmed so that a limited area is illuminated at any given time," said Walter.

"To protect the specimens and artifacts susceptible to more intense light, I presume." The darkness was eerie, but as my eyes adjusted to the low-level lighting and the magnificent sight that loomed before me came into focus, my discomfort was transformed into supreme awe of the surroundings.

There were rows and rows and rows of floor-to-ceiling metal warehouse shelving, like that found in a Home Depot, but instead of construction supplies, the steel shelves were stocked with riches beyond comprehension. I couldn't see too far in, but it was like walking into Noah's Ark, except that pairs of animals had been replaced with every specimen, article, or representation of science and culture this planet had to offer since the beginning of time – and from what I could make out, in duplicate, triplicate, and even quadruplicate in some cases. I felt like I had died and ascended to a spectacular Shangri-La created especially for the most ardent of history and science lovers.

"Amazing," said Marco. "I mean, I've been in every corner of the Museum, inside every single storage area, behind every closed door, but this place..."

"It is a matter of the scale and of everything being situated on one level here rather than distributed on different floors as they are in the curatorial center," said Walter.

"The weight load, huh?" said Marco. "They had to go vertical in the downtown space."

"Exactly."

"It really makes you realize," I said, "that the sampling of collections we have on display at the Museum is so infinitesimally small."

"Well, it is time to put those tongues of yours back into your mouths, so to speak, and to start documenting things," said Walter.

"Oh, right." I dug into my bag and pulled out my phone.

"Did you not bring a real camera?" asked Walter.

"No need. The quality of pictures produced by phones these days is pretty extraordinary. And for a point-and-shooter like me, this is the best option – all auto adjust, built-in flash, and I can email the pictures directly from the phone."

"I suppose," said Walter. "I just believe a device developed to carry our voices could never replace a piece of equipment specifically aimed at taking pictures."

"I'm sure most photographers agree, but you can't beat convenience." I drew the phone upwards and quickly snapped a shot of Walter.

He immediately covered his face with his hands. "Oh, dear. Please do not do that."

"Wouldn't you like me to send a picture of you to Brenda?" I chuckled.

"Don't you dare! She would never approve of such narcissism."

I took shot after shot of the view from the entrance, zooming in and out to get different perspectives. A panoramic shot would be great, I thought, so I fiddled with the phone's settings. While doing so, I inadvertently photographed the floor. I was about to delete the image, but when I glanced at it on the LCD screen, it gripped my attention. I stared at the phone more intently, then peered at the ground, back at the phone, and again at the painted concrete surface. Walter and Marco were a few steps ahead, so I bounced forward and tugged on the back of Marco's jacket. As he revolved towards me, I drew my index finger to my lips, then rotated my phone's screen towards his face. He pulled back, and then zoomed in towards the device, eyes widening. Our glances ricocheted off each other several times while Walter forged ahead, oblivious that we had stopped following him.

Marco crouched down and skimmed his hand along the surface of the floor. Before our eyes were paint splotches similar to those we had found on the concrete outdoors and on Marco's car during our last visit to the area, the same type of marks we had followed to this same building that rainy night. Inside they had barely been visible to the naked eye because of the grey on grey palette and the low-level lighting. It was very different than what had been done to Marco's vehicle, which was tantamount to vandalism, and obviously executed to attract our notice. Why the subtle version here? Was the painter being playful, or was this a test of some sort?

"Helloooo back there," bellowed Walter. "What are you up to? This is no time for lollygagging."

"Just tying up a loose shoelace," said Marco.

"Oh, indeed. Safety first."

"And I need to take photos, remember?"

"Yes, yes. Understood. I will attempt to adjust my pace accordingly."

I swiveled back towards Marco. "Should we tell Walter?"

"Not yet. This might be nothing."

"Nothing. This is pretty deliberate."

Marco popped up out of his crouching position. "C'mon," he whispered. "Let's follow the path and see where it takes us. We'll include Walter only if necessary. We can't have him losing his job."

Walking forward again, I stopped dead in my tracks. In turn, Marco stepped on my heel and my foot came right out of the shoe.

"What the heck? Are you okay?" asked Marco.

"Yeah, yeah." Once more, I grabbed my useless sling-back and slipped my foot back into it. "I should have used my brake lights. I just can't get over this place. I mean, look at all these dinosaur bones," I said gazing at countless shelves loaded with monumental femurs, colossal vertebrae, and massive skeleton bits and pieces of everything from feet and tailbones to skulls and rib cages. Each piece sported a large tag with a series of numbers on it, but I noticed that in one area instead of hand-written numbers, there were bar codes, evidence of the Museum's move to digitization.

"I know what you mean. It's like a graveyard for the animals in *Jurassic Park*," said Marco.

"But these aren't from a film. They're from real creatures that occupied the Earth, and it looks like we have the remains of every dinosaur that ever populated the planet."

"C'mon," said Marco. "Let's catch up to Walter. He's following the trail, and he doesn't even know it."

After having snapped several pictures of the disassembled ancient monoliths resting peacefully on the shelving, I sauntered forward, every few steps looking down, noticing the light spray of grey paint. "This is fantastic, Walter. These pictures will be an amazing addition to our photographic library. Stewart will be over the moon."

"I am delighted to add to his level of satisfaction. This way please," motioned Walter with his extended arm. "We will be turning down the next aisle. As a student of European history, Kalena, you may find yourself even further gob smacked, as the British say."

Suddenly a shiver swept over my body, and I began to rub my arms and hands.

"Yes, it is a bit like strolling about in a massive walk-in freezer. Remember that in the galleries, many collections are housed in temperature- and humidity-controlled cases. The intention here is to maintain similar conditions, so things are kept on the cooler side, and the humidity is kept as stable as possible, particularly for some of the collections we are about to encounter. But, despite all these efforts and precautions, the massive amount of rain we have had this year has created some challenges for our curatorial staff," said Walter.

"There is a touch of damp in the air." I trembled once again.

"Paintings are the most susceptible to damage, so there is one area upon which we will be encountering soon enough, that is more carefully climate controlled. But what say you of this section?" Walter waved his arm like a graceful game-show hostess directing our attention to a section that looked like the vestiges of a medieval battleground. There were scatterings of armor strewn across multiple levels of shelving, most of it in pieces. The bulk of it was what one might consider standard European protective coverings, but I could discern some more exotic armor, probably from countries like China and Japan. There were even intricate and highly ornamented wooden shields, plates, and spears that I presumed hailed from Africa and South America.

"Whoa!" roared Marco. "My nephew and niece would freak if they saw this. They love this stuff."

"Funny how kids are drawn to the sediments of war and symbols of extreme violence. I'm not sure where that comes from," I said.

Marco looked at me with a bewildered expression.

"I mean, you couldn't pay me to watch *Game of Thrones*," I said.

"Are you serious?" remarked Marco.

"People are getting hacked to bits—"

Walter stepped in and moved us away from each other

as though sending us to opposite corners of a boxing ring. "Now boys and girls, shall we continue?"

"Sure, sure. No one's going to win this round." Marco grinned, and the three of us proceeded down the passage, but he was scanning the area towards the lofty ceiling. "There aren't any cameras covering some of these aisles," Marco said.

"That is not something we divulge to the public. As you know, although surveillance equipment has come down in cost considerably over the years, it would be an enormous expense to fully equip this building," said Walter.

"Yeah, budgets are tight. And I guess the Museum wants to make sure the most valuable stuff in the main building is monitored properly," said Marco.

"We are coming to yet another fascinating area of the facility. Unlike your niece and nephew, it is this zone that stirs something in me. And it is one of the more recent additions to the building."

Turning yet another corner and still following the subtle trail that had been laid out, one could not help but release a gasp.

"Holeeeeeeeee," said Marco.

"This is straight out of some Sci Fi B movie," I said.

"It is something," said Walter.

Before us were shelves full of jars – large jars, small jars, roundish jars, square jars – all containing clear liquid and specimens of every conceivable sort. I turned on my phone's flashlight app, and the illuminated sight before me was truly haunting. Hundreds, probably thousands of fish, sea life, and land creatures floated lifelessly in their ghostly containers. Those whose bodies were turned in our direction seemed to be staring directly at us.

"All of these specimens are suspended in alcohol. If ever there was anything you wanted to learn about aquatic creatures, this is certainly the place to do so. Everything is organized by genus and species. They are whole specimens, and they have been stained to feature various elements. As you can see, the fish turn translucent when preserved, but with the dyes, one can make out the nervous or circulatory systems, for example."

"Cool," said Marco.

"I seem to recall we had no choice but to move all this off site?" I said.

"Yes, indeed. Because of their extraordinary weight, they cannot be stored on upper levels without adding costly structural supports. At the same time, if they are stored below grade, there is a heightened risk of explosion."

"And those things over there, how come they aren't made of glass?" asked Marco, pointing to metal canisters evenly distributed throughout the area.

"Those cylinders contain a specific kind of gas that, should some alcohol fumes escape and combust, the containers would release a formula that would minimize the damage from a critical incident. I should add that maintaining a steady, cool temperature in this warehouse is just as, if not more important, for these collections as the others. Steady temperatures help maintain the integrity of the jars' seals by limiting expansion and contraction. It also prevents the proliferation of this kind of thing." Walter tilted a jar about a foot in diameter towards us displaying mold growing on the lid. "This is a problem with which the Museum struggled incessantly when these collections were in the main building. To date, it's proven to be less of a problem here."

"That whole combustibility thing, you would think

they'd keep the temperature even colder here."

"Effectively not, Kalena. There is no evidence that sub-flash point temperatures reduce the danger of fire," said Marco.

"Huh?" I said.

"Short version," said Marco, "is that cold temperatures don't necessarily reduce the risk of fire or explosion."

I gaped at Marco.

"Getting your Ontario Security License involves a pretty big dose of health and safety training."

I raised my phone to snap photo after photo as we sauntered through rows containing jars occupied by squids, snakes, octopi, lizards, small mammals, birds, and even insects. The selection seemed so vast and all-inclusive that I was expecting us to run across shrunken heads and human brains at any moment. But not once did I allow myself to lose the path of translucent paint splatter below our feet. It was almost as if Walter had been robotically programmed to follow the earmarked route.

After we turned yet another corner, we encountered a most curious construct ahead of us. Built into a corner of the warehouse was an independent structure, a building within a building. Its walls did not reach the ceiling, and it sported a roof. It had the appearance of an over-sized vault, and it looked as though it was hermetically sealed.

"This must be where the paintings are stored," I said.

"Spot on, Kalena. This is the only part of the storage site that is both locked and alarmed."

"And you have access?" I asked.

Walter pulled out a set of keys while smirking like a mad scientist. He lumbered closer to the door and then halted abruptly. "What is the meaning of this?...I don't understand."

Marco and I dashed forward to join the stuttering librarian and saw that the door to the vault had been splattered more obviously with the grey paint. Walter's gaze dropped to the ground, and Marco and I looked at each other.

Walter turned 180 degrees and scuttled back in the direction from which we had come, his stare fixated on the ground. When his pace accelerated, I shouted out, "Walter, STOP!"

"I must get to the bottom of this. Don't you see? The building has been compromised. We must discover the origins of this trail."

"The front door!" exclaimed Marco.

"Pardon me?"

"It starts at the front door," I added. "Well, actually, outside the door. It begins a ways away and leads to the building."

Walter advanced towards us, glaring, and beginning to look as though he was about to blow a gasket. "I knew it. I knew it. I knew you had some ulterior motive for coming here, but I tried, I tried so hard, so very, very hard to give you both the benefit of the doubt."

"We didn't know this was going to be here, honest," I said. "We were surprised ourselves. I only noticed the paint on the floor when I accidentally snapped a picture of the ground."

"Marco, I am most disappointed in you. As soon as you noticed this you should have called Malik."

"I thought it was premature."

"WHAT? There has been a clear breach here, and you did not think it was appropriate to call our head of security?"

"I think we should go inside the vault." I said.

Walter's head snapped in my direction. "Are you mad?"

"There's no sign anything else has been tampered with – no empty spots on shelves, or anything like that," said Marco.

Walter hesitated and then blurted out, "I must be out of my mind." He marched to the paintings vault and inserted the key. After turning the door handle, a piercing alarm sounded and Walter slipped past the threshold. He fiddled with something, the alarm stopped ringing, and the lighting inside switched on.

Marco and I dashed into the doorway simultaneously, our shoulders colliding.

"Uh, sorry," I said.

"Uh, sorry," he said.

"Would you two cease clowning about. I swear."

"Get a grip, will you, Marco?" I said with just the tiniest hint of a smile. Marco rolled his eyes in my direction. But Walter was right, it was time to get serious.

"So, this part isn't much different than the painting storage in the main building," I said as I assessed the space. The floor and the ceiling each sported a pair of wide-set rails that held in place an impressive number of brushed aluminum screens. Each panel ran almost the full height and width of the room, leaving just a narrow passageway through which one could meander. I guessed that the room ran about a fifth of the length of the warehouse, so it was quite expansive. Every ten screens or so, there was enough of a gap to slide a section of panels so that one could walk between the compressed area of screens.

Framed with sturdy metal along all four sides of the edging, the screens were also kept rigid by two pieces of steel that cut each large rectangular pane into four sections. The result was a relatively lightweight, sturdy moveable wall system upon which paintings were hung in as dense a configuration as possible. Had the dividers been twice the height, they would have had the semblance of eighteenth-century French salon walls saturated from top to bottom with painted canvases displayed for public viewing. The only thing that broke the clean aesthetics of the space was an old desk and chair in one corner of the room likely set up for curatorial staff who might be conducting research or tagging the enclosed collection.

While standing beside Walter, I noticed his shallow, rapid breath deescalate. "I don't see any paint markings in here, do either of you?"

Marco and I both scoured the ground. "Not that I can see," said Marco. "Kalena, can you shine a light down here. Maybe they changed the paint color to match the beige floors in here."

I launched the flashlight app on my phone, directed its glare towards the ground and panned it around. "Doesn't look like it...Whoever it was, I guess they couldn't get past the alarm in here or didn't want to risk setting it off."

"Very odd that our intruder would go to such pains to direct us here and then...drop it," said Walter.

"I agree," added Marco. "Something doesn't make sense. Let's walk the whole distance of this aisle. I have a feeling if any more clues were left, they won't be buried somewhere that would take forever to find."

"You mean, in case we're idiots?" I asked.

"Could be. But someone really seems keen about us finding something," said Marco.

"Or us finding something missing," I said.

"Let's do a quick sweep but let's put some of those on

first." Marco bounded over to the desk and grabbed three pairs of white cotton gloves.

"Splendid idea," said Walter. "Aside from compromising the integrity of a possible crime scene, the gloves will prevent us from leaving any deposits of oils or metabolic wastes, such as salts and urea on any of the paintings."

"What are you looking at me for, Walter? I don't have any urea on my hands," I said.

"I don't know what that is, but it sure doesn't sound appetizing," said Marco as he tossed gloves at each of us. "I'm feeling a bit O.J. Simpsonish." He was struggling to encase his hands with the one-size-fits-all gloves.

"Shall we move forward?" asked Walter. "Perhaps you should proceed first, Marco."

Marco squeezed ahead and, behind him, Walter and I aligned in single file. Our pace was more considered as we scoured the narrow aisle for some kind of tell-tale sign. The three of us were completely unfamiliar with the inventory housed here. How could we possibly make a determination if something was missing? Then something glistened on the floor ahead of us.

"Do you see that, Marco?" I asked.

"Yippers."

The next few steps we took felt as though we were crossing through a worm hole and everything had been reduced to slow motion. We then halted and stood like petrified trees, hypnotized, our gazes fixated on the patch of floor at our feet.

"This is big trouble, isn't it?" I asked.

"The biggest of the big," replied Walter.

CHAPTER THIRTEEN

The symbol before us painted in gold and probably applied using a stencil, based on its relatively clean lines, was, I felt, going to create a time-consuming whirlwind of activity for which I had neither energy nor patience. I was still trying to whip up a supply of commemorative medals for a museum opening. What had I been thinking? I wasn't thinking, actually.

"This thing is from the Rotunda ceiling as well," said Marco, breaking me out of my reverie.

"Bravo!" said Walter.

"It's the winged lion of St. Mark, the emblem of Venice," I said, now fully present in our immediate circumstances. "My Renaissance art history background comes in handy once in a blue moon."

The depiction of the lion on the concrete floor was in the same hues of gold, rust, and bronze as the Museum's version on the Rotunda ceiling. The lines were simple, stylized, and mirrored works created at a time in European art history before artists had mastered the theories of perspective – as a result it had a two-dimensional sensibility to it. The mythical creature had one full wing behind its head and body, while the second one was folded in. To fit into the square outline, the lion's tale was curved above its hind quarters and tucked in under the expanse of the extended wing.

"I should point out," interjected Walter, "that the lion

on its own is the symbol of Venice, but when illustrated, as it is here, with one paw resting upon the bible, it is technically the symbol of St. Mark. This reduced version is too small to show the Latin phrase normally depicted on the book's cover."

"Do you think that phrase could be a clue? What is it, Walter?" I asked.

"PAX – EVAN TIBI – GELI MAR – STA CE – MEVS which translates into 'may peace be with you."

"All very interesting, guys" interjected Marco. "But am I the only one who's noticed that the tail looks like an arrow? I mean, lion's tails don't normally curl up over their backs like that."

The three of us paused in silence for a few seconds when, without warning, Marco leapt over to the moveable screen at which the lion's tail appeared to be pointing and started to separate the adjacent panels in opposite directions.

In an instant, there was a two-foot gap on either side of the targeted panel. Walter and I gathered in with Marco, but there was no suspicious opening in the arrangement of mounted paintings on either screen. Instead, what stood out was what appeared to be a painting, about 2' x 3', sealed in layers of bubble wrap and paper. And then I remembered Benny's video, of the person walking in the rain with an object that looked like a covered canvas...and they were scrambling in the direction towards the Museum's off-site storage – not away from it. Whoever it was hadn't stolen anything. They had brought something into the building and then led us right to it.

CHAPTER FOURTEEN

Marco reached into his pocket and pulled out a Swiss Army knife. But the gesture elicited a pained squeal from Walter.

"Walter?" I looked at him in puzzlement.

"I...I...I just don't know if we should open it. How will we explain our actions when we talk to Malik and the...uh...authorities?"

"We'll tell them exactly what happened. When Kalena was taking pictures of the vault, we noticed the symbol on the ground, got suspicious, found this wrapped painting and that's that. I'm keeping the gloves on so I won't leave any of my own finger prints."

"But we might be compromising important clues for the police," said Walter.

"It's not a murder scene. We won't go to prison for this," said Marco.

Walter shot a grieved expression towards Marco and then lowered his eyes. "If we must," he said.

The package appeared to be attached to the screen by hooks that were mounted on the outside of the bubble wrap encasement. Marco tenderly lifted and then pulled the painting towards himself and gently lowered it to the ground, setting it down softly.

"Doesn't look like I'll be needing this after all," said

Marco as he deposited the knife back in his pocket. The painting was painstakingly wrapped with the edges of the tape at the corners left hanging so one could simply pull on them to open up the protective covering.

Cautiously, Marco clasped the tape between his fingertips and tugged the bubble wrap away from all four corners of the object. Underneath was a layer of translucent paper wrapping.

"Whoever left this here certainly knows how to take care of a painting," said Walter. "They have used glassine."

"Museum quality paper, then?" I asked.

"Yes. It is manufactured by supercalendering. After pressing and drying, the paper web is passed through a stack of alternating steel and fiber-covered rolls which flatten the paper fibers to face in the same direction. The result is a product that is air-, water-, and grease-resistant."

Too much information, I was thinking, but I didn't want to piss off Walter at this point.

"This is like a giant envelope," said Marco, while shifting the painting forward to demonstrate that the paper was sealed. "Guess I will need the knife." Marco allowed the package to lean on his leg, and once again removed the Swiss Army knife from his pocket.

"CAREFUL!" screamed Walter.

Marco and I both jerked and the item started to fall away from its resting place against Marco's leg. Quick to react, Marco snagged the parcel before it met the ground. I released a deep sigh.

"Please don't do that again, or I'm going to have to seal your mouth with duct tape," I said.

"Apologies, apologies. I promise to restrain myself," said Walter.

Marco unfolded a few of the knife's attachments, including a small, sharp-edged blade. After reinserting the knife's unneeded accessories into the casing, he sliced into the paper along one of the shorter sides with the precision of a forensic scientist cautiously cutting into a cadaver.   Once he'd slit the whole of one side, he took hold of what appeared to be a frame, and with great delicacy, slid a painting out, then set it to rest on the floor, leaning against one of the moveable panels.

"Whoa," I said.

"Is that all you have to say, Ms. Art Expert?" asked Marco.

"Well this is a little outside my expertise. The painting looks like it was produced long after the Italian Renaissance, like by a couple of hundred years."

Marco smiled smugly at me. "Well, at least I get why our intruder used a symbol for Venice as a marker. No doubt about where this scene is set," he said, focused on the painting.

Marco was correct about that. What we witnessed before us was a representation of a Venetian canal, easily recognizable because of the plethora of gondolas and characteristic Venetian architecture. At first glance, it seemed the city had been captured at dusk, but upon closer inspection, trapped beneath centuries-old darkened varnish most likely were warmer and vibrant tones of greens and blues of the water and skies. The breadth of the canal was in the foreground, and it tapered back to a point, creating an elongated triangular shape. It wasn't a part of Venice I could identify with my meagre first-hand knowledge of the city, other than possibly one of the domes of San Marco in the distance.

"Looks like it could be a Canaletto," I said, hazarding a

guess. I turned to Walter. "You're awfully quiet."

"Yes, well this is such a coincidence that I find myself rather speechless. As you know, before Brenda left for London, we escaped briefly to Los Angeles. One of our stops was the Getty Center where they had an exhibit of Venetian *vedute*."

"Ve-what-ey?" said Marco.

"*Veduta*, is the singular," I said. "View."

"Oh yeah, sure."

"It is a highly detailed, usually large-scale painting, but can be smaller, of a cityscape or some other vista," added Walter.

"Are you saying you saw this in in the Getty?" I asked.

"No, not at all. But I do not believe it's a Canaletto. Very close, however. I think it may have been painted by his nephew, Bernardo Bellotto, who exploited his uncle's fame and occasionally appropriated his appellation. Having two artists from the eighteenth century use the name Canaletto created some confusion in subsequent centuries. But while in Los Angeles, we beheld a most exquisite painting...also a view of the Grand Canal, but it had a tediously long name. If you could deploy that phone of yours and look up Bellotto, please, it could shed some light on this matter."

I raised my phone, tapped the icon for Google Voice, and spoke into the device, clearly articulating all the syllables, "Ber-nar-do Bell-o-tto Grand Can-al." Within moments the search results populated the screen. "Is this it? *View of the Grand Canal: Santa Maria della Salute and the Dogana from Campo Santa Maria Zobenigo,*" I said using my best Italian accent.

"Now that's a mouthful," chortled Marco.

"Yes, on both counts. That is indeed the painting we

saw. But what is relevant for us is that I recall a most interesting story about one of his other paintings..."

Walter continued to ramble while I pressed the link to another site in the search results that had caught my eye – 'Additional Missing Works of Art | Monuments Men Foundation.' "Oh man," I said.

"Excuse me," said Walter.

Quickly navigating deeper into the site, I scrolled through the pages until I came upon a painting that matched the cityscape in front of us. My throat instantaneously contracted, and my voice crackled as I spit out, "It's Bernardo Bellotto, all right...his *View of the Grand Canal in Venice*."

"Is it part of the Museum's collection?" asked Marco.

Walter looked at me knowingly. "I do not believe that would be possible."

"How come?" asked Marco.

"Because according to this site," I continued, "it's the property of the Borbone-Parma collection, but it was taken by German soldiers from the Villa delle Pianore in Lucca, Italy, in the spring of 1944. This painting went missing during World War II, part of the Rape of Europa, as it has come to be known." I paused. "And it's never surfaced since then."

Walter moved closer to the painting, smoothing his gloved hand over the top edge of the frame. "Until now, that is."

CHAPTER FIFTEEN

The plan had originally been to return to the Museum by lunch, so all I had with me was the Giddy Yoyo chocolate bar. But it was neither the time nor place to eat a chocolate bar nor to bellyache about my aching belly. It also didn't seem appropriate to alert anyone that I was entering a mild state of delirium.

Malik had arrived on the scene around 1 pm. There were a few satellite office areas scattered throughout the warehouse, and our head of security sat the three of us down in front of a desk, then planted himself behind it, in interrogation mode. I thought this was a simple site visit...take a few pictures...in and out, he had said. We thought the same thing, too, sir, I had replied.

Prior to this, I had never called Malik Roumanos 'sir' as we had a relatively casual rapport, both having worked at the Museum forever. He was of Arabic origin but had come to Canada in his youth by way of Australia, so he had a slight trace of an Aussie accent. He had once told me his name meant 'leader and ruler,' and he certainly represented the connotation well. Tall and lean with dark features all around, he had a stately presence. He commanded a great deal of respect at the Museum, and he was known for his firmness, which was a prerequisite for his position. I also knew him to be fair and compassionate. But kindness was not in order for this day's conversation.

Why are the three of you wearing gloves, he had asked? Oh, these, we had answered, raising all of our hands into the air like dolts. We put them on as soon as we entered the painting area...in case we were tempted to touch any of canvases, and, well, we just hadn't removed them yet, Walter had answered. Did you notice the trail of paint leading to the vault, Malik had asked. A trail of paint, I had responded. Hmm, Malik had said. Why didn't you call me as soon as you saw that symbol on the ground, Malik had asked. We thought it was a practical joke, sir, Marco had answered. You know how those curators like to kid around, he had said, like those signs they have in the Bug Room back at the Museum. And so you took it upon yourselves to open up a sealed package in an area of the warehouse that houses the most precious of our artifacts, Malik had stated. The three of us had all looked down at our shoes. And you suspect this painting was part of some Nazi plunder. Yes, we had nodded. And how did you arrive at that conclusion, Malik had asked. Kalena did a Google Voice search on her phone. Quite marvelous isn't it what one can do with a phone in this day and age, Walter had answered. Malik shook his head. And you believe it's authentic, Malik had asked. Well, obviously we have no way of knowing, I had responded. But it looks genuinely old...or it's a really good fake. Hmm, Malik had said. Are you going to call New Scotland Yard, I had asked. All three men had turned towards me at once. Well, that's what they do in the movies, I had said, grinning. Not the right time for levity, I had decided. I don't know if we call the police at this point, Malik had said. There's no standard protocol for this kind of situation.

Marco and I had seemed to be on the same wavelength as neither of us had chosen to bring up Benny's video or our previous adventure. After all, we had no way of knowing if there was a direct connection between those events and this painting, I had tried to convince myself.

Maybe we should have one of our conservators have a look at the piece, I had suggested. At least they could determine the approximate age of the painting and tell us if it's an amateur copy. Walter interjected saying a specialist in the period would need to do an analysis. That might involve a call to the Art Gallery of Ontario. Hmm, Malik had said. If the three of you didn't look like a trio of Mickey Mouse wannabes wearing those white gloves, it would probably be easier for me to take your suggestions more seriously. At that particular moment my stomach had grumbled rather loudly, and we had all burst out laughing. But soon we had settled back into a more solemn demeanor.

Of all the museums in all the towns in all the world, she walks into mine, I had said. Once again, the three of them had turned their gaze towards me, clearly not getting my reference to *Casablanca*. I mean first of all, every museum on the planet is concerned about people stealing from the collections, not putting a stolen item into it, I had said. And of all the museums around the globe, why did this end up here? Extremely, good question, Malik had responded.

* * * * *

Marco rode back to the Museum with Malik at his boss's request. Suspecting that Malik wanted to separate us in the way that police detectives question persons of interest in different rooms to trip them up on their stories, I felt uneasy. But had I objected to these transportation arrangements suspicion might have been raised. So, I surrendered. Walter and

95

I journeyed back to the Museum almost in uninterrupted silence, and the stillness gave me the space to ponder the circumstances with a little more objectivity. By the time we reached the Museum, I had decided that Marco and I should fully disclose everything to Malik, including everything from Benny's discoveries to our interpretation of the various symbols. Marco and I had nothing to gain by keeping certain facts to ourselves, and transparency seemed to be the best strategy, at least for maintaining my job.

Upon arrival at the Museum's Shipping and Receiving dock, the area was congested and there was no room for Walter to park. The Director and the Chairman of the Board were the only individuals with designated parking spots for their vehicles on site. So, Walter dropped me off near the Staff Entrance and drove away in search of a spot somewhere on the nearby University of Toronto campus. I was feeling faint. My head was throbbing, my blood sugar was low, and my body was sensing the cold and damp more than ever.

Inside the Staff Entrance, opposite the Security Desk, there was a mature woman with hair dyed coal black, lips painted 1950s red, and with an insipid skin pallor incapable of complimenting the saturated colors of her hair and lips. But the woman stole my admiration with an outfit that could have been torn directly off actor Diane Keaton's body. She wore a black and white checkered trench, open at the neck line, with the starched collar of a white shirt popping out. Around her neck was a choker with four strands of pearls, stripe-like with alternating rows of white and black. Her wide-legged and cuffed trousers appeared to be of a luxurious black neutral tweed, and they were long enough to just cover a pair of adorable black-and-white Oxford flats. To top off the brilliant look, she sported a small portfolio case, black with the tiniest white polka dots. I wanted it. I wanted her whole damn outfit, actually.

The woman looked familiar, and I wondered if she was perhaps a member of the Museum's board. Then as I approached the Security Desk, the guard announced loudly, "This is her, Dr. Zelinka. This is Kalena Boyko," almost startling me out of my still soggy shoes.

I swiveled around to face the woman. Of course. When I had Googled her during my search for a medals artist, I had seen photos of her on her Wikipedia page. I wondered if she was even aware she had a Wikipedia page.

"Dr. Zelinka," I said, "we don't have an appointment, do we?" I pulled out my cell phone.

"You may put that thing away," she said. "A woman of a certain age makes her own schedule. I was at the university on a matter, and I decided this was the most opportune time for us to meet."

By this point, my legs were quivering from hunger, but I was certain a lecture on professional courtesy would be futile. "Very well," I said. "I'll need you to sign in and follow me."

"I have already done so. Please take me to your office immediately. I have been held hostage here long enough."

I turned my head to the guard and pursed my lips, and he responded with a good-luck wink. He handed me Dr. Zelinka's temporary security badge, and I, in turn, passed it to the visitor. She snatched the pass and attached it to her portfolio, which sported a handy-dandy clip. "You should actually put that around your neck," I said.

"I do not think so."

I sighed. "This way, then. I'll be taking you through the school entrance and cafeteria hallway."

"You are not informing me of anything new. I have been a member here longer than you have been in this world. Proceed."

Dr. Zelinka's curmudgeonly behavior was testing my already paper-thin patience. But after a few steps, I adjusted my pace to her slightly slower amble, and despite some darker thoughts, I tried not to put the woman in danger as we wound our way through throngs of rambunctious school children scurrying through the long and wide hallway. "My office is just ahead," I said pointing towards the Mugwump.

"GOOD HEAVENS!" Dr. Zelinka screamed. "Where are you taking me?"

"The door to my office is just around the other side of the Mugwump." A smile was brewing inside my body and a laugh dying to escape.

"This is outrageous. What kind of a museum artifact is that?"

"It's a movie prop, from one of David Cronenberg's films."

"It's that Department of Contemporary Culture, isn't it? I knew it was a mistake as soon as I heard the Museum would be creating such a ridiculous section. Somehow, they think this will bring more young people into the Museum. They have no trust in the younger generation to appreciate the traditional collections–"

"Wow, look at that!" screeched a teenager who raced over to the Mugwump.

"Cool." "Wack." "That is so awesome," rang out from what must have been other members of the teen's school group.

"This is unfathomable," my visitor grumbled. "Since I stopped teaching at the university, I seem to have lost touch with what is happening to the youth of today. Their parents should be taught how to raise their young properly."

"Oookay...well this way," I said, edging through the crowd of adolescents and scooting in front of the mythical creature from *The Naked Lunch*.

Once inside the office, Dr. Zelinka forced her way to the chair behind my desk and sat down.

"Umm, you're sitting in my chair." I quickly rolled over a chair resting in the corner and positioned it to face my desk. "You can have a seat here."

The former prof grumbled and reseated herself while I took my rightful place. She then opened up her portfolio, pulled out some papers, lunged forward, and set them on my desk.

"I...what?" I said. "Our first meeting was to discuss the design elements that His Royal Highness has requested. I, uh, have some graphics for you and a contract. These look like...well, finished drawings. I mean they're beautiful renderings for the commemorative medal, but..."

I examined the details etched onto the weighty paper. One sheet depicted a stylized jet soaring in the air, while the second sheet was an incredibly detailed rendering of the exterior of the new Saudi transportation museum with a palm tree in the foreground, its frond hovering over the roof of the building, like a natural canopy. She had obviously done her homework, and she clearly had a phenomenal talent for designing medals and coins. I was in awe...and horrified.

"These are truly remarkable, and if it was up to me, I would approve these on the spot."

"Of course, you would."

"But the Saudi Prince has very, very specific ideas about what he would like represented on the medals." I could feel my face flushing. "So, I think we have to prepare ourselves for the possibility that he might reject these designs."

"Nonsense. I have made creations for the Queen of England, and they were accepted without hesitation."

"Yes, I believe you have already mentioned your work for the Queen."

"This is my offer to you and His Royal Highness. I do not do revisions."

Great. Just great.

* * * * *

Shortly after escorting my high-maintenance visitor out of the building, I sprinted to the cafeteria to pick up a very late and very much welcome lunch. My order included two generously-sized and extremely dense pieces of 'flourless' chocolate cake (somewhat of a misnomer as the cake was made from almond flour), drowning in a thick chocolate icing. That Giddy Yoyo chocolate bar would remain in my purse as an emergency supply.

"I don't recall these slices having so much whipped cream on them," the cashier said while rotating her head in the direction of the almost empty bowl of whipped cream at the end of the ice cream sundae bar.

"Oh, really," I swiftly handed over my payment and skedaddled.

My inbox had been inundated with emails while I had been gallivanting around the off-site storage and uncovering stolen works of art. So, while devouring my lunch, I sifted through the plethora of correspondence I had received. At first, I wasn't certain I'd be able to demolish both pieces of cake, which by the time I got to them were floating in a puddle of melted cream. But as it turned out, it wasn't an issue.

After responding to the most urgent emails, I scanned Dr. Zelinka's drawings, loaded high definition PDF files on to our FTP site, and sent Harry the link so he could get them in front of the Prince for approval – yeah, right. It was past midnight in Saudi Arabia, so I knew I wouldn't receive a reply before the end of the work day and that a response from the Prince would come on his terms and not on my deadline's demands.

I was pondering my next step when a telephone call came through from the Security Desk. "Kalena Boyko," I answered.

"Hey, it's me. Can I give you a ride home? We need to talk."

I stiffened.

"Are you there?"

"Yeah, yeah. Please just tell me now, do I still have a job?" I asked.

"Yeah, nothing like that. I just want to give you details on what Malik and I talked about. It was kind of unexpected."

I looked up at the digital time-keeper. The hours from all four time zones seemed to blend together into one big panel of green lighting. "Let me know as soon as your shift is over. I'd like to get out of here at a decent time today."

"Why don't I pick you up on Yorkville, just around the corner from Avenue Road?"

"In the boat?" I asked. "And then drive through Yorkville in that eyesore of yours?"

"Aw, now you're hurting my feelings," Marco snickered.

"Why don't we do Bloor and St. George instead? It's further from the Museum, and we're less likely to attract attention in that Charger than if we were to cruise through Yorkville between the Ferraris and Lambos."

"Okay, okay. You're funny sometimes."

I doubted Benny worried about what kind of a car she was seen in.

* * * * *

Before leaving the building to rendezvous with Marco, I first escaped to the Museum's ceremonial entrance, its glorious Rotunda. I grabbed a hold of the top end of one of the brass railings and seated myself on the landing with feet resting on the stairs. Like the ceiling above me, the rest of the Rotunda was a wonder I usually took for granted. I remembered reading in a press release that it's still considered one of the city's architectural showpieces, not just because of its obvious splendor, but also because the stone used in both the building and decorative elements were quarried in our home province of Ontario. I was savoring the magnificence when I heard footsteps approaching. My hands slid over the smooth surface of the stone beneath me as I tried to rise to my feet.

"Do not get up," said Walter. I sank back onto my rear as he neared me. He gripped the next rail a few feet away and proceeded to settle himself on the landing, but he misjudged the edge and slipped down to the next step. He swiftly pressed into his palms and nudged himself back up onto the landing.

"You okay?" I said.

"Yes, of course," he said, rubbing his lower back with one hand. "I too enjoy coming here to immerse myself in this grandeur."

"It wasn't that long ago when this was the busiest hub of the Museum."

"Indeed. I know there were multitudes of objections to depriving this area of its traditional role as the main entrance, but I for one am content it has become a bit of a haven. And although this stone has withstood the footsteps of more than one hundred and fifty years, I suspect it will survive longer with the reduction of daily wear and tear."

"You're probably right," I said, a little sleepily.

"The Rotunda was designed by the architectural firm of Chapman & Oxley, but the concept was that of our founder and first Director, Dr. Trick Currelly."

"You don't say?" I said.

"These marbles are quite splendid," said Walter, nodding his gaze towards the floor. "All local, you know."

"I do know."

"The four pillars by the crest poles were turned from single blocks of marble. The green, buff, pink, white and brecciated marbles...and the blue sodalite in the center of the sunburst, they all originated from quarries near Bancroft. It was an important center of marble quarrying in the first three decades of the twentieth century."

"I've been there," I said. "Not to the quarries, but to Bancroft. On my way to Ottawa, once." A sweet memory of a road trip brought an unexpected smile to my face.

"The walls, on the other hand," said Walter ripping me out of my reverie, "are made of dolostone, or Queenston Limestone. And yes, I know, you have been to Queenston, as every good Ontarian has."

"Are you bored with me?" I asked.

"Not at all, not at all. Queenston Limestone was also

used on the outside façade, from the base to the window sills on the first floor. The sandstone, however, came from a quarry near the village of Terra Cotta." Walter whipped his gaze towards me.

"No, I haven't been there." I grinned.

"What brings you here, by the way, in such a pensive mood? Well, other than the events of this morning," asked Walter.

"I don't know." I tilted my head upwards, absorbing the view of the Rotunda mosaics. "I guess, I naively thought there might be some clues here." As I looked back down, I glanced at my watch. "Oh, my goodness!" I gripped the rail and sprang to my feet. "Apologies, Walter. I have to run. I'm meeting...I have to meet someone."

"Oh, oh," said Walter, his voice sounding a bit startled. "Adieu, then. I suppose I should depart shortly myself. I must say this day certainly knocked the wind out of my sails."

"Then have a restful evening," I said, walking away from the librarian. "And say hello to Brenda for me, if you're Skyping her later."

"I most certainly will. I most certainly will." Walter's second iteration of the phrase tapered off to almost a whisper. Perhaps he was contemplating what he was going to tell his soon-to-be fiancé about the day's shenanigans and his involvement.

When I stepped out of the building, I had umbrella in hand, but miracle of miracles, it wasn't raining, not even spitting. So, I gleefully tossed the collapsible device into my bag and snaked my way towards St. George Street via the quieter route, behind the Museum and the university buildings. The first landmark en route was the Royal Conservatory of Music, home to the city's sublime Koerner Hall. It gave the area a most delightful luminescence, with its stunning glass curtain wall allowing the interior light to flow onto Philosopher's Walk.

It was just minutes before I reached St. George. Fortunately, it was already past high rush hour, so the mobs of people flooding in and out of the St. George subway station had dwindled considerably. There were, however, still a number of cars stopped in the no standing zones on both sides of the street, but Marco's car was not among them.

We'd failed to specify the precise spot for the rendezvous, but then I figured I'd hear his colossal clunker rumbling its way towards me from blocks away. But my eyes were inexplicably drawn to a classic Lincoln Continental with black tinted windows parked across the street from where I was standing. It looked as though it could have been the end product of one of Marco's fixer-upper projects.

Leaning against the vehicle was a thin man wearing an over-sized black leather, car-length coat and dark pants. He sported aviator sunglasses, and the mirrored lenses reflected the light from the bright street lamps. There was a glow from the end of a cigarette in his mouth, and, after every few puffs, he removed the cigarette to blow smoke rings into the chilled late-autumn air. Oh, no! It couldn't be. Could it? This couldn't be a coincidence.

The man noticed me staring his way, then dipped his head and peered over the top of his sunglasses. He dropped the cigarette, stamped out the butt, then tilted his head to one side as if motioning me to come towards him. Suddenly, I felt like I had a whole butterfly migration fluttering in my stomach. When I failed to move, he jutted his head forward and shrugged his shoulders. The next thing I knew the window on the passenger side of the Lincoln slid down and

Marco poked his head out. "For crying out loud, Kalena. What are you waiting for? C'mon, get in the car."

There was no mistaking the figure now. The driver of the car was precisely who I thought it was. It was Bob-just-call-me-Bob.

CHAPTER SIXTEEN

It had been many, many months since I had seen this weaselly man. In our one and only encounter, he had introduced himself saying, "I'm Bob, just call me Bob" as though his surname was top secret. From that moment on, I always referred to him as 'Bob-just-call-me-Bob.' He was a former neighbor of Marco's, and I suspect he was the individual who inspired Marco to become a security guard. What was most intriguing about this man was the fact that his family had been in the security business in Toronto for more than half a century, and he seemed to possess a lot of insider knowledge about the Museum, including some little-known information about a decades-old, never-solved jewelry heist that had taken place at the institution some decades ago. He had shared some intel with Marco and myself that helped us expose some reprehensible activities in which one of our senior executives was involved and which could have badly tarnished the Museum's international reputation. But there was something about this seedy character, who was slipping into the driver's side of the car, which made me feel edgy.

I scurried across the street, opened the rear passenger door, and plunked myself onto the seat. "Cheezus," I said to Marco, breathing rather rapidly, "I didn't know you'd be picking me up in another car...or be with someone else, for that matter."

"Howdy, to you too." Bob turned on the car's ignition,

and unlike most of Marco's vehicles, Bob-just-call-me-Bob's car purred like a satisfied kitten.

"Sorry, that was rude of me. Nice to see you again. I didn't recognize you at first."

"No worries, little lady. I do try to just blend in with the surroundings."

Like driving a Mafioso-like car and wearing sunglasses at night. Not conspicuous in the least. "I'm just a little puzzled," I said.

"About why I'm here with you and Marco?"

"Well, yes."

"Looks like some debriefing is in order. Marco, you go ahead. I need to keep a 360 lookout, make sure we're not being tailed," said Bob while spying me in his rear-view mirror.

I swiveled around in my seat rapidly, glanced out the back window and then out the side and front windows. There wasn't a single car around us in any direction. I straightened out and attached my seatbelt. "Okay, what's up then? Honestly, I'm so beat. I really just want to get home to my cozy bed."

"It has to do with my ride back to the Museum with Malik and some of the things he said."

"Like what?"

"Hold on, missy. I'm just going to pull up over here." Bob had driven us to the southern edge of Toronto's Annex area, a neighborhood that got its name from its annexation to the City of Toronto in the late nineteenth century. He parked right next to a green space I recognized as Taddle Creek Park. It was unmistakable because of the unique avant-garde sculpture in the center of what was probably a very busy dog park during the day.

As soon as we pulled up to the curb, Bob sprang out of the car and lit a cigarette. He exhaled a smoke ring, then leaned inside the vehicle, "Why don't we go sit on one of those benches by that big pitcher thing. It must be about twenty feet high."

I muttered under my breath, and Marco rolled his eyes at me as he exited the car. Was he annoyed with me or with Bob's tobacco addiction?

Bob-just-call-me-Bob had already propped a foot on one of the backless benches and was hunched over with his elbow resting on the raised thigh. While approaching him, I paused to see which way the breeze was moving, ensuring I was upwind of the billowing smoke, and took a seat. With shoulders huddled, I shoved my hands into my coat pockets and tucked my body into as small a footprint as possible. Marco slipped into a spot between Bob and myself, unzipped his coat, removed his hat, and sat back as though it was a steamy Caribbean night.

Bob pivoted slightly and pointed at the sculpture with his cigarette. "That is the weirdest piece of public art, if you ask me."

"It is actually very clever," said a female voice from behind us.

I zipped around. "I thought that voice sounded familiar." I rose to my feet, and as Benny neared us, I ran and hugged her like she was my long-lost sister. "This is an unexpected reunion."

"Marco told me you had a very exciting day," Benny said trying to loosen herself from my grip.

"That's an understatement." I finally released Benny but leaned in towards her. "I'm sure glad you're here," I said in a hushed tone.

Bob drew a last puff on his cigarette, tossed it to the ground, and stomped on it. "Nice to see you again, Miss Benny."

"You two've met?" I asked.

"Once…when I was at Marco's home for Thanksgiving. Bob dropped in for a little while to visit with Marco's father."

So, she had met Marco's family.

"Back to this fountain," she continued. "Like most water features, it is *bellisimo* when the water is actually flowing."

Benny's lovely, long locks were unbraided and rippled gently in the soft wind. She wore over-the-knee black suede boots, with a heel you could easily run in, over black leatherette tights embossed with what appeared to be a velvet paisley pattern. Her lime green tent jacket just skimmed the top of her thighs and was closed at the neck with a single oversized black button.

This was not the drainer I had met that first night. This was a woman who could walk down the Via Veneto in Rome and turn heads of all genders. She had that gift Italian women have of pairing a few fashion-forward, but not necessarily expensive items so brilliantly that it made them look like they had walked off the pages of *Vogue*. There was no point in envying her – one's sense of style is as innate as one's intelligence.

"Oh, I get it. The water streams out of the top of the pitcher and fills the wading pond," said Marco, interrupting me out of my admiration.

"*Di preciso*. The over-flowing pitcher is made up of approximately four kilometers of stainless steel rod and is meant to represent the length of Taddle Creek."

"It's so embarrassing that you know so much more

about something that is a stone's throw away from the Museum than we do," I said.

Benny giggled. "Please do not feel troubled. It is my vocation to know about this. I teach my students about these matters in my graduate tutorial. Taddle Creek is another buried treasure in Toronto. It rises from a small pond fed by a creek. You can still find the pond in Wychwood Park. From there it flowed southeast, across Bathurst Street and then southward to this area and finally to Lake Ontario."

"Well I do know the creek is what created the hollow that forms Philosopher's Walk. I even traipsed through it to get here tonight. It's hard to believe those grassy slopes were once filled with water."

"The creek was first called Ziibiing by the Anishinaabe people. It was an important waterway for transportation and food and was known to be a meeting place for both the Anishinaabe and Haudonausonee peoples. It had a significant spiritual importance to the peoples that lived here before the Europeans invaded. Can you imagine how lovely this whole area would be if the waterway was daylighted?" pondered Benny. "Instead, what was once an oasis has been submerged and is used to transport the city's sewage. It is a *tragedia* on many levels."

Bob-just-call-me-Bob took out another cigarette, flicked his lighter and lit up. "Well how else are cities going to deal with all the crap, literally?"

"This is actually a most archaic solution for sewage. Cities around the world are unearthing their hidden waterways, returning green spaces back to their urban inhabitants, and dealing with issues of sewage in progressive ways that are healing to the environment and more effectively control flooding in urban areas. You should come to one of my tutorials." Benny shot Bob a sly wink.

"Well that's not going to happen. Unlike you folks, I'm too busy dealing with the criminal elements in this city, making this a safer world so all of you can run carefree through fountains like this."

"Oh, Bob," said Benny, "you do amuse me."

Bob turned up one side of his lip in, what I suspected, was his best effort at a smile. "Anyway, we are here for a specific reason, not to figure out how to create a utopian society. Marco, you want to start us off?"

"Yeah, sure. Well, first things first. Malik has asked us to keep our lips zipped about everything that happened today. He's going to speak to Walter separately."

"Well, it's not like I was going to contact the *Globe and Mail*," I said.

"It's not the newspapers he's worried about, but staff morale," said Marco.

I tilted my head.

"Malik may have been a young man still living in Australia when those opals were stolen from the Museum back in '81," Bob-just-call-me-Bob chirped in, "but I'm sure he heard about the toxic atmosphere that suffocated everyone at the Museum after the jewel heist."

"Marco told me about that," said Benny, "that the thief you call *Il Gattopardo* was involved and that he had hid in the Museum until after closing to steal the jewels."

"But someone had sliced the wiring to the case, and investigators were pretty certain there an insider involved," said Bob.

I was suddenly propelled back to a conversation I'd had

some time ago with the enigmatic Geoffrey Ogden and I began to feel nauseous. "That was never proved." I lowered my head. "And it led to a beyond-tragic suicide by someone who was being blamed but, who everyone now thinks was totally innocent."

"That suicide was unnecessary," said Bob.

What an odd thing to say, I thought to myself.

"Anyway," said Marco, "the last thing Malik wants is for staff to start accusing each other of trafficking art confiscated in the last World War."

"But Malik can't possibly think he can keep this under wraps. I mean, he has to go to the authorities."

"Yeah, yeah, he is," Marco said looking at me assuredly. "It's just he's going to work with them on the sly—"

"Sub rosa, as we say in the biz," said Bob.

"Uh, sure. And besides, Malik has a pretty strong suspicion it was an outsider who dropped off the painting at the warehouse," said Marco.

"Why would he think that?" inquired Benny.

"There was an animal claw mark on the back of the frame."

"A leopard's scratch? Marco, why didn't you say anything to me?" I asked.

"I didn't catch it." Marco dropped his head. "It was Malik who spotted it, and he didn't mention anything until we were on our way home."

"Wow. Wow and wow." I fixed my gaze on Bob. "So, you're saying a world-famous art thief who's evaded the authorities for decades decided to give the ROM a piece of stolen art. That just sounds so twisted and, frankly, unlikely."

Bob's expression turned into a kind of smirk. "That's

what I'm here to shed some light on." Bob pulled out a cigarette but then broke into such a violent hack I thought he was going to cough up a lung.

"Are you ill?" asked Benny. "I do not know if it is my imagination or this nighttime lighting, but your skin, it looks a little yellow, no?'

Bob took another few moments to recapture his breath. "Bah, it's just the nicotine. Ignore me. I've been coughing like this for decades."

"Seems worse these days," said Marco.

Benny and I exchanged 'that can't be good' looks.

"There's a fact that very, very few people know about The Leopard, even in the industry," Bob continued, "something that has ALWAYS been kept out of the media, so authorities could easily distinguish if an art heist was actually perpetrated by the master, or by a copycat."

Benny, Marco, and I gave Bob-just-call-me-Bob our full attention. "Go on." My foot started to tap on the ground rapidly.

"Well, our infamous cat burglar seems to have a strange sense of humor, or irony or something." With cigarette now lit, Bob inhaled a particularly long drag and went into smoke-ring-blowing mode, starting with a small loop and then exhaling successively larger ones, forming a pattern in the air that could have passed for a transitory work of art.

"Any time he stole something, he'd leave behind a piece known to have gone missing in double-u, double-u two."

"What?" My word echoed through the empty parkette. "But that must mean *Il Gattopardo* has access to a pretty sizeable cache of confiscated art."

"Yup," said Bob. "Works stolen during the war were usually taken en masse."

"This is kind of imponderable. But...it has to be more than The Leopard being a cheeky thief. I mean, he's managed to avoid the authorities for so long. He doesn't sound like someone who's dying to get caught. Yet, it's risky behavior bringing in a work of art to a location from which you are stealing," I started to massage my forehead just below the hairline.

"There could be a few different factors at play," said the compulsive smoker.

"Such as?" asked Benny.

"Well, art gone missing during the war is probably more heavily documented than any other art, so it's a lot more challenging to fence except, well, to folks like the Russian mob who could care less about the provenance of a piece. Or..." Bob dropped his cigarette, stomped it out, now having amassed a pile of butts. "Or maybe it's just time to get rid of the wartime loot, could be sick or something, or just wanting to clear his conscience. Guilt deepens over the years, I've heard."

"But what if *Il Gattopardo* stole something from the warehouse he can sell more easily on the black market and left the Bellotto painting as some kind of contorted recompense?" I said.

"Well, first of all," chimed in Marco, "even though the paintings at the off-site storage are the more valuable pieces there, the fact they're in a warehouse and not in the main building means they're not hot-ticket items. I seriously doubt anything there would be worth his while."

"And secondly?" I asked.

"Well why would he have gone to all that trouble to lead someone to a painting he left behind and then not give any hints about what he might've taken? At least that's what Malik thinks. And I think he's probably right."

"Gotcha," I said.

"But Malik's not going to take any chances. He's already organizing the curatorial staff to do an inventory check. He's telling them it's a test of the bar code tracking system."

CHAPTER SEVENTEEN

While taking a short ride on the Line 2 subway underneath one of Toronto's main east-west arteries, I sleepily leaned my head against the window. My mind jumped to my upcoming work term in the London office and I contemplated how the English capital seemed so much more civilized in comparison to Toronto, especially in terms of its public transit. Toronto possesses just a few subway lines servicing a population of close to three million, while Greater London boasts nine million inhabitants. The Tube and its interconnected rail lines humble Toronto's system. Granted, London had a much earlier start in developing an underground transit network while Toronto's unexpected and unparalleled growth spurt has taken place on a considerably more condensed timeline, most of it, actually, occurring in the 21st century. And the urban development is not slowing down. I'd read recently that a population roughly the size of Montreal is expected to move to the Greater Toronto Area in the next 25 years.

Our troupe of unlikely crime solvers had lingered in Taddle Creek Park for some time before I had finally made my way onto the subway. I had received multiple offers for a ride home from each of the members of the Taddle Creek Park gang, but spending more time with any of them, even the charming Benny, was the last thing I craved. Instead, I had opted for public transit. I would soon be transferring to a bus and, at this time of evening, the bus ride had a calming effect upon me.

Not having to carry on a conversation also provided me the opportunity to contemplate the discussion I had had with Geoffrey about his family's involvement with *Il Gattopardo*. He had reluctantly confessed to me that his grandfather had once happened upon the thief in the middle of stealing jewelry from the family estate. Instead of reporting him to the police, Geoffrey's grandfather had blackmailed The Leopard into doing a job on his behalf. The family patriarch had lost the Ogden Opals in a poker-bet-gone-bad. The winner of the game, and new owner of the pearlescent jewels, was the ROM's own founder, who subsequently had added them to the Museum's collections.

The loss of the gems, however, had so badly broken Geoffrey's grandmother's heart that her well-intentioned husband later made an even worse decision than putting up the opals in a poker game. After catching The Leopard in that compromising position in his home, Geoffrey's grandfather had coerced the thief into 'repatriating' the opals illegally for his wife from the Museum – and the seasoned cat burglar had done a smashingly good job.

What Geoffrey's grandfather had not counted on was that a Museum staff member (the father of my former colleague Richard Pritchard) would be wrongly accused of being the insider who had assisted *Il Gattopardo* with lifting the opals. Nor could anyone have predicted that the allegations would lead to Richard's father's suicide – on the premises of the Museum itself, in one of its subterranean areas – as we had touched on in Taddle Creek Park. With the opals now sullied with blood, Geoffrey's grandmother rejected them, and her husband had The Leopard release them onto the Black

Market in Hong Kong. Most of the stones eventually found a home in a Hong Kong museum.

Geoffrey had entrusted his family's dirty secret with me, and I knew it was information I could never relate to anyone – not to Marco, nor Malik, and certainly not to Geoffrey's best friend, my boss, Stewart, who knew absolutely nothing about the dark episode. It was something I was going to have to take with me to the grave.

Re-counting the course of events to me had shattered Geoffrey – I had seen the distress in his eyes, heard the quiver in his voice, and saw his body language transform before my eyes. But I would never forget sensing there was something Geoffrey was withholding from me, that there were other things he had deliberately abstained from communicating. I had no shred of evidence that he hadn't disclosed everything, but for some reason I suspected his grandfather, and possibly Geoffrey himself, knew the identity of The Leopard. Or were there other vital details that Geoffrey had left out deliberately?

When I finally finished my journey and reached the lobby of my building and passed through to the elevators, I was exhausted and impatient. I started pressing relentlessly on the elevator up button.

"You know that's not going to get the elevator here any faster."

Startled, I sprang away from the elevator doors and almost toppled into the voice's owner.

"Sorry, didn't mean to scare you," said the six-footish, attractive man with wavy black hair. He had backed up, arms raised as if ready to catch me if I didn't regain my balance.

"Oh, hi Mex," I said to the neighbor who occupied a unit at the end of my hallway. "I didn't hear you sneak up on me."

"Clearly." Mex was probably just a few years younger than me. He had once shared that his mother was Asian and his father Jewish, and as a child, he had often been mistaken for being Hispanic. His school friends had nicknamed him Mex, and although he had a high-powered job in one of the investment firms in Toronto's financial district, everyone still called him by his boyhood moniker.

The elevator doors opened and we entered. "Can you believe we haven't had any rain for, like five hours?" I giggled.

"Unbelievable," said Mex. "I don't know about you, but this humid weather is doing wonders for my skin." He caressed his face with his hands, and I cackled. "By the way, I finally popped the question to Fiona."

"Seriously? That's fantastic. Congratulations."

"And we bought a house just on the edge of Parkdale."

"So, you two are going to gentrify a fixer-upper, I presume."

"Wouldn't have it any other way. I'm keeping my condo, though. I'm going to rent it out."

The doors opened on our floor. "Cool. I trust you'll be screening for tall, handsome men, single, straight, close to my age."

"I'll do my very best." As we reached my door, Mex kept on walking. "Enjoy the rest of your evening...and, most importantly, stay dry."

"It's my highest priority." I threw Mex a lethargic wave goodbye, unlocked my door, and stepped inside. Immediately, I started to peel off my clothes, then pulled out a pair of stretchy and super soft-to-the-touch tights decorated with Indian motifs including horizontal patterns of flowers and architectural elements as well as a variety of painted elephants, all in black and white. Next, I unfastened my bra and slipped it off while keeping my comfy black camisole in place, à la Jennifer Beals in *Flash Dance*. The liberation of my upper body was nirvana.

The door to my washroom was closed as always – according to Feng Shui principles, energy from other parts of the home won't drain down the toilet when there is a barrier. But when I nudged the light switch to the on position, I could tell from the crack under the door that the lights had not been illuminated. Damn. Really?

During the summer, the operability of the light switch had inexplicably been compromised by humidity. If I fiddled with the switch enough, I could usually coax the fluorescents to kick in. Then in the early fall when the weather was drier, the problem had disappeared and so did my plans to hire an electrician to replace the electrical box. But with the return of particularly damp weather that mimicked the mugginess of high summer in Toronto, the issue had resurfaced.

Repeatedly and rapidly, I flipped the switch on and off. Nothing. Then I slowed down my movements and drew my ear close to the switch, like a master safe-cracker listening for the tumblers of an old-fashioned safe's locking mechanism to fall into place. There was a spot where, if I stopped on it precisely, I would hear a click and the light would usually be triggered. But my efforts failed. I gave the plate a smack. Nada! Murmuring, I rotated towards the wall behind me and flipped on the bright kitchen fluorescents to cast light onto the surrounding space, opened the door to the bathroom, and steeled myself for having to wash in the dark.

But then I noticed the toilet emitting an unusual noise. Up with the toilet seat lid, which was also always kept shut in order to maintain a harmonic energetic balance, and there was water trickling from under the bowl's rim. Suspecting the handle had paused in the wrong position, I pushed it down hoping a flush might clear the incessant flow. As the flush cycle ended, there was a more aggressive rushing of water coming from the tank. I cleared off my collection of Storm watches, then pried off the weighty ceramic lid. All of a sudden, I was blasted by a shower of cold water that completely soaked my upper body, almost right down to my waist as if I had been standing over top of a whale's blowhole at the moment the creature cleared its breathing passage.

I slammed the lid back onto the tank and quickly took a whiff of my chest. Clean water, at least.

* * * * *

"Hey, baby bro'. Is that actually you and not your voice mail?" I said. "I must have caught you on the other side of the world."

"Good guess, sis. I'm in hot and humid Singapore."

"Oh, wow. You didn't tell me you were going there."

"The trip came up really suddenly. I actually haven't told Mom and Dad I'm here or they'd probably freak."

"Probably, especially as I'm sure they don't even know where it is, unless it came up in a Jeopardy question."

My brother chortled.

"But don't tell me. It's positively awesome there, although pretty clammy, I imagine."

"Bingo! But AC is blasting everywhere. I just got out of a meeting and I feel like a popsicle. What about you? What's up? Is everything okay on the dark side of the Earth?"

"I'm just having a really, really stupid moment and if I call Mom and Dad, they'll tell me to move home again."

My brother broke into a rowdy laugh, then settled down. "Don't take it personally. They do the same thing with me even if I just tell them I have a hangnail. But you sound really down. Are you feeling crappy again?"

Lying in bed, on one side, I tumbled over on to my back. "Naw. No more cluster headaches. I changed my brand of spring water. But I've had the craziest week, like really *Twilight Zone*. Then the stupidest thing happened to me, and it broke me – I literally came undone."

"Like what?"

"My toilet."

"Uh, huh."

"When I came home tonight the toilet literally attacked me – mercilessly."

"You must know you sound a little cray-cray."

"I swear, the cock and ball went berserk, and the toilet transformed into a freaking fountain from hell."

"Ball-cock. It's called a ball-cock. Cock and ball is a torture technique, à la *50 Shades of Grey*."

"Whatever. What moron named toilet parts after male genitalia anyway?" I could just imagine the eye-rolling happening on the other end of the line. "But it gets better. When I tried to cut off the water supply, the shut-off valve was seized and water was gushing everywhere. I had to force the tank lid back on, but not before I was drenched. Then I called the Security Desk and, get this, they wouldn't call the superintendent because it was so late."

"Oh my god, sis. This could only happen to you."

"I finally started screaming and told them I was likely to flood the whole building riser if they didn't get someone up pronto."

"So, I take it the super turned up."

"With a ginormous wrench in hand. He managed to turn off the water, but he can't fix anything until tomorrow. So, I have no functioning toilet."

"Are you peeing into a cup?"

"Not yet. Luckily there's a bathroom on one of the underground levels in my building, but clearly, not very convenient if I have to go to in the middle of the night."

"Developed world problems."

I sighed. "I know."

"I suppose I should bring home some Singaporean chocolate to make you feel better."

I squealed with glee. "You better believe it. There's an amazing chocolatier there, Laurent Bernard, a French chocolate artisan with a to-die-for shop."

"You boggle my mind. How do you even know that when you've never even been to Singapore?"

"You need to ask me that?"

CHAPTER EIGHTEEN

'Heavy rains flood roads, Toronto breaks weather record,' read the title of an article on the CityNews web site. I sipped my home-made smoothie composed of an organic berry and banana base and an abundance of freeze-dried organic powders ranging from turmeric and a 14-mushroom mix to spirulina and goji berry. As a non-coffee drinker, it served as an effective afternoon pick-me-up.

I scanned the multitude of tidy piles of paperwork that covered the outside perimeters of my desk, then continued reading the days-old e-article.

'Heavy, persistent rains and strong winds are wreaking havoc on the Greater Toronto Area, with flooding and power outages reported across the region.

Police closed Lake Shore Boulevard West in both directions for several hours from British Columbia Road to New Brunswick Way due to flooding.

The Bayview extension was also closed south of River Street for several hours before reopening after 7 pm.

"Right now, we have the highest water level that we've ever seen in recorded history, and it is expected that it will continue to keep rising for a couple more weeks at least" said a representative of the Toronto and Region Conservation.

She said water levels have yet to peak and precipitation from the other Great Lakes could add another five to 10 centimeters to Lake Ontario before levels recede.'

125

Holy rainfall, Batman, I thought to myself. That's plain insanity. In more than 20 years of living in Toronto, I'd never thought of my home as a metropolis at risk from such flooding. What on Earth was going on these days?

I shut down the browser, picked up my phone, and tapped the Lumosity brain games app. I had barricaded myself in my office the last few days, and, while perfecting the art of low productivity and avoiding such matters as warped art thieves, prima donna coin artists, and single-minded Saudi princes, I had managed to successfully edge my way into Lumosity's 99th percentile in almost all categories, with the exception of speed. I blamed that minimally lower score on long fingernails, painted with Pacifica's 7-Free Purple Haze nail polish, hampering my keyboard tapping abilities rather than considering the possibility of any kind of diminished brain capacity.

BRRRRRRRRRRING. I grabbed at the phone receiver with spastic hands. How the hell did the volume on the ring tone get turned up so high on my phone?

"Kalena Boyko speaking."

"Good day, Kalena. You're a popular woman this afternoon. There's someone here at the Security Desk to see you and someone also dropped off a package for you. I was going to run it over to Shipping and Receiving, but since you'll be coming by to sign in your guest, I'll just hold it here."

I quickly launched my calendar. My schedule was clear of meetings for the afternoon. Who could it possibly be? "Who–?" The line disengaged. Whatever.

From my purse I pulled out a small makeup bag and retrieved a mirror. The indelible circles under my eyes were a moot point, so I gave my hair a quick comb-through to spruce

126

myself up. But ugh, I wasn't dressed in a particularly professional manner today – dark grey cotton jeggings, a past-the-hips length periwinkle cable knit sweater, and a pair of black Camper flats. I paused. It had to be Dr. Zelinka with another one of her impromptu visits. I couldn't deal! I just couldn't deal!

I mustered as much fortitude as possible, soldiered on, and passed through a long hallway and a few doors to the Staff Entrance. On opening the final portal, the wind was siphoned out of my lungs. No, no, no. What was he doing here?

Wishing I could make myself invisible à la Harry Potter, I managed a feeble, "Geoffrey, what an unexpected surprise."

Geoffrey edged towards me to plant a kiss on my cheek, but I extended my hand keeping him at distance.

"Well done. Professional all the way," he said in a hushed tone. He tucked a beautiful weathered leather attaché under one armpit and gently wrapped both his hands around mine, sending a flutter straight to my heart.

The guard at the desk kept his gaze tilted downwards, as if intending to give us some privacy. Thank goodness Marco was not on duty here for once. He and Geoffrey were like oil and water, an incompatible combination of elements.

I slipped my hand out of Geoffrey's and put both hands behind my back. "Hey, wait a minute. We issued you a staff badge so you wouldn't have to be signed in."

"Indeed, but I'm coming via Saudi, and I didn't stop in the UK to grab my Canadian bag."

"You have bags packed and ready to go for various destinations?"

"I was trying to be droll. I simply forgot to pack it. I don't have someone like you back home to keep me neat and organized."

Despite stepping off a plane from the Middle East, Geoffrey's impeccably fitted suit was pressed, the part in his hair was strategically placed, his shirt was fresh, and he looked far too handsome to possibly be legal in any country. In fact, he made Toronto's Bay Street brokers look like farm hands. I looked down at my sweater and leggings. Farm hand.

I donned a subtle smile and tilted my head to one side. "Shall we go to my office?"

"Hold on, Kalena," blurted out the guard. "You don't have to sign for the package, but you will need to log your visitor. By the way, I like your accent, sir. British, I guess?"

"And here I thought you were the ones with the accent," said Geoffrey.

"Huh? Oh, I get it."

I picked up the pen on the counter and started to fill out the log when my gaze darted towards the box, around 8" x 8" x 8," wrapped in kraft paper and secured with a few turns of string around all four sides. "Why wasn't this dropped off at Shipping and Receiving? I thought you folks weren't supposed to accept deliveries here."

"I'm afraid I can't say. We had a quick shift change, and I believe it arrived just before I took over duty here."

"Is this from you, Geoffrey?"

"Well now I feel remiss for not arriving bearing gifts. It is not from me, I am afraid."

I picked up the box. Its weightlessness gave me the impression that the container might be empty. I turned it upside down, and attached with scotch tape was an image of what looked to be another symbol from the Museum's mosaic ceiling. My throat clenched. Swiftly, I turned the box right-side up again.

"You've suddenly taken on a rather supernatural pallor. Are you well? Do we need to summon a detection dog to check out the package?" asked Geoffrey.

"Don't be silly. I'm not expecting any letter bombs."

"That was not my intended implication."

"Let's go, shall we?" I marched forward, almost frantically, and Geoffrey fell behind.

"You would think there were British bulldogs nipping at your heels," he said.

I glanced back at Geoffrey and noticed that even for someone of his six-feet-plus stature, he was taking unusually long strides to keep up. "Well, I have plenty to do today, and I wasn't expecting a guest."

Geoffrey gently grasped me by the upper arm, drawing us both to a halt. "Honestly, I didn't come here to make you feel uncomfortable. This visit is mission-driven. I need to deliver some news, and I thought an in-person encounter might soften the impact."

I hesitated. "You're getting married, aren't you?"

"Now you're being silly? Who could I possibly have met that would make me forget about you?"

I burst out laughing, and Geoffrey looked genuinely puzzled. "You are a smooth one," I said. "Let's not forget you run in a very posh circle that includes some pretty impressive and stunning women."

"Like you, you mean? I've always been sincere with you. I am truly disappointed that the distance between us has made it impossible to develop something more meaningful."

I sighed, but suddenly Geoffrey's earlier statement registered. "What have you come here to tell me then? Has the Prince rejected the design for the medal?"

"Let's dash to your office, shall we?"

We walked briskly in silence until Geoffrey side-stepped the Mugwump. "Well that's certainly an interesting guardian you have at your portal. Dare I ask?"

"It's a figment of William S. Burroughs drugged out mind."

"I say."

I opened the door, passed over the threshold, and dragged the visitor's chair from the corner of the room, positioning it in front of my desk. I then dropped into my own seat and poised myself in grilling position.

"So, were you there when the design was presented to the Prince?"

"I was. I truly believe what your artist created is sophisticated and regal and would have made a wonderful memento for the museum opening. And I tried to convince the Prince of the same."

"My own personal lobbyist."

"Unfortunately, despite my heartiest efforts, I was not able to convince him to accept our offering, despite consuming enough black tea for a lifetime. I won't be sleeping for days – they drink a rather strong brew there."

I lowered my chin a tad. "I appreciate you going to bat for me, really I do. I knew before I sent the mockup it would be hopeless. But I was kind of hoping for a miracle, ya' know."

Geoffrey chuckled, rather irresistibly.

"What do I do now? I'm at a bit of a loss, and we are so short of time."

"Well, as it turns out, I do come bearing gifts after all." Geoffrey opened up his attaché and removed a small portfolio. "The Prince had a court artist sketch something."

"They actually have court artists? How very Renaissance."

"Painters, sculptors, architects, landscape designers, and more. They take their royalty and patronage very seriously." Geoffrey handed me the sketches, observing me closely. "Yes, I know. But they are the clients," he said.

"And we give the clients what they want, not what they need, which in this case appears to be a narcissistic glorification of the monarchy." The obverse was a frontal portrait of the Prince covering the whole surface of the medal. The reverse depicted a side profile of the Prince in the foreground, head tipped upwards, peering at a small speck of a jet in the sky in the background. "Blimey."

"Blimey, indeed. But I do have some additional news," said Geoffrey.

"Be still my beating heart. Do I need smelling salts?"

"Perhaps. Stewart has already spoken to your metals conservator, Dara, I believe her name is."

"Dara Green?"

"Yes. She will help organize production of the medal based on this design. She has many connections in this field, and since the Museum is in between large exhibitions, she said she could take on some of the coordination with you."

"Great...I guess."

"I thought you would be elated with this news."

"Sorry, I don't mean to sound ungrateful. It's just that you two have once again had to step in to deal with...never mind."

"That is completely absurd. We were the ones who put you on the spot, especially with Brenda in the UK and Stewart in the US. He's so impressed with how you have been managing on your own. You should not in the least see this as a failure in any shape or form. And by the way, Stewart thought the design you sent was extraordinary and no one was more disappointed than he at the Prince's decision."

"Well, that's good to hear." Suddenly, the package on my desk drew my attention.

"Would you like to open that now? If it's anthrax, we could both go down together…a little Romeo and Juliet scenario."

"How romantic. But I'll brave it on my own, thanks," I said.

Geoffrey glanced at his watch.

"You have another flight to catch?"

"I still have a few moments remaining to chat about philosophy, spiritual journeys, Toronto sports teams. Whatever your pleasure."

"Well, there was something I wanted to ask you, but you must promise you won't flip out," I said.

"You are wondering if I have ever fathered any children. The answer is no, at least not of which I am aware."

A giggle was unpreventable. "Surprisingly, that was not the question. It's about, well…"

"Come now. Do tell."

"It's about *Il Gattopardo*."

Geoffrey threw his head back, then methodically realigned his cervical spine, one vertebra at a time. "I do hope you are talking about the book, or the movie, not the thief."

I grinned.

"I thought after the discussion we had the last time I saw you it was clear this subject was closed forever."

"Please…it's kind of a strange question, but I need to know the answer."

Geoffrey closed up his soft leather briefcase and

pressed himself forward in his chair to rise.

"When he tried to pillage your family home and your grandfather caught him, had he brought something with him that he intended to leave behind?"

Geoffrey reseated himself. "I have no clue as to what you might be referring."

"Well, more specifically, did he have any art with him that had gone missing during World War II?"

Geoffrey stiffened. "Honestly, where do you come up with these notions?" He started to lift again from the chair, but I reached over the desk and took a hold of his arm.

"I've rattled you."

"There are some things best left unspoken."

"I need a straight response for once. Please don't try to weasel out of answering."

"What you don't understand is how this line of inquiry could damage my family."

I bored a hole through Geoffrey's eyes, and this time I took a hold of his hand and held it firmly.

Geoffrey turned his head and peered towards the doorway. "The object with which Grandfather James caught him red-handed was...not a work of art that had been in the family for generations, but, something my grandfather had dubiously acquired during the war."

Immediately, I released Geoffrey's hand. "What do you mean dubiously?"

"You must understand what it was like during the war and what a chaotic time it was even when peace was declared. It was a free for all, societal rules were suspended. It was havoc, sheer havoc."

"And..."

"And there is a persistent mythology that the Germans

were the only ones pillaging during the war, but everyone was guilty of it. Perhaps not on the same scale as the Nazi plunder, but everyone was engaged in this type of reprehensible activity, including the French, the Americans, the British, and I suppose even some of your Canadians muddied their hands." Geoffrey smoothed back the hair on one side of his head, as if there was anything out of place, and avoided looking at me.

"You know, there's a whole new film genre that's emerged in recent years – movies about World War I and World War II that provide a more balanced perspective."

"Balanced?"

"There are no clear heroes or villains when it comes to war," I said. "Sure, the aggressors can be blamed for initiating catastrophic violence, but inevitably atrocities are executed by all involved in a war. There's some great films like *Land of Mine*, *Frantz*, *Suite Française*, and *Alone in Berlin* that show how the average German citizen was often a victim of global politics as was the average person living in an Allied country."

Geoffrey threw me a quizzical look.

"What?"

"It amazes me how you can transform any conversation into a discussion about film."

"Well my references just don't come from film. My mother was forced to work in Germany during the war, and she was actually treated well by the people who employed her. Well, maybe employ is not the right term. She didn't exactly get paid. But she did get room and board."

"Fortunately, humanity is accessible to all of us."

"As is darkness. My mother also personally witnessed Allied looting after peace had been declared. She saw them ripping down art off the wall in the hotel where she worked.

She said afterwards, when things were really difficult, she had had moments where she regretted not snatching things herself, but it just hadn't crossed her mind to act so unethically."

"Your mother sounds like an extraordinary woman."

"You don't even know the half of it."

"You must think my own family sub-standard when it comes to character."

"It's not for me to judge. But, can I just step back a bit. You told me your grandfather blackmailed *Il Gattopardo* into stealing the Museum's opals after he had found the cat burglar in your family home."

"Yes."

"Well, it seems to me that The Leopard had more blackmail material on your family than vice versa considering they had stolen art in their collection."

"Indeed. But remember, the man had entered our home illegally. I do not know the precise conversation between my grandfather and *Il Gattopardo*, but I suspect that when Grandfather asked the thief to steal the opals from the Museum, it had less to do with blackmail than with the thief delighted with a new challenge."

I gaped at Geoffrey.

"I simply cannot say anymore. Please believe me, I have already betrayed my father's most profound trust by telling you as much as I have."

"I understand, but I have one last question."

"Truly, Kalena?" Geoffrey sounded exasperated.

"I know we talked about this before, but I'm not sure you were entirely forthcoming. Did your grandfather know who *Il Gattopardo* was? Did he see his face? Could he identify him?"

"That's three questions...But I can truthfully say I am not sure. He always insisted he did not know the thief's true identity – masked bandit and all that. However, he may have," Geoffrey looked down to the floor, "he may have wanted to protect my father and the rest of the family by denying he had detailed knowledge about The Leopard. But we'll never know."

Geoffrey once again cast his gaze at his wrist. "Now, I really must depart or I will miss my meeting in Boston, and that would set Stewart off." He stood up rapidly, but then paused. "I do have a quick question for you."

"You do?"

"How is that security guard of yours doing, Marcus?"

"Marco. And he's not MY security guard. But he's doing great. He has the most amazing girlfriend. I think she's my sista frum anotha motha."

Geoffrey chuckled. "I'm surprised. I thought he was sweet on you."

"Protective is a better description."

"Hmm, interesting."

As Geoffrey approached the door, I hopped out of my chair and stepped towards him.

"No need to walk me out. You said you had a multitude of other things to do."

"You mean like contacting Dara and getting those medals into production."

"Or opening that package." Geoffrey winked.

Before I knew it, Geoffrey had stepped into my personal space and flung his arms around me. He hugged me so very tightly, the kind of embrace one might receive from a love going off to war. He lowered his head and nuzzled his face into the side of mine.

"Don't ever underestimate how much I adore you."

I tried to pull away gently, but he drew me nearer.

"I don't know what you're involved in this time, but please take caution. Do not be reckless. When big stakes are involved, people can be far more dangerous than one might suspect."

Geoffrey planted a most gentle kiss on the nape of my neck, his favorite erogenous zone, as he had once confessed to me, and it sent a vibration throughout my body, weakening my determination to resist. But he released me as suddenly as he had seized me, turned around, and walked out the door. Tears trickled down my cheeks. Oh, it was all too futile.

CHAPTER NINETEEN

It took some moments and a few tissues to compose myself. I wasn't certain if I had been grieving for an unfinished love story or if it was because, for a moment, I had felt desired again. When a marriage ends as a result of infidelity, it takes an imponderable toll on one's self-worth, and often a woman's immediate response is to barricade her heart from the world – or cut off all her hair.

I was grateful to Geoffrey for stirring something in me, no matter how transitory. And I cherished him for respectfully walking away from the whisper of potential love. He was much more of a gentleman than I had ever given him credit. Damn. Damn this sometimes unkind universe.

Having returned to an emotional equilibrium, the draw of the package resting on my desk became overwhelming. But goddammit, what was I thinking? If there were any fingerprints on the wrapping paper, they were now thoroughly contaminated with mine. I had probably messed up some valuable forensic evidence.

I reached for my phone to call Malik. If he wasn't my first call, I knew I would never hear the end of it. But there was no answer, and I didn't want to leave a voice mail message. Next step was to hunt down Marco...and Walter. Having Walter around was often better than the Internet, and he was definitely more amusing. I called the Staff Entrance and asked the guard if she could radio Marco to swing by my office. Next, I rang Walter and asked him to drop by – urgently. And I waited.

That damn digital clock indicating the times across the globe seemed to glare down at me with a malevolent green glow. Then the door swooshed open. First entered Marco, and closely tracking behind was Walter.

"What IS going on?" Marco asked.

"Hello to you too."

"Well, you had me hunted down, not so subtly, I might add. Everyone's going to be wondering why you summoned me, and I suspect I'm going to have to make something up to keep people from talking around here."

"Indeed, Kalena," said Walter. "The rumor mill in this institution is most rampant. Please explain yourself."

"First of all, I want you two to know that I called Malik first, and I couldn't reach him."

"I heard he's underground, in the tunnel area. He's with the Head of Facilities checking for seepage from all this rain."

"Ah, yes," said Walter. "When Taddle Creek is awakened, it leaches into the basements of the buildings that sit on top of it, including our revered institution. Usually the concern is in the spring, but our weather is so topsy-turvy this year."

"You mean Taddle Creek might break through and flood the Museum?" I asked.

"God, I hope not. That would be some scene," said Marco.

"It is not likely to reach such catastrophic proportions, but it could penetrate the lower chambers of the building and create unwelcome humidity," said Walter.

"So why were you trying to reach Malik?" asked Marco.

"This," I said, indicating the package on my desk.

Walter backed away.

"Relax. It's not going to explode. Walter, you don't happen to have any curatorial gloves on you? I think I've left enough fingerprints on this paper as it is."

From a back pocket, Walter plucked a pair of white cotton gloves and handed them to me.

"Can you give us a hint what's going on?" said Marco.

"Patience." I donned the cotton hand wear and cautiously turned the item upside down. "This was delivered to me at the Staff Entrance today. Take a look at this."

Marco and Walter leaned in together, like synchronized divers, to examine the underside of the box when Walter unexpectedly whipped a magnifying glass out of a pocket on the inside of his jacket.

"Well, I certainly made the right decision calling Ghostbusters. Well done," I said.

Walter pivoted towards Marco. "What is she going on about?"

"Never mind. This looks like it might be another symbol from the Rotunda, eh, Walter?" said Marco.

"No doubt about it. It is one of the symbols from the section representing classical cultures of the Mediterranean." Printed in color, trimmed down to about 2" x 2", and on what appeared to be standard photocopy paper was an image in rich hues of gold, bronze and copper of a standing canine animal suckling two young human children. It included part of the decorative rectangular border.

"This one's pretty straight-forward." Marco looked at me with an 'oh-yeah' expression on his face. "It's Romulus and Remus," I continued, "the legendary founders of Rome being nursed by their wolf mother. Though it doesn't really bear much of a resemblance to a real wolf. I suspect the Roman artists who created the renditions upon which this is based didn't actually have much interaction with wolves."

"Kalena, would you kindly launch Google and do a search on 'ROM Rotunda mosaic Romulus and Remus?"

I popped over to my keyboard and instantly typed in the words. Walter speedily joined me in front of the computer monitor.

"Scroll down a few results, please," said Walter. I obeyed. "There, that one," he said, pointing at the screen.

"The one with the typo? Romulus and Remus 'murtured' by the wolf."

"Precisely."

With cursor on the link, I pressed the enter key, and the exact photo that was taped to the bottom of the package appeared on the screen.

"For frig's sake, how did you do that?" I asked.

"Although our Marketing Department uses a service to keep track of all postings on the Internet about the Museum, I occasionally do a little patrolling myself to see what is being said out there in the cyber world," said Walter, lifting his hands and waving them, as though the Internet was some kind of voodoo. "This particular page stood out because of the paltry attention to spelling. I simply cannot believe no one has corrected the word since this was posted several years ago."

Marco and I exchanged grins. "Do you think the person who loaded this photo has anything to do with this package?" said Marco.

"Highly unlikely. I recall researching the identity of this person, and it was a student who had come to the Museum on a school visit with their high school class."

"So, someone just randomly downloaded this particular image from the Internet," I postulated.

"So, what are we waiting for? Let's see what's inside." Marco tapped his foot vigorously.

I grabbed a pair of scissors and carefully cut the twine wrapped around the package and placed it aside. Then, I withdrew an X-ACTO™ knife from my desk drawer, carefully sliced the clear packing tape that had been used to seal the paper, and, continuing with great attention, removed the paper while touching as little of the surface as possible. The box in which it was enclosed was nondescript and could have been bought at any office supplies store or post office. There was more tape on the box, so I sliced the edges to free the flaps. Next I peeled the top cardboard tabs away, revealing black solid foam. "This looks like the stuff used inside Pelican Cases."

"The ones we use to transport museum artifacts?" said Marco. "Kalena, didn't you once chase around a certain someone at Pearson Airport carrying a Pelican Case. You were convinced he was *Il Gattopardo* absconding with the world's oldest piece of chocolate?"

"What? I have never heard this story," said Walter.

"And that's all you'll ever hear about it," I said. Especially since I had completely misunderstood the situation and made a fine fool of myself.

Walter groaned. "Well, whatever is inside here has been packed with the same kind of precious care as the painting we found at our off-site storage. We are dealing with someone who understands the principals of the conservation of objects, someone who is truly fond of these pieces and their safety." Walter went to touch the black matter and then as quickly withdrew his ungloved hand. "This is definitely Plastazote®."

"It looks like regular packing foam," said Marco.

"It does, but this foam uses a polymer combination that not only gives it increased stiffness, but it is temperature resistant and more moldable and lightweight than other such foams. Its engineering is perfect for housing museum artifacts as it offers a superior performance, and there's no chemical agents in the foam."

"Enough about the foam. I'm digging deeper." I said.

"I'm on pins and needles," said Walter. "God protect us from Malik's wrath for doing this."

I meticulously removed the top layer of the foam, which, when fully removed, was hollowed out in the middle to form a recessed circular hollow housing an object.

"My, my," said Walter.

We were looking at a curved piece of hemispherical translucent glassware enclosed in a metallic covering that stood slightly away from the glass body. It was not a solid piece of metal but rather a delicate open latticework with interlocking circle and diamond shapes. Walter drew the magnifying glass closer to the object, blowing up our view of the most exquisite miniature leaves located on four points of each circle. It was now more evident that the extremely fine metalwork was intended to mimic a vine encasing the glass. Though elegantly wrought, the forms of both the glass and the metal were irregular enough to suggest it was produced far long before industrialization.

"Oh, no," I said peering intently at the work. "It's cracked. Oh man, I hope I didn't do that."

"If this is what I think it is, those cracks were most likely incurred centuries ago," said Walter.

"You think this is from ancient times, like from ancient Rome?" I asked.

Walter nodded his head slowly. "Around the 4th century, I believe. Could you please hand me the gloves? I would like to lift the glass slightly to confirm my suspicions."

"Are you sure you want to do that?" I said while removing the gloves.

"I am quite used to handling ancient artifacts. In fact, the volumes in the rare books section of our library are far more delicate than this. And I will assume full responsibility."

Walter clad his hands with the gloves and, as if dealing with something volatile, lifted the cup-like object out of the foam that had been so painstakingly carved out to protect it. It appeared to be about six inches in height and the diameter at the top part of the ware looked to be around eight inches. There was a two-tiered lip at the open end of the glass that was not encased by the wire cage. And, there were more cracks in the glass than had been evident upon first viewing.

"Is it an antique wine glass? If it is, it's pretty huge. But you couldn't ever put it down because of the rounded bottom...Or maybe it sat in something?" surmised Marco.

Walter softly lowered the glass back into the foam. "Excellent deduction. It is what is known as a cage cup, because of the wire lattice around the glass. Indeed, when these were first discovered, it was thought they were wine vessels. But it is now believed, because of the metal fittings, that these glasses were intended to be suspended. Current thought is that these were used for candles in burial sites and were not used for wine at all. Ms. Boyko, I am once again going to ask you to consult Google. Back to the site that we looked at when we located the painting."

"The Monuments Men site?" I asked.

Walter raised his eyebrows. "It is looking more and more familiar, I am afraid."

I typed in a few search words, brought up the website, and started scrolling down the list of still-missing objects until I came upon a heading that read 'Roman Cage Cup.' "Zowie kapowie!" The image looked exactly like what was sitting in front of us. I clicked on the picture to increase its size. "That's it. There's no mistaking it. It's identical right down to the crack patterns in the glass."

"What does it say about it?" asked Marco.

"Well, it's the property of the Altertumsmuseum in Mainz, Germany. Hey, I've been there, well not to the museum. I once did a Rhine river cruise from Köln to Mainz." I glanced at Walter and Marco who were staring at me blankly. I read on. "The museum's now called the Landesmuseum. Seems that at the beginning of World War II the cage cup, along with other archaeological items, was taken to Erbach, in Germany's Odenwald forest. It was seen there by an employee of the museum in Mainz in 1943, who noted then that the cup was partly damaged." I wiped my hand across my brow in a 'whew' gesture.

"In 1945," I continued, "the items were transferred from Erbach to the Central Collecting Point in Wiesbaden. Then in 1945 or '46 the director of the museum in Mainz checked the objects with an officer of the French occupying forces at the Collecting Point. All the objects were still there, but it seems that's the last information the museum has about the whereabouts of what was its most valuable and famous object...like EVER. All the other items that had come from Erbach were eventually returned to the museum."

"Except this one," said Marco.

"Except this one," echoed Walter.

"Seems kind of weird that it went missing once the war had ended and the French were in control there."

I parted my lips to speak, but then stifled myself.

"Not so odd at all Mr. Zeffirelli," said Walter. "It would not be the first or last time that Allied troupes pillaged. Perhaps out of a sense of retribution, but of course, that does not excuse such theft."

"Or they just did it out of plain greed." I started to flick my fingers as though I had a nervous tick. What were the odds of having the same obscure conversation with two different parties within the same hour? My mind began to race in a million different tangents.

"I am not surprised that this particular item was looted," said Walter. "These cage cups are extremely rare. If my recollection is correct, only about 50 of them have survived and only a few in near-complete condition, such as this one."

"Oh my god, I can't believe I was carrying this thing through the hallways so carelessly," I said. "You would think that whoever sent this would have at the very least put a big orange 'Fragile' sticker on the package."

"Which brings us to another very important matter that none of us is addressing," said Walter.

"Like what?" I asked.

"The fact that this was addressed to you. YOU were specifically targeted to receive this."

I reached for my chair with unsteady hands and sat down.

"And you were the one that someone wanted to find that painting in the warehouse," added Marco.

"That's ridiculous. Someone would have to have had ESP to know I'd be going to Eastern Road. I'd never been there before, and you two, Stewart and Malik were the only ones who knew I was going there."

"They don't need to have ESP, Kalena," said Marco. "They probably have access to spyware technology."

Geoffrey's parting words began to reverberate in my head, and I shuddered – 'when big stakes are involved, people can be far more dangerous than one might suspect.' "This is just way too coo-coo for cocoa puffs for me to wrap my head around."

Without any warning, the door to my office flew wide open, and Malik literally tripped in. The three of us glaciated.

I bounded to my feet and pointed at Walter. "It was all his idea."

"Thank you for that," said Walter, most stoically. "I appreciate the support."

Marco and I erupted into inappropriate laughter. "What brings you here anyway?" I asked, getting a grip.

"After leaving the dungeons below, which is one of the few places we don't get a cell signal, I saw the missed call from you, and I just so happened to be passing by your office."

"Oh, yeah. I did call."

"What is going on here? And what was all Walter's idea? Walter, why are you wearing white gloves again?"

Walter instantaneously clasped his hands behind his back.

"Does this have anything to do with the package on your desk?" said Malik, staring at me.

"Uh, yes, it does," I said. "We kind of received another gift."

"If it's like the one you found at the off-site storage, I don't think I want to know about it. I just received a report this morning confirming the painting you found at the warehouse is indeed real. It won't be long before contact is made with the Bourbon-Parma family to return the painting."

"Who are they?" I asked.

"An Italian offshoot of the French Bourbon lineage. The family's more than 300 years old, and they also have ties with Luxembourg," explained Malik. "The painting was taken from them during the war."

"I am certain they will be most delighted to have the treasure back in their collection," said Walter.

"Please don't tell me this story hasn't ended," said Malik.

"I'm afraid not," I said. "Someone sent us—"

"You, Kalena. They sent YOU," said Walter.

I rolled my eyes. "Someone dropped off a package for me that just happens to contain an ancient Roman artifact."

"Which happens to be another piece of art that's been AWOL since World War II," said Marco, "and on the Monuments Men list."

"And it is a rather rare specimen...let me correct that, an extremely rare piece that went missing from a German museum, actually," said Walter, "whilst the French were in charge."

"Say what?" Malik took such a deep breath I could actually see his rib cage lift and pause before it dropped again. "Kalena, what have you got yourself mixed up in?"

"Me? This isn't my fault. I have no idea what's going on or why I'm being targeted."

"Okay, let's back up a bit. Where and how was this box delivered?"

"I'd received a call from the Staff Entrance advising me I had a visitor and also that a package had been dropped off for me."

"You never said anything to us about a visitor," said Marco.

"It wasn't relevant. It was just a coincidence," I said.

"Well it could be...relevant, that is," said Marco.

"Wait a minute," said Malik. "The officers know they're supposed to direct ANY deliveries to Shipping and Receiving."

"That's exactly what I said, but the guard said it had happened just before the shift change, so he didn't know the circumstances."

"And who was the visitor?" asked Malik.

I glanced at Marco. "Well. Um. It was Geoffrey Ogden, from our London office."

Marco's eyebrows lifted. "You never mentioned he was here."

I shrugged my shoulders. "Like I said, he just happened to be in the wrong place at the wrong time. The delivery had already been made."

"Are you sure of that?" inquired Malik.

"Are you suggesting he had something to do with this? There's no way," I said, a bit too emphatically.

Marco muttered something under his breath, and I threw him an evil glare.

"You're undoubtedly right. I hardly think Stewart's partner in London had any role in this, but we can't rule him out entirely," said Malik.

"He's en route to Boston as we speak," I said.

"That's convenient," said Marco.

"I'll go through the camera tape first. We should be able to eliminate him using the video footage we have from that entry point. And if luck is on our side, we might also be able to identify who the courier was."

"What do we do in the meantime, I mean with all this?" I said, pointing at the desk.

"I'm afraid you have a long day ahead of you. We side-stepped some of the usual police procedures with the painting, but now it's clear we're dealing with a serial offender–"

"That is a strong term," said Walter, "for someone who appears to be more of a Robin Hood-like character – returning stolen art," said Walter.

"Well it's definitely something I've never encountered in my long career in security. And whether it's a good deed being done here, whoever is behind this has access to a stockpile of stolen materials. The painting was one matter, but with the provenance of this object being German and having gone missing under French watch, this could very well open some very old wounds and result in some pretty uncomfortable international relations." Malik looked ever so grim.

"You mean no one wants to admit that anyone but the Germans were involved in this kind of activity?" I asked.

"I would think so," responded Malik.

I brought my hands to my cheeks and stroked my fingers down my jaws.

"You should probably tell Stewart what's going on," said Malik.

I stiffened. "I don't know what I would say to him or know where to start."

"I can make the call if you'd like, I don't mind," said Malik.

"I'd appreciate that," I said.

"Shall do. In the meantime, I need the three of you to stay here. Walter, call your department and let them know you are indisposed for the rest of the day. Marco, I'll get the

150

remainder of your shift covered. And whatever you do, don't touch that cup or the package or anything on your desk. We're going to have to do a sweep of this office." Malik ambled over to the door. "And keep this door locked. Make sure no one else comes in." Malik propped open the door. With his back facing us, he paused, shook his head, and then hurried away.

"Brenda is going to have a conniption about this when she gets wind of it." Walter looked rather desperate.

"Is anyone hungry? I have some President's Choice Organic Chocolate Digestive Biscuits stashed away. I can make some tea."

Marco and Walter groaned.

"Do you think we might get a trip to Italy or France or Luxembourg out of this?" I was grinning like a scary clown doll.

Marco raised his hand and mimicked the frenetic movement and screeching sound of the stabbing scene in *Psycho*.

CHAPTER TWENTY

"Hi Mom," I said in Ukrainian.

"Kalynychka, how did you know it was me? I didn't even say anything yet."

"Because you always answer the phone, even when Dad knows that 98% of the time the calls are for him."

"You are so funny, dear. But yes, he relies on me quite a bit. What did you do tonight? Did you go to your dance class? You must enjoy your life while you are still young. Don't get old like us."

"It happens to everyone. I don't have the secret to being young forever. Yes, I went to my dance class." I peered at the gym bag in the corner. It hadn't been touched for days.

"No wonder you sound so tired. When are you coming to see us? Did you know your brother was in Singamore?"

"Singapore. Yes, he told me a bit about it."

"I don't understand. He didn't even tell us he was going. What if his plane went down in the ocean? We would never have known."

"You don't have to worry. It's far safer to fly than it is to drive."

"Oh, that's just something those airline companies say so people aren't afraid to take planes."

"Yes, Mom."

"What about you? Are you planning to go somewhere without telling us?"

"I was maybe thinking of going to Iceland, but I would tell you."

"Iceland? I don't even know if we have a Ukrainian word for Iceland."

"Icelandia," my father yelled in the background. "There is a Ukrainian word for every country in the world, Mama. Icelandia."

"Why would you want to go to Icelandia?" my mother continued. "It sounds very cold. Would you go with someone?"

"I'd probably go on my own. I don't think I have any friends as interested in going there as I am."

"God almighty, Daughter. Why would you want to go somewhere without any companionship? Why don't you try one of those dating sites I keep hearing so much about on TV? There must be one with Ukrainian men."

I dropped my head limply. "Yeah, maybe, I don't know. I have to go. I have to get some things ready for work tomorrow."

"Oh, okay. Maybe the next time you call your father will surprise us and answer the phone."

"Probably not," my father yelled.

"We'd have to alert the Ukrainian newspapers so they could write a story about it," I said.

My mom giggled sweetly. "Well don't go to bed too late, my little frog."

"Good night, Mom."

Oh lord, what if the Toronto papers do write up the story about the found artwork? My parents would make me quit my job for sure and lock me in my old room in their home in Hamilton forever and ever.

CHAPTER TWENTY-ONE

"Wow, this place is truly *speciale*. I feel so at home here."

"I thought you'd like this spot. I'm lucky I live so close to it."

"I'm surprised Marco has never mentioned it."

"He probably doesn't know about it. People in Toronto tend to hang out in their own neighborhoods a lot."

"For now, I am most happy with this slice of *Roma*. Thank you for inviting me. I am glad we have this chance to catch up."

"I hope Marco won't mind us getting together," I said. "I'm sure he'll think it's kind of weird."

"If he were to have any objections, I would not pay any attention to him." Benny winked. "This is such a cool bakery café. And a clever name – *Forno Cultura*. It would loosely be translated as 'wisdom from the oven.'"

"I love it here. The master baker is a third-generation baker, but his training is in architecture."

"It shows. All this metal and glass, and so much wood, the color of bread. And look," said Benny pointing towards the windows, "it is interesting how the light from the street above floods this basement space. The view of people's legs as they pass, it is like performance art."

I chuckled.

"And the way they have used a thin layer of glass to separate the customers from the artisans making all the breads and pastries, it is almost like watching a Venetian glassblower at work in a studio."

"Another great thing is they use organic flour. I actually try to avoid bread, but I've been told that although the flour is free from preservatives, the bread keeps unexpectedly long."

"Stay away from bread! How is that possible in here?"

"I admit, I'll sometimes have their breakfast sandwich, with eggs, sundried tomato, and black olives."

"That sounds so good. I'm glad I do not live close by. I could never resist these sweets – all these cookies, cakes, and puddings. And the biscotti. And look at those *coronetti*."

"You're so right. The *coronetti* are amazing. They're so flaky and buttery. And the ones with dark chocolate, they're so dense they make your eyelids flutter. I love that the pastries aren't too sweet. It allows all the subtle flavors of the ingredients to unfold beautifully on the tongue," I said.

"Well what are we waiting for? Let us get something to 'gnosh on' as you North Americans say. We can eat and talk at the same time, can we not?" asked Benny.

The two of us pushed ourselves away from the high table facing the window and hopped off the tall wood and metal stools. Once at the counter, I became woozy with gluttony, but I harnessed my piggishness and settled for a couple of the olive and chocolate mini cakes. I knew them to be sweet and bitter and softly salty (from the whole black olive stuffed inside), but as moist as pudding. I took two pieces as they were two-bite cylinders, so it was a respectable portion of food, I thought. Not craving a warm drink, I ordered a *limonata* to complete my order.

I returned to my seat promptly, but Benny was taking her time making a much more considered selection. Besides all the wares at the counter, she carefully scrutinized all the trays stacked in multi-tiered bakers racks tucked into various pockets of the café. When eventually she came back to the table with a coffee, she also had a ricotta and raisin *frollo* and a *sfoglia glassate*, a puff pastry slice furled around poppy seeds and almond butter.

"Before you put those down," I said, "maybe we should move over there, I said, grabbing my cakes and Italian lemonade and directing with my chin to a couple of stools in a slightly more private area.

"*Concordato*. It is a busy place."

We seated ourselves on the same side of a table for two, cornered in on two sides by bakers' racks, still with a view to the work area and to the street, but we angled ourselves so we could face each other when speaking.

Benny gently split one of her pastries. "First of all, I want to thank you so, so very much for not mentioning my name in any of the interrogations. I hope it does not create any problems for you. I could never forgive myself if you went to prison for, how do you call it, obstruction of the course of justice."

"It was a no-brainer. As soon as Malik left my office that day, Marco mentioned you were applying for a Permanent Resident Card and none of us wanted to risk you being denied the status."

"I am grateful, but I am the one who pulled you into this mess by showing you that video clip."

"Please don't give it a second thought. We had a long talk about it and none of us thought that sharing the video would enhance the inquiry in any way, you know, because it was so dark. And we don't know if that was the person who actually entered the warehouse–"

"So, what was it like, being questioned by the Canadian Security Intelligence?"

"Well, first of all, I was so relieved we didn't have to go to Ottawa. I had no idea they had offices in downtown Toronto, right on Front Street, about ten minutes from here. It's by the CBC building. Who knew? I've probably gone by it a million times and never realized it was a CSIS headquarters. It looks like an ordinary building."

"I suspect that is intentional. Just like your Museum warehouse. It is meant to be somewhat *invisibile* to people who pass by."

I nodded. "The rooms they took us into were pretty nondescript, too. I think I was expecting something very different. Clearly, I've been watching too many British TV police procedural shows lately. I thought I'd have a couple of high-ranking officers on one side of a table with a portfolio of photos, documents, and a slide show and making an audio recording."

Benny chuckled and some of the pastry flakes that had stuck to her lips, floated to the table like down feathers. "So, it was not like that?"

"Nope. It was actually pretty chill, and they seemed to go out of their way to make me feel at ease."

"After all, you are not the criminal."

"I know, but like I said to Malik, I have no idea why someone would pick me to hand off stolen art-work. How would anyone doing this even know who I am? I'm just a dull, little museum administrative employee who tries to lead a quiet and simple life."

"Dull is not a way I would describe you, and from what Marco has told me about your previous adventures, you do not lead as quiet and simple a life as you suggest."

157

"Well, I've had my moments, I guess." I thought back to when I took down a huge chocolate fountain during a gala event at the Museum attempting to thwart what I thought were the efforts of The Leopard to steal some Museum arti-facts. "But still, this is freaking me out. Just walking into the CSIS building made me feel guilty, like I had walked into a priest's confessional." I took the second mouthful of my two-bite chocolate dream and swallowed it more quickly than the first.

"I am sure I would feel the same way."

"Honestly, my conversation with Stewart was a lot more stressful."

"Oh, no. Why? What did he say?"

"I mean, he didn't flip out or anything. But he was going to interrupt his contract with the museum in California and come back to Toronto."

"Would that be so bad? It does seem like you are carry-ing a big burden here, from what Marco has told me."

"I just don't see what it would accomplish. And if he left, he might jeopardize his relationship with the client – and it's a very lucrative contract – it's kind of keeping our depart-ment afloat. Luckily, Malik called Stewart right back and ba-sically said the same thing, so Stewart decided to stay put."

"Well that is good if that is what you want. But Marco told me you have not been sleeping well. He is very con-cerned about you."

"He doesn't need to be."

"But he is very...very fond of you."

I squirmed around on my stool, shifting my weight from side to side. "I guess we've developed a kind of brother-sis-ter-like relationship."

Benny erupted into laughter. "I am not sure that is the

best way to describe the chemistry I have sensed between you."

There was a build-up of heat in my face.

"You must not feel uncomfortable." Benny smiled. "I know Italian women are often thought to be tempestuous, but I do not think I am one of them. It is just that when he was telling me about that man from England…"

"Who, Geoffrey?"

"Yes. He did not speak about him with much kindness. I could only guess he felt some sense of jealously towards him. Marco mentioned Geoffrey is interested in you – those are his exact words."

"He's definitely reading too much into things," I said.

"No, I do not think so. You seem to blush when we speak of both Geoffrey and Marco."

"Now YOU are reading too much into things. But I don't understand why Marco tried to insinuate that Geoffrey was somehow involved in all of these events. It's almost mean-spirited."

"But I understand Geoffrey came to visit you at almost the exact moment the artifact was delivered to the Museum?"

"That was sheer coincidence. Malik went through the tapes, and there's no evidence Geoffrey ever had the package in his possession. The videos from different cameras show him arriving in a cab, no suspicious bundle in hand, and leaving in a cab. The box seems to have been dropped off by a kid wearing a hoodie…a young boy, maybe nine or ten, based on his height, walked in, slipped the package onto the Security Desk and walked straight back out without a single person noticing him. There was no camera capture of his face, nothing distinct about his clothing. Nothing that was in any way helpful to the investigators."

"I see. So, it seems someone probably recruited this boy off the street," said Benny.

"Probably."

"And Geoffrey is not implicated. Well that is good then. May I ask you something quite personal?"

"I think you're going to ask it no matter what I say." I grinned, and Benny replicated the expression.

"Is the reason you have not explored things with Marco because you believe you might be too, how shall I say this, mature for him?'

I gulped some *limonata*, coughed, and let my throat settle. "You know, I recently saw a movie from the 60s I'd never seen before – *Girl with Green Eyes* – and I heard a line that made a lot of sense to me. A young Lynn Redgrave, you probably don't know who she is, she's a British actress."

"I do know her. Her sister, Vanessa Redgrave, is an activist and the family is well-known in Italy, especially by the authorities."

"Really? Well, Lynn Redgrave quotes a line to Rita Tushingham that Peter Finch had said to her off camera – 'old men and young girls are all very well in books, but nowhere else.' The same applies to old women and young boys."

"We humans often feel situations are more complex than they need to be."

"Sometimes you can't help thinking about the future when it comes to relationships," I said. "Let me ask you something now. Have you and Marco ever had a discussion about children?"

Benny suddenly looked uncomfortable. "Marco and I are still getting to know each other. I do know he loves his sister's *bambini*."

"Well, I'm older than you probably think. You know how they say 'the 40s are the new 30s,' but our reproductive systems don't benefit from that."

"You are in your 40s? I would never have guessed. But women are having children much later than ever. I had a cousin who had a child when she was 42 and then another at 44. She never looked or felt better."

I reduced the volume of my voice. "I can't have children...at all...I am what they used to refer to as 'barren.'"

Benny was silent for a few too many seconds. I continued. "I had some health issues when I was in my mid-30s." I tossed my head back. "Oooooh, it's such a long story."

"You need not say anything more if it hurts your heart to talk about it."

"It's not so much that. It's just that when I tell people what happened to me, they tend to think I'm crazy. But you can't make up stuff like this."

"What was it?"

"Well...we were trying to get pregnant, my ex-husband and I, but I was having some problems with my immune system. I kept getting sick all the time with colds, flus, infections, on a regular basis. The doctors couldn't figure out what was going on with me. I had so much blood drawn out of me for testing at the time that I could have started my own blood bank."

"So, it was not cancer or something like that?"

I shook my head no. "But the doctors kept prescribing me more and more antibiotics to deal with the different infections. Instead, my immune system grew worse and worse."

"Well, yes it would. Antibiotics kill off too much friendly bacteria in the body, and so often one develops secondary

161

infections. One must always take probiotics with antibiotics."

"You're a smart cookie. I didn't understand that at the time. I blindly trusted that the doctors knew what they were doing."

"*Povera cara*. It is hard to imagine this still happens so much. What followed next?"

"Well, it seemed like overnight, but it wasn't – I guess it was over a period of a year or two, my immune system got weaker and weaker, I got sicker and sicker more frequently. I even developed what's known as 'sick building syndrome.' I could just walk into a building with poor fresh air intake, and I would begin to feel wretched."

"Did you develop environmental sensitivities?"

"You do know something about this, don't you?"

"My mother is a naturopath."

I nodded my head. "I became allergic to all my toiletries, shampoo, soap, makeup, and to cleaning products, you name it. I had to replace everything with organic or 'green' products, and sometimes I couldn't even tolerate those."

"And your husband, was he supportive?"

"He was at the beginning. But one night I woke up completely soaked after having night sweats, and he thought I had AIDS. I reminded him I'd already been tested for the HIV virus, but he started to change. Especially when..." I lowered my head.

Benny took a hold of my hands.

"It turned out I had gone into premature menopause. I was having hot flashes at age 35. Can you believe it? I had some kind of bizarro auto-immune disorder, and it impacted my endocrine system and ultimately my fertility. My body became incredibly toxic."

"This is some kind of nightmare."

"It doesn't end there. I started developing all kinds of food allergies and problems with water."

"Water? But the body cannot survive without water?"

"Tell me about it. I was beginning to feel like I was an alien living in a human body and that the nutrients on this planet were unsuitable for my foreign vessel."

"But what did you do? What were you drinking?"

"It turned out there was something in tap water that my body found unfriendly – could have been the chlorine or fluoride. I still don't know for sure to this day. Then I tried filtering tap water, but that was even worse. The carbon filters used in home purification systems are made from organic products, like corn or coconut, so I don't know if that had anything to do with it. But it turned out to be a disaster as I had an even worse reaction to 'purified' water. I was having hot flashes every few minutes."

"This is unbelievable. You must have been frantic."

"I was definitely confused, but I was trying to go on with my life as best I could. I finally tried distilled water and that at least calmed the symptoms of my hyper-menopause. Eventually I switched to bottled spring water because distilled water leaches the body of minerals."

"And your husband, things were still poor with him?"

"It turned out he didn't have much patience for a frail alien being. He wasn't keen on the fact that my health issues were interrupting his hedonistic enjoyment of life. You know, eat, drink, and be merry. I stopped drinking alcohol entirely, began eating organic food and I became a compulsive food-label-reader. And once it was clear I couldn't produce a mini-him, he decided to trade me in for a younger, healthier model – in secret, of course, and while we were still married."

Benny squeezed my hands, and I noticed her eyes welling up.

"Don't cry for me, Argentina."

Benny released my hands dramatically. "Men! They can be such *imbecilles*." She started muttering something in Italian so rapidly that had the conversation been on screen and subtitled, an audience would not have been able to keep up. "And here you are," she said breaking back into English, "at risk from an element our bodies cannot do without, from *acqua*. You could be dead in the water, under the water, from the water, whatever the expression is, and your husband, all he could think about was himself." She switched back into agitated Italian.

I interrupted. "As horrible as it was, I was never close to dying."

"*Non è importante*! A partner in life is supposed to be stronger for us at such times. When you love someone, you must do it with all your heart and stand with them no matter what, even if they might be–"

A huge bang boomed through the café, and cups, glasses, cutlery, and bakers racks all wobbled from the vibrations of the explosive sound. Everyone jumped out of their shoes, some shrieked, others had their shoulders hunched up, all uttering versions of 'what was that?,' 'what happened?,' 'was that a bomb?'

The lights in the café cut out, and it became eerily quiet. The subtle humming, previously unnoticed, of various pieces of equipment and appliances had halted.

"Oh, for fuck's sake," yelled one of the employees. "Power's totally down."

"*Dio mio!*" exclaimed Benny. "LOOK! What is happening?"

It was pouring cats and dogs outside, but at the same time there was a fountain of sparks flowing from an unseen area above the line of our window view.

Another employee started to make her way towards the exit, but she froze at the top of the small set of stairs. "Oh, man. Better settle in everyone. We won't be going anywhere until someone comes and tells us it's safe," she said.

Another rumble of questions and comments spread through the crowd of customers. "Why, what's going on?" "Is the power out on the whole street?"

Everyone including Benny and me edged closer to the front of the establishment to get a better perspective of the street from the subterranean windows. "Oh, please don't let it be a horrible accident," I prayed under my breath. But when more of the street became visible, I was astonished.

"This is fucking crazy," bellowed the profanity-loving employee. "Looks like lightning hit the streetcar wires. They're hanging all the way down to the sidewalk."

"I can't stay here; I've got to get home to take my dog out or he'll be peeing on the carpet," complained one customer. "I knew I should have stayed home," said another.

"Listen folks," said an employee. Those wires are live, and it's pissing rain. You could get yourself killed. At least here we're safe and cozy, so I suggest you take a seat."

Benny turned to me. "Do you always have such excitement in your neighborhood?"

"Can't say that we do. I was saving this for you, actually."

"Who knows how long the power is going to stay off. Free coffee and tea while it's hot – for everyone!" yelled an employee behind the counter. "I imagine police and hydro crews will be here any–"

Layers of sirens sounded as we heard responders coming closer and closer to the café. The volume was deafening; I had to cover my ears. Finally, the screeching ended. We couldn't see any of the vehicles, so I assumed they had parked further up the street.

"This is *meravigliosa*," said Benny.

"What's so wonderful?" I asked, a little puzzled.

"In Italy, such people as are in here would have already poured into the street. Police and firemen in the different districts would have been arguing about who should interrupt their afternoon espresso and, in the end, no one would come for some time. You Canadians are not only polite, but very level-headed and obedient to systems and rules and regulations. It is so splendid to see people working in such harmony."

"Obedient civil citizens we are indeed," I said. "Let's hope CSIS believes that of Walter, Marco, and me."

CHAPTER TWENTY-TWO

I tilted my head upwards towards the glass ceiling, then soaked up the inspiring stone, metal, and wood elements that surrounded me. Although my current location was far more magnificent in grandeur, it triggered the memory of my recent adventure at the more modestly ambient *Forno Cultura* with Benny over the weekend. Eventually, she was able to get home via the Bathurst Streetcar, and, fortunately for me, the power had not been severed to my building, even though I lived just a block away from the incident.

Traffic remained hampered even into Monday morning rush hour as streetcar wires were still being repaired and buses had taken over the route. But soon enough I made my way into work and now found myself enveloped by classical music piped through speakers in the stunning space occupied by the 'b espresso bar' within Toronto's Royal Conservatory of Music.

The structure literally married the gap between the original Conservatory building and its resplendent addition, one which was a most welcome embellishment on the Bloor Street/University Avenue area landscape. About three stories above me was a pergola-like ceiling/roof with its faux lattice work made of steel and glass panels that kept the outside elements where they belonged. I was seated at one of the modern white and steel tables nestled against the rock-faced masonry that forms the exterior of the heritage part of the building. On the other side of the narrow passage from where I sat rested the trendy bar and café that melds into the spectacular Koerner Hall, a grand performance hall designed by Toronto's own KPMB Architects.

This spot had always been one of my favorite respites when I needed to escape the Museum, and yet, it was situated just steps away, on the other side of Philosopher's Walk. And today, I felt like I needed to be outside the Museum confines to perform the unpleasant task at hand. I savored the few moments I had alone to enjoy my organic chamomile tea in peace. But within moments, I heard the tap of determined feet against the natural stone tiles that composed the café's flooring. I had to dig deep for the smile I sported on my face.

"Well, I see you did not think to order something for me."

"I, I wasn't sure if you were a tea or coffee drinker. I wanted to wait for your arrival–"

"No matter, I will not be here long. There is much work to be done and so little time," said Dr. Zelinka.

As abrupt as she was, I could not help admiring her fashion sense once again. She wore a knitted dress with grey and black vertical stripes, the black lines being about double the width of the grey ones. As she removed her black coat, which resembled the form of a dress with its cinched waist and pleated skirt, the sleeves of her dress revealed themselves to be made of a stretchy grey lace. Her hosiery was black with the narrowest of grey stripes and to her outfit she had added a pop of color with suede lavender shoes with a one-inch chunk heel. I doubted there was any point asking her if she would leave her whimsical shoes to me in her will.

"I'm glad it turned out to be such a lovely, sunny fall day

today, especially after all that rain we had over the weekend," I said.

Dr. Zelinka slivered her eyes. No chance of cracking a smile on that face.

"I actually have some news that I'm sorry to have to deliver–"

A figure stepped up to our table. "Kalena, what a coincidence," she said. "I know we were supposed to meet in an hour, but maybe we can chat here when you are finished with your esteemed guest."

"You look very familiar to me. I have seen you somewhere before," said Dr. Zelinka.

"I had the pleasure of taking one of your classes many years ago, Dr. Zelinka. My name is Dara, Dara Green. I work in the ROM's Conservation Department."

I remember when I first saw Dara's name in the Museum's directory; before I had met her, I thought perhaps she might be of Ukrainian origin, as Dara, meaning 'gift' in my mother tongue, is a fairly common Ukrainian name. But she was not East European at all. Her family hailed, in fact, from Barbados. She had once told me she was mostly of African descent, but suspected she had some of the island's indigenous blood in her mix as well. She was an exotic, natural beauty who underplayed her look by wearing oversized athleisure clothing with her signature blacktop runners.

Dara had long ago come to Toronto, where she had studied at the University of Toronto and was most fortunate to have landed a position in the Conservation Department as a metals conservator. Jobs such as these are so specific that people in these positions tend to be lifers, and I suspected Dara would spend her entire career at the Museum. But her appearance at the café was entirely unexpected this morning, and I found myself gripping my tea cup so tightly my fingers were turning white.

"Yes, I do remember you," said Dr. Zelinka. "Your work was somewhat rudimentary, but I thought you had potential for improvement."

Dara's eyes met mine. I prayed she could read the 'shut up, shut up' signals I was trying to send through them. "That's kind of you to say so," she said. "I've done well for myself at the Museum, actually. But I was so very sorry to hear your design for the Saudi medal was not accepted. I thought it was some of your most elegant work. It's a shame we'll be doing such a disservice to your art with the much simpler design."

Someone just put a bullet through my brain – right now – this very instant!

Dr. Zelinka jerked her head towards me. "What is this mad woman talking about?"

Suddenly, my horrified expression was mirrored in Dara's face. "Uh, oh, I'm...I see I've jumped the gun a bit. I better leave you two to discuss...the situation." Dara one-eightied and sped out of the building so fast I thought she might leave a wake of stone dust in the trail behind her.

"This is some sort of error. Call up your Prince this very moment. I must speak with him. No one has ever rejected my designs, let alone have me replaced with some hack. I have created masterpieces for royalty and have been honored with international awards. No, this is a mistake." She leaned over, picked up my phone, and waved it in my face.

I took a hold of my phone and had to almost rip it from her hand. "I'm so very sorry. It's impossible to call the Prince. I don't communicate with him directly."

"Then there is clearly a language issue. Does anyone on

170

your team speak Arabic?"

"We have a staff member there who does speak Arabic. But the royal family members speak English fluently." I noticed that people in the café were peeking at us out of the corners of their eyes. "Please, calm yourself. You must not consider this a rejection of your design, it's a matter of different cultural and artistic aesthetics."

"They have uncultured taste, these people."

"That's not really an appropriate assessment. It is not our place to impose our Western sensibilities on other cultures."

Dr. Zelinka harrumphed with her entire body. She sprang to her feet and gathered up her belongings. "I can see you are not taking this seriously. But it is of no import. Someone in your position has no authority to deal with such significant matters. I will speak to your Director about this immediately."

"He's aware of the situation," I said.

"Pardon me?" There were daggers flying out of Dr. Zelinka's eyes.

"He's been briefed on the matter. He's currently in Los Angeles and he specifically asked me to deliver the unfortunate news to you myself. He, too, has deep regrets about the turn of events, but the Prince is the client, and we must respect his choice."

With steam coming out of her nostrils, Dr. Zelinka spun around and clicked her way out of the building without looking back. I leaned forward and rested my forehead on the table.

"Are you okay, miss?" said a voice.

I slowly peeled my head off the surface to find one of the café's staff beside me, and I drunkenly rolled my upper body over to one elbow. "Yeah."

"Can I get you anything?" asked the diminutive young Asian woman.

I perked up. "Do you have any more of your decadent brownies?"

* * * * *

I took two brownies to go. After that verbal beating, unfortunately, I still had to meet with Dara to mobilize the medal production. But I was planning on keeping both pastries for myself. Even though I knew Dara had not spilled the beans maliciously, I didn't feel like a reward was in order. I returned to the Museum taking the back route – a short jaunt down Philosopher's Walk and then a quick left over to the Staff Entrance.

When I turned the final corner, I was startled to see Dara propped against the wall, looking like a sad dog. Immediately, she pushed herself away from the wall and stood erect. "I'm soooo sorry. I didn't mean for things to unfold that way. I hope I didn't leave you with too much of a mess to clean up," said Dara.

My heart unthawed instantaneously. "Aw, you know, her reaction was totally wackadoodle. And I think she's possibly racist. She made some comments about Middle Eastern culture that were seriously politically incorrect."

"I'm not surprised. She's an amazing artist, but I don't think she belonged in academia. I heard about so many confrontations with students and faculty. I think she was encouraged to sever her ties with the university sooner than she expected. That probably made her more insane than she already was."

172

"We'll send her blessings of love and compassion then, shall we?" I winked.

Dara threaded her arm through mine. "C'mon let's go up to the Conservation Department and bang out a production schedule. It's going to be super tight, but I'm used to fast turnarounds in this place," she said, edging me towards the Staff Entrance.

"Well there's a new twist I just learned about this morning, by the way."

Dara halted in her tracks. "Like what?"

"The Prince wants an additional 200 medals, plated in gold, for his VIP guests."

"Wow."

"And they want presentation boxes for all of the medals."

"Double wow. I'll see what I can do about the gold-plated medals – they're always trickier. More things can go wrong in production. But the boxes, that's your gig."

"I was afraid of that. But you have no idea how grateful I am that you're managing production. You're a lifesaver – literally." I lifted up the paper bag in my hand. "I've got brownies."

"Good girl. You're going to be needing a lot more chocolate in the next few weeks."

CHAPTER TWENTY-THREE

'**37** billion of treasure hidden around Europe' read the title of an article I was reading on my mobile while riding the Queen Streetcar. It was, not surprisingly, an overcast day with predictions for rain. I was on my way to meet Walter, Marco, and Benny, and even though we were planning on being indoors for most of our time together, I was hoping the precipitation would hold off until we were securely indoors. Cancelling the outing that Benny had organized had been on my mind that morning, but she had gone to considerable effort to get special permission for the three of us to join her on a photo session she had wrangled at the R.C. Harris Water Treatment Plant, one of the city's most striking landmark buildings, to which public access is, for the most part, restricted. Benny, bless her heart, thought it would be a fun and relaxing way for us to spend the day, what with Walter and I being lovers of architecture. Marco, well he apparently only agreed to join us after some ranting. But I'm sure he found Benny hard to resist.

Unconsciously, I dipped my hand into the container of addictive Alter Eco Organic Salted Caramel Truffles. Made of malty Ecuadorian cacao, rich coconut oil, and a sprinkling of Fleur de Sel Guerande salt, I tried to unearth an uneaten truffle among the discarded wrappers. I was certain there were at least a few uneaten ones...or had I really eaten all ten truffles in my hour plus streetcar ride? My hand found one last small orb, unwrapped it, and popped it in its entirety into my mouth. These irresistibly creamy truffles melted exceedingly quickly.

Refocusing on my phone, I scrolled further down the article. 'While some of these cultural treasures were saved by Allied units, around $37 billion of loot is still missing. And the hunt is still on.'

$37 billion – that's mind boggling. As I read further, the emphasis of the article was on precious metals, like the $93 million in silver and jewelry hidden somewhere in the hills surrounding the castle of Wewelsburg in northeast Germany and $100 million in gold apparently dumped in Lake Walchen near Munich. But the more I Googled about lost treasures, the more I realized the volume of confiscated treasure still evading authorities was imponderable, that copious amounts had been destroyed or literally lost, and, most interestingly, how little information seemed to be available about possible Allied troop involvement, other than by the Russians, that is.

Apparently, the Soviets had done a highly commendable job of pillaging Germany at the conclusion of the war. In fact, in 1998, the Russians had gone so far as to pass a federal law on *Cultural Valuables Displaced to the USSR as a Result of the Second World War and Located on the Territory of the Russian Federation*, which allowed Russians to keep illegally stolen art and museum pieces and to prevent any restitution to Germany. Didn't that violate International Law?

After a tad more searching, I did find a reference to a few measly pieces of art, apparently won in a poker game by some American G.I. – hmm, that sounded like a familiar story – that were eventually returned to their rightful owners by the Monuments Men Foundation. But overall, I was sensing a conspiracy of silence about any possible Allied misdoings.

My intuition was telling me that the works turning up in my life were not from a German source. And they weren't likely to be Russian bounty since the Russians had basically 'legitimized' their right to keep anything they had confiscated from the Germans, even if initially stolen from another country.

I lifted my gaze to the barren trees I passed en route. Most of the leaves had now fallen and had been swept away by recent rains and wind. 'Winter is coming.' When I arrived at the eastern-most end of the Queen Streetcar line and descended, I was grateful to be wearing my lavender lace rain coat and sporting my lavender umbrella. Extending my palm outside of the umbrella's scope of coverage, I realized I didn't actually need it. There was the lightest of rain drizzle, but I decided to stow away the collapsible implement inside my black pleather purse.

The walk, slightly east and south from the streetcar stop, to one of Toronto's not-so-best-kept architectural secrets was brief, but I started shivering instantly. It was at least 15 degrees colder here than it had been back near Bathurst and King. It was usually colder by the lake, but it became clear to me I had stepped smack dab into a kind of heat inversion. I didn't understand why these inversions formed, but I did know that in these instances the warmer layer of air closer to the surface of the ground somehow gets pushed up into the atmosphere and is replaced by a much colder layer of air.

Just ahead I spotted a metal gate befitting the art deco edifice that loomed behind it. I remembered having read that the security entrance was a modern add-on and that the steel and cast aluminum piece, along with its mechanical components, had cost a considerable bit of coin.

The gate had a sense of whimsy and elegance with its scallop-like design. And stamped right through the lower bar of the gate, allowing the light to pass through, were the words 'R.C. Harris Filtration Plant.' The swing part of the gate was not connected post to post, but left a gap of several feet at the western margin, allowing easy access to the grounds by pedestrians. At the same time, it was evident any vehicle short of a tank would not be able to plow through the metal defender.

After passing onwards, my colleagues were nowhere to be seen. But as soon as I pressed towards the edge of the top of the hill where stairs lead to a lower plane, I could see my three Musketeers huddled at the base of the steps under one large golf umbrella donning the Museum's logo. It could only belong to Walter.

"Why didn't you text us when you'd be arriving?" blurted out Marco on my approach. "We could've waited inside." Even he looked a little chilled.

I tossed a smirk at Benny. "Sorry, I was doing a bit of research on my phone during the long ride here and got pre-occupied." Redirecting my gaze to Marco, I added, "you should know by now the best way to keep tabs on me is to give me a lift."

"Oh, oh. I'm so very sorry for the oversight. I thought you had your own vehicle," said Walter startling me. "A Smart Car, I believe Brenda had mentioned to me."

"I didn't mean you, Walter. Anyway, dead battery issue. I just need to call roadside assistance. The battery's in the most ridiculous spot ever, under the floor on the passenger side, if you can believe it. It's impossible for a normal person to boost it."

"I could've helped with that...if I'd known about it," said

Marco.

"You've been too busy trying to get Geoffrey arrested."

Walter and Benny exchanged wide-eyed glances. "What kind of research were you conducting," said Walter, "if you do not mind me asking?"

"Nothing important. I'll tell you about it later. Have you already done the intro?"

Walter's expression transitioned into one of confusion.

"You know, the traditional history lesson we get anytime we meet at a new spot. Or maybe Benny's going to do it this time, since this is her gig." I winked at her.

"Oh, no, no. Walter's English is much better than mine. *Dopo di te*, Walter."

"We do have time, don't we Benny?" I glanced at Marco. His arms were crossed.

Benny withdrew her phone and scanned the screen. "*Certo*. I have not yet received a text from our guide."

Under my breath I mumbled, "And Marco was riding me about my arrival time because?"

"What did you say?" asked Marco.

"Nothing." I exaggerated a smile. "You know, I was here once a really long time ago for an art exhibit."

"That must have been before 9/11," said Walter.

"Good guess. Actually, it was so long ago, I couldn't find any reference to it on the Internet."

"Maybe it never happened," said Marco.

"Ha, ha. They had these monumental canvases and art installations set out throughout the building, kind of like Ai Weiwei's work. Really interesting pieces."

"Yes, I was told about that," said Benny. "That would have been something to see. Do you have photos?"

"I honestly can't remember. It was before the day of cell

178

phones, before Marco was born."

"Interesting," said Walter. "Well, if I may proceed, this is one of the city's grandest treasures, in my opinion. The facility was named after the city's former Commissioner of Public Works and was designed in 1929 by Thomas C. Pomphrey, but did not open until 1941. As we can see, the edifice is a huge compound of buff brick, stylized frescoes, and arching windows. It is hard to fathom that this Art Deco building is a fully functioning water filtration plant providing the city with 45% of its water supply. Water is also chlorinated here and then pumped to various reservoirs throughout Toronto and region."

Marco moved away from the shelter of the umbrella and plopped himself down on a step. Benny drifted over and stood beside her seated paramour.

"Marco, what is the matter with you today?" asked Benny, nudging her knee into Marco's upper arm.

"Nothing. Go on, Walter."

"The entrance is modelled after a Byzantine gate—"

"*Interessante*," remarked Benny, "that it has that Byzantine connection, like the ROM's Rotunda."

I nodded.

"The use of Byzantine elements in architecture and décor in the first half of the twentieth century was very trendy. I cannot wait to view the opulent interior. It has been nicknamed the *Palace of Purification*. Such a shame the public cannot see the interior regularly. The buildings' limited access is a hangover of heightened security following 9/11. More recently, they have reassessed matters and certain parts of the plant can now be visited during such events as Open Doors Toronto. But I understand from Benny we will be seeing areas still off-limits to most, and without any crowds.

179

How fortunate are we?" The glee in Walter's voice was a testament to his nerdiness.

Marco started to push himself up.

"Let's not forget the films and TV shows that have used this place as a location," I said.

Marco plunked back down.

"Correction, it's actually in literature where it's been most prominently memorialized," I added.

"Indeed," said Walter. "In Michael Ondaatje's *In the Skin of a Lion*. The book is a vivid exposé of the life of the migrant workers who constructed the plant. The novel was nominated for a Governor General's Award for English Language Fiction in 1987. But the filming history at this site is definitely your forte."

"They aren't exactly Oscar-nominated films," I said. "*Undercover Brother* and *Strange Brew*...and more recently, *Regression* with Ethan Hawke and Emma Watson. But this place has also turned up in a lot of television series, like *Flashpoint*, *The Pretender*, and *Robocop*."

"*Scusi*, Kalena. I am glad you have shared this information with us, but we must now meet our escort. It seems she is inside waiting for us."

Marco sprang up like a fireworks rocket set alight. "Let's get the heck out of here."

"Our guide is a communications coordinator with the city," said Benny. "We are starting here at this smaller building. It is the pump house."

My three comrades darted ahead while I lagged behind, snickering at the fact that the four of us lacked the nimbleness of Aramis, Athos, Prothos and d'Artagnan. But as unlikely a quartet of characters as we were, we had formed an unusual bond and our tolerance of Marco's inexplicable crankiness was an indication of our unspoken camaraderie.

"Wowza," I said. "This architecture is so breathtaking."

Benny turned around, "I agree. People always ask of me how I could have left behind the magnificent architecture in Italy and then I see a treasure like this, and I think to myself that you Canadians so often underestimate the beauty in front of your eyes."

"Perhaps," said Walter, "but this structure is not exactly along the beaten path for most Torontonians to admire."

"I suppose you are right," said Benny.

No sooner had she finished her sentence than a petite woman with jet black hair, pulled back into a high pony tail, and wearing minimal makeup appeared at the entrance. With a convivial warmth she smiled and seemed to have spotted the camera slung over Benny's shoulder, "Hello, I'm Camila Cardozo. You must be Benny," she said.

"I am. It is so nice to finally meet you in person. Again, I cannot thank you enough for allowing us here and taking time out on a weekend."

"It's always fun to come here and show it off. My job has constantly entailed weekend work. I knew what I was signing up for." That explained why, though a Sunday, Ms. Cardozo was dressed in business attire including a two-piece indigo suit with a collared, ultramarine shirt underneath the jacket. I pondered whether she always wore water hues when touring people here.

We introduced ourselves and once formalities were concluded, Camila turned to the four of us. "I'm sure this cold is settling in your bones. But it seems to be lifting a bit with this wind coming in. What bizarre weather we're having today. In any case, I won't keep you out here long. I just wanted to point out a few of the exterior features."

I glimpsed over at Marco, expecting to see eyes rolling into the back of his head, but suddenly he seemed all ears.

"I'm sure you've noticed the yellow brick and Queenston Limestone."

"It is very skilled stonework," commented Walter. "Stunning even, I would say."

Benny had raised her camera and was already snapping shots.

"Did you notice the ornamentation?" said Camila gazing upwards. We all stepped back a few feet. "Those are stylized turbines serving as pilaster capitals."

A strong burst of wind stirred up and whipped a section of my hair in front of my eyes. I pulled it back, but another blast just blew it forward again.

"Shall we head indoors? This wind might be blowing in a storm." said Camila.

"I'll say." I turned my back into the stinging gust and noted that Walter had done the same. Then suddenly a piece of paper sailed by me and latched onto Walter's back, like one of those nightmarish alien creatures in a sci fi movie that adheres itself to its human prey with nefarious intentions.

Leaning into the wind while trying to keep the hair out of my face, I snatched the piece of paper that had clamped onto my colleague. It took only a millisecond of a glance before my heart felt like someone had pressed the 'pause' button on it. Before I could solidify my grip on the sheet, the wind seized it and swooped it into the heavens.

"OH, NO!" I screamed. The others jerked to a standstill. I swished the hair out of my eyes and gasped. Around me a flurry of papers were hurtling in the air and I sprang to seize another sheet. It was identical to the one that had flown away. As if mind-melded, Walter, Marco and Benny all scurried to gather the flying debris without me having said anything. But, one by one, I saw their facial expressions transform.

"I appreciate the effort, but don't worry about those," said Camila. "Flying garbage is, unfortunately, one of the consequences of being near the lake and in such a wide open space. Those sheets will all land somewhere nearby and the city's cleanup crews will gather them."

"I'm sure," I said. I peered around. Walter seemed to be quaking underneath his tweed overcoat. Marco was scanning the grounds, and Benny, she just looked thoroughly spooked. Was this really happening again? Who could possibly have known we would be here? Why hadn't we noticed anyone nearby releasing these reams of paper?

CHAPTER TWENTY-FOUR

As Camila ambled closer to the portal, Marco raced ahead of her and opened the weighty door. She passed over the threshold with Benny and Walter at her heels.

"Well, aren't we the gentleman today?" I said to Marco. But before passing inside, I turned around and scanned the myriad of papers scattering about the lawn. With the lake made choppy by the wind, the sheets eerily mimicked the whitecaps of the unusually large waves that had formed. I was reminded what a powerful force Lake Ontario could be. It had mercilessly swallowed many a ship and seafarer over the centuries.

Rotating back towards Marco, I opened my mouth to speak.

"Don't," he said. "It's not the place."

"But, something's really wrong here."

"No kidding," he said, gently urging me ahead.

"Do you think Benny could be involved with this...or Walter?"

Marco guffawed. "Now you've completely lost your marbles."

"Who else—"

"Just get inside," said Marco, more sternly than I had ever heard him speak to me.

"Okay, okay."

We passed into a small vestibule, and I noticed the

highly polished railings right away. At the base of them, the brass curved into a shape that looked like a nautilus. The stairwell, though small, was a stunning mixture of light and dark marbles, and along with the intricately twisted metal spindles supporting the railing, I found myself mesmerized by the attention to detail of the architectural elements and their intrinsic harmony.

"As you may have noticed, this elaborate foyer is centered on the drinking fountain niche. It deliberately divides twinned symmetrical routes to the pump room." Camila was gesturing like a flight attendant. "It really doesn't matter which route we take. We'll end up in the same spot."

Camila scampered up the stairs to the right, and we followed. On the ascent, I noticed the edges of a piece of paper wedged into Walter's pocket, but I was distracted by a loud droning that battered us more and more. There were several signs warning visitors not to stay in this area for more than 30 minutes – I presumed because our ears could be damaged by overexposure to the deafening sound of the pumps below.

The main pump 'ballroom' was separated by a wall of glass panels and a couple of doors leading out onto a balcony. Camila opened the closest door, and we were walloped by the unmuted sound of the pumps. We followed onto the walk-out balcony which offered an expansive surveillance point.

My knees trembled, as they always did at heights, but I carefully scoured the view. I didn't know what I was looking for exactly, but what I saw were rows of round teal machinery, probably taller than my 5'5,'' shaped similarly to giant nautilus shells, and laid out in orderly ranks on the orange-tiled floor. Peering directly across to the ceiling area, there was a steel bridge that spanned the room housing a ginormous pulley system with a monumental hook hanging ominously right over the middle of the room. Overall, it was a visual spectacle that reminded me of a movie set one might see in a Guillermo del Toro film – flamboyantly colored, cinematic, and almost surreal. But the whirring of the pumps was already starting to aggravate me.

"Those are what pull in water from Lake Ontario," screeched Camila, "and then, after the water is purified, it's redirected to other distribution locations throughout the city. They're the original pumps, by the way. They were really built to last. I'm not exaggerating when I say they don't build them like this anymore. We'll see them up close in a few minutes." She motioned for us to follow her back from where we had come.

We crossed the open area and were led to another section. "So, this was originally the plant's control room," said Camila, reducing the volume of her voice substantially. "It's slightly smaller than a school's gymnasium, and these days it's almost empty, as you can see."

There were a few antique odds and ends in the corners of the room and a few pictures hanging on the walls. "Currently, it doesn't have a utilitarian purpose, but that wasn't always the case. In that 1940s picture over there, you see evidence that it was once filled with NASA-like gear, heaps of electronics, blinking indicator lights, and massive dials."

Benny returned to snapping pictures, then ambled over to me in one of the corners of the old control room, presenting to me the digital LED screen on her camera. Walter also moseyed our way and joined the huddle. Speaking under her breath, Benny said, "The image on the paper, it looked like an Egyptian motif."

Walter nodded yes.

Across the room, Marco was at Camila's side, but his eyes darted our way. Spontaneously, he began a conversation with our guide that we were unable to discern.

"It is the Egyptian falcon," continued Walter in a sotto voce, "associated with the all-seeing Eye of Horus and with the god Ra. It's clutching the symbol of the fullness of life in one of its claws."

"It's an image from the Museum's mosaic ceiling, isn't it?" I said.

"Definitely. It is very distinct. A side view of a falcon with its two wings extended, one above the other, almost as though it's hiding something in its feathered span."

"Is that supposed to mean something's been hidden here?" I said.

Walter shrugged his shoulders.

Camila and Marco rejoined us, and we exited the room together. Just outside the doorway lay a piece of paper on the otherwise pristine floor. My stomach clenched as Camila stooped down to pick it up. "What is this?" We could all see it bore the same image as the papers that had been soaring about the facility's grounds – it was adorned with the stylized image of the falcon.

"Oh, I am sure that must have fallen out of my pocket." Sweat was forming on Walter's forehead.

"Hmm. Well, this place is so immaculate we don't even have garbage bins lying about."

"Here, I'll take that," said Marco. He seized it unceremoniously from Camila's hand, crumpled it into a ball, and stuffed it into his coat pocket.

"Oh, okay," said Camila. "Thank you, I guess."

As a group, we had to have been coming across like a

bunch of fried lunatics, and Benny was probably wishing she had never invited us. Unless…she had ulterior motives and actually wanted us to be there.

We shifted into another space. "This is the current control room, which you won't be able to take pictures of, unfortunately," Camila said turning to Benny, "for security reasons." It was austerely furnished with a large desk and a few computer monitors. "Everything's regulated by a single person. In fact, the whole plant now is so automated it's run by just two people 75% of the time."

"That is most efficient," chimed in Walter. "Where is the current controller?"

"Not far, I'm sure. Perhaps on a break."

With the building as underpopulated as Antarctica, it seemed anyone could roam the halls unencumbered. I wondered if there were innocuous cameras throughout, but I was unable to discern any. Surely there had to be some kind of Big Brother presence in the facility.

"Let's head downstairs again and check out the pumps up close and personal, shall we?" said Camila.

Once back on the ground level, we wandered onto the most highly polished clay tile floor one could imagine. It was so shiny, you could almost see your reflection in it, and so spotlessly clean you could eat a meal off it. At this point, I was tempted to pull out the silicone ear plugs I carried with me at all times. I used them during my daily gym classes where I found music was played at an uncomfortably loud volume.

But the sound here was definitely many decibels more powerful than what I was exposed to in my workouts. Benny on the other hand was having a field day, seemingly oblivious to the painful drone. And she was getting a workout and a half running from one end of the cavernous space to the other.

Finishing up the extent of the pump house, we were led to our point of entry. Marco ploughed forward to open once again the hefty doors, and we stepped back outside. It felt as though the four of us quietly gasped in unison, each visibly looking dumbfounded. There wasn't a single sheet left in the area. The lawn was as paper-free as we had originally found it, as if we had dreamed it. A shudder waved through my body. I wasn't sure if it was because of the chill of the outdoors nipping at me again or if my intuition was nagging me to pay attention.

Camila marched us around the pump house and towards another building that we were soon bypassing.

"Aren't we going in here?" I asked.

"I'm afraid this building is not part of any tour. It's not as mysterious as you might think. It's the Alum Tower and it houses two gravity-fed alum flocculant hoppers and some head pump equipment."

"Huh, what?" I said.

Walter chirped in. "Alum, or aluminum sulfate. It is used to remove unwanted color and turbidity—"

I put up my hand.

"Stirred up sediment," continued Walter. "Simply said, it clarifies the water."

"Thank you for that explanation," said Camila. "Very thorough."

"Is that really safe for humans?" I asked.

"There are toxic versions. This isn't one of them," she answered. "Shall we move on to the main building?"

"If it's not toxic, why won't they let visitors inside the building?" I muttered under my breath. Walter shot me a scolding glance, and I decided to zip it.

Camila was gaining some ground, so we scampered to catch up. She paused and directed us to the largest and most photographed edifice of the complex. "The filtration building's south entrance is just up ahead."

"It is even more impressive at this proximity than it is from the lake," said Walter. "I have sailed by here, and although the proportions from a distance are imposing, this is, as Kalena would say, 'beyond.'"

"You're right about that. But you never struck me as a sailor type," I said.

"There are many things about me that might surprise you."

"Is that right?" I dipped my chin and looked out of the corners of my eyes at Marco, but he appeared to be ignoring me.

"I love these fountains, don't you?" said Camila pointing out one small north-facing and one slightly larger south facing-fountain decorated with exquisite yet simple Art Deco motifs. Though of a different period, these outdoor fountains reminded me of the type of small waterworks one might haphazardly encounter in the streets of cities like Paris and Rome.

I must have been lingering too long as Camila was suddenly herding me towards the other Musketeers. Still, I managed to inhale the vast lake-facing view of 'The Palace' and its expressive yellow brick and Queenston Limestone. The row of arched windows in groupings of five seemed to stretch endlessly along its east-west axis. For Toronto, this was a massive building, which could have only been built at what, back in the day, was the eastern edge of urban development. Today, the city sprawls much further east melding seamlessly with what were once suburbs.

Inside, Camila lead us promptly to a small laboratory where there were ten identical kitchen faucets continuously pouring water into a single elongated basin.

"This is pretty strange," I said. "It looks like something Dali would have dreamed up."

Camila chuckled. "I agree. But each faucet serves a specific purpose as each one is connected to a different point in the purification process. It allows the staff to take a sample of water from anywhere in the plant to help them calibrate their testing equipment."

"Intriguing," said Walter.

From all angles, Benny was taking photos galore of the sink-gone-wild. You could tell she was going to get some unique perspectives.

Camila snatched a couple of paper cups from a supply resting off to the side and situated one underneath the first faucet. "This is raw lake water." Then after heading to the other end of the basin, she filled a second cup. "And this is the plant's final purified water." We all strolled over to her and peered inquisitively at the clear liquid in both cups.

"I don't understand," I said. "From looking at it, you can't tell the difference from the raw water and the treated water."

"That's exactly the point. The common perception is that Lake Ontario is really dirty but, in fact, it's very clean, spotless actually, and there's minimal purification work. Most of what is done at the plant is to simply filter out some sand and grit."

Walter extended his hand towards Camila. "May I try both cups of water?"

Camila speedily dumped the water from the cups into the sink. "Uh, no. We can't allow that."

Walter looked a little frazzled, and I whispered into Benny's ear, "I'm not so keen to try even the purified water." The Alum Tower was haunting me.

"What was that?" said Camila.

"Uh, well, I, uh, only drink spring water," I said.

"Oooooh," she said. Camila forged ahead with a bit of attitude in her body. "We are so fortunate this building was constructed when it was. Can you imagine a municipality funding this kind of opulence and ornamentation these days?"

"Not imaginable even for a museum or art gallery in this age," stated Walter, clearly soaking everything in as we strolled through one of the twin hallways. "Opulent, indeed."

"Oh, wow," I said as we entered the central rotunda. I remembered it had taken my breath away the first time I saw it, and it was no less impressive on the second visit. "This is too gorgeous. I mean, this is an effing water filtration plant."

"*Vero.*" It wasn't long before Benny was darting everywhere along the splendid floor.

"Careful not to slip," bellowed Camila. She rotated back towards us. "I'm so proud when I show off this area. You can see that the floor is in a compass pattern, and it's composed of beige and black terrazzo fields, Valternache inlays—"

"Val what?" asked Marco.

"Valternache – it's the green and black marble. And the honey-colored marble is Rosata Clair," continued Camila.

"I just love this ceiling." I sighed all the way down to my toes, feeling as though I had been transported to an Italian Renaissance villa. For a breath, the tensions melted from both body and spirit.

"I am in agreement, Kalena," said Walter. "It is completely incongruous to our colorful Museum Rotunda ceiling, but the simplicity of the polygonal ceiling dome embossed with those geometric patterns is extraordinary in its subtlety." With head tilted skywards, Walter rotated 360 degrees on the spot. "It is glorious how the room is top-lit through the milk glass spider's web skylight." He lowered his gaze a touch. "And balances exquisitely with the spider's web skylights running down the length of this hall. Had the upper decoration been anything but monochromatic, this spectacular centerpiece would have been lost in an overabundance of lavishness."

"It's so wonderful to have visitors who understand the components of design. Let's step a bit closer here, shall we?" gestured Camila towards the room's tour de force. "This signal pylon is centered directly in the middle of the room."

"As if inspired by an Egyptian obelisk," Walter said.

"An Egyptian obelisk," I said, fists clenched, and sharing gazes with my companions that suddenly turned nervous.

"It was intended to have that kind of classical monumentality, but it has a very modern utilitarian purpose. You can see the various monitoring lights and dials, which, at a glance, can give readings of the time of day, the rate of filtration in millions of gallons per day, and even the depth of the water in the reservoirs."

The pylon was an elegant work of art on its own. It mirrored the floor in composition in terms of bands of Valternache and Rosata Clair marble, but it was also inset with chrome and bronze panels that were so highly polished you could see your reflection. I walked to within inches of it, then peered around one corner. What was that? I squinted hard.

"Um, Camila." I grabbed her arm firmly and she jumped. "I thought I saw some movement down there."

"It's possible one of the few staff got curious about us

and stepped out."

I twisted my head towards Walter just as he lifted his arm and pointed. "Look, about half way down the hallway. It looks like it could be a piece of paper."

"My eyesight's not that great," I said. "Marco, Benny, can you see it?"

"I have eyesight like an owl in the dark," said Benny.

"Why does that not surprise me?" I said.

Without warning, Benny took off like a sprinter at the sound of a starter's pistol. Marco, Walter, and I looked at each other and had a moment. It wasn't a Musketeer moment. It was a Three Stooges moment. It was a 'what the fuck do we do?' moment. "Oh, for crying out loud," I said and then peeled after Benny. In nanoseconds, Marco surpassed me in leaps in bounds. I rotated my head and saw Walter yards behind. "Really, Walter?"

Through his gasping Walter retorted, "I am not wearing proper footwear for this pace of movement."

"Wait, what are you doing?" shrieked Camila. "We're headed that way anyway, there's no need to gallop." And then I heard the click of her heels on the marble floor. "We really need to stay together as a group."

Up ahead, Benny had come to a halt, then Marco. They gazed at the ground and then glanced back at us. "*Veni, veni. Pronto.*"

First, I caught up with the pair, then Walter hobbled up, then Camila. She gazed downwards and stooped over.

"NO!" I cried. "Don't touch it."

Camila jerked up and leaned away from me. "What is going on here? You people are starting to creep me out a bit. It's just one of those sheets of paper we saw flying around outside...which is kind of odd, actually. I'm not sure how it ended up in here."

"Our behavior must seem a bit unusual. Please excuse us." Benny's calming tone sounded as though she was trying to put Camila under a spell. "It is a little complicated. But we think that perhaps we are being led towards something."

"Led to what?" Camila said furrowing her eyebrows.

Benny turned to me. "Are you sure you saw someone?"

"It was more like a shadow," I said.

I noticed Marco tilting his site line up at the skylights. "It could have just been clouds passing by," said Marco.

"I, I don't know. It's possible, I guess."

Walter rotated towards Camila. "Out of curiosity, where are you taking us next? I presume you have a standard route for your itinerary."

"You do have moments of brilliance," I said, giving Walter a punch in the upper arm. He looked at his limb and massaged it.

"On Benny's adamant request, I'm taking you to an area I'm not usually able to include on a tour. You folks will have to be extra careful, and you MUST stay with me."

"Let us proceed then?" said Walter.

"Lions and tigers and bears," I muttered under my breath.

Camila once again bent down to pick up the paper, but then straightened herself out. "We can get that on our way out."

I couldn't tell what was going on in Camila's mind.

"We're going to walk to the end of this hallway, but I'm sure you'll be very curious about what you see behind this long row of glass panels," said our guide.

It was dark on the other side of the transparent wall save for the distant arched windows. One, two, three, four, five, I counted. These were obviously the windows we observed from the exterior when we walked along the south end of the building. Below them, in long pools of what appeared to be black water, was the eerie reflection of the windows lit by the outdoor light. It was a haunting image and I found myself leaning in, almost pressing my nose to the glass.

"Oh cool," said Marco. "Swimming pools. But I didn't bring my bathing suit."

Benny shot him a cute smirk.

"Well, not quite. These are the filtration beds. There are forty of them in total, all symmetrically aligned. And this is where the plant's dirty work happens. After the lake water is treated with the coagulant to gather remaining residue—"

"The alum," I said.

"Correct...It's pumped on top of these beds, which are basically huge expanses of anthracite—"

I rotated my head to prompt Walter.

"Otherwise known as charcoal," he said. "Now I see why they're so dark."

"It is so very strange," said Benny. "It reminds me of a science fiction movie I once saw. These look like the breeding grounds for some alien life forms."

Goosebumps had formed on my arms, but not because of Benny's comment. I had not previously been aware that tap water was processed through charcoal filters. Suddenly some things were making sense to me – I was having a major ah-hah! moment. This carbon filtration had to be the source of my body's reaction to city water and why it had made me feel ill. I must have developed a strong sensitivity, if not an outright allergy to charcoal, but I now understood that, even though the amounts of charcoal in tap water were likely minute, every time I drank water from a faucet, I was adding a

196

toxic-to-me element to my hyper-sensitized body…over and over and over again, and heavily taxing vital cleansing organs like my kidneys.

Camila continued. "Water dribbles down and leaves gritty debris and impurities in the charcoal. Meanwhile the clean water continues to trickle down even coarser layers of rock until it settles in an underground reservoir. And then the chemicals are added."

"Like non-toxic fluoride and chlorine." I couldn't resist.

Camila almost sneered at me. We weren't going to be BFFs after this. "And then the water is ready to be pumped off to the city."

I grasped the fact that chlorine is used to kill deadly bacteria in a water supply being used by millions of people. Fluoride, though, is a more controversial additive as its sole purpose is to reduce tooth decay. This chemical is more toxic than lead and just slightly less toxic than arsenic. It's all about dosage, and the reality is that every human being has a different level of tolerance to chemicals. If one has a weak immune system, like in my case, it can result in serious environmental sensitivities, and one is less likely to fare well over a lifetime of ingesting such substances.

This was not the moment, however, to get into a debate about water purification methods as I was already feeling like I was messing up Benny's experience. But I couldn't help pondering whether there were now improved ways of purifying water. Just because we had been doing it this way for almost a century didn't mean it was the way we should continue to do it. It would be arrogant of us to completely discount new innovations and technologies, which might even be healthier for the planet. After all, most of us weren't Flat Earthers. Some of the most incorrect and longest-held views by various civilizations throughout history had taken unnecessarily long to be overturned due to closed-mindedness and obstinacy.

Camila snapped me out of my reverie when she reached into her purse and retrieved a pair of keys. She then walked to one of the doors to the filtration bed area and unlocked it. "Remember, no running allowed."

"You hear that, Walter," I said. "Behave like a sensible adult."

Walter tapped his hand to his sternum. "Who, me? Oh, you are jesting. Very droll."

We stepped inside to the silent space. What a contrast it was to the deafening pump room we had visited earlier. Benny raised her camera and began again to shoot the creepy setting. There was something mesmerizing yet ominous about the rows of filtration beds, the countless columns, the sheer expansiveness of the space. I was reminded of the *Yerebatan Sarnici*, also known as the Basilica Cistern in Istanbul, or rather under Istanbul. The Turkish cistern provided a water filtration system for the Great Palace of Constantinople, among other buildings, and supplied the Topkapi Palace from the mid-fifteenth century into modern times. Perhaps it had been an inspiration for this plant.

A chilling stillness befell us. Benny had inexplicably stopped taking photos. She seemed to be squinting off into the distance, but then looked through her viewfinder and adjusted the lens. She took a deep breath and straightened her spine as though ready to go into battle. "There's something there."

"Please, not another piece of paper," groaned Camila.

"No, there's an object between two of those pillars, in the middle there."

"What? Where?" asked Walter. He lifted his chic geek

glasses to his hairline. "Oh dear, that didn't help considering I am short-sighted."

I rolled my eyes.

Marco shifted over towards Benny, and they looked at her camera's LED screen together. "Can you enlarge it any-more?"

"It's not a dead body is it?" Camila said, her voice squeaking a tad.

"Nothing like that. But you guys stay here," said Marco.

"Not on your life," I said.

Marco, Benny, and I hightailed it as though there was a rolling boulder behind us.

"What? What?" said Walter. I turned my head momen-tarily and saw the librarian glued to his spot, but flagging his head from side to side like a bird.

"Just come on, Walter. We're probably going to need you," I hollered.

Camila bellowed. "I told you you're not supposed to run in here...It's a liability issue. You could fall in and drown...and I'd lose my job."

"Sorry, Camila," I wailed without turning around. "We'll be careful."

We beelined it towards the centrally located filtration beds and Marco halted at the end of one of the causeways, almost triggering a domino-like pile-up, but we miraculously managed to keep from tumbling over each other. The click-clack of heels behind us continued.

"What is that?" asked Benny as we all stared at the same miniscule pitch-black object almost in dead center of the platform separating two water beds and just to the side of one of the columns supporting the expansive concrete arch hovering above our heads.

"Is it a bomb?" said the gasping voice behind me. Camila had finally caught up to us.

"Even less likely than it being a corpse," answered Walter.

"How could you possibly have seen that from so far away? I don't think it's even four inches tall," I said.

"The magic of camera lenses. It sees everything," said Benny. "And it is all so symmetrical here, with all these pillars, and arches, and railings. It was enough of a difference to make me think something was out of place."

"Well, are we going closer?" I asked.

"No! Not this time." Marco extended his arms out like a crossing guard preventing children from reaching the other side of the street. "We're not going to disturb the crime scene one bit."

"Crime scene?" Camila was so visibly flustered now that I felt sorry for her.

Walter withdrew a phone from an inner pocket of his overcoat. "If you do not mind, I'm going to step forward. I will be very, very careful. I promise you, Marco."

"What for?" asked Marco.

"Well following our interviews with CSIS, they mentioned a very interesting app that was recently launched, and I would like to see how well it performs."

"CSIS," yelped Camila.

"I'm surprised to see you with a cell phone, let along using an app," I said. "What's it all about?"

"It is quite remarkable. If you take a picture of a work of art, it goes through an international database to see if it is registered as a lost or stolen work. It's not foolproof, but perhaps worth a try."

"Is this through the Monuments Men Foundation?" I

asked.

"I do not believe so; although I imagine they must have participated in the development of the application by providing their data. It's an international art theft crimes group of some sort that spearheaded this effort. Apparently, it has taken them years to create."

"Let's give it a go," I said.

"*Sono d'accordo*," said Benny.

"Well, okay. Just maybe walk to the side and come back along the exact same path," said Marco.

"Yes, sir." Walter treaded forwards, oddly lifting his feet high above the concrete, but landing them ever so lightly. He reminded me of a caricatured cat burglar in an animation. I grabbed Benny's arm with one hand and put my hand over my mouth with the other – this was no time for laughter.

Marco was less amused than I and just tossed his head back. Camila, well, she looked like she wished she hadn't gotten out of bed this morning. But then something made the hairs on the back of my neck stand up, and I leaned in towards Marco. Discreetly I said, "Interesting that Walter suddenly has a cell phone – after not having one all these years – and on top of that, he's downloaded an app on art theft. Something is rotten in the state of Denmark."

Marco sighed then focused back again on Walter. "You almost done there, buddy?" His words echoed in the cavern-like space.

Walter appeared to take a couple of shots and then commenced walking backwards, legs lifting high again as if trying to plant his feet in the exact spots he had been in moments ago. I doubled over, but I couldn't suppress the laughter any longer, and once I started, the others joined me. Even Camila added some giggling to the raucous howling that was now reverberating around us.

Walter grounded both feet, then rotated his head. "What is so amusing?"

"Just ignore us," I said breathlessly, in between peals of laughter. What was I thinking earlier? If Walter was involved in an international art theft ring, then I was the Prime Minister of Canada.

Walter finally rejoined us, and I gave him a big hug.

"What was that for?" he asked.

"Just for being you."

Walter's ears reddened instantaneously. "Um, well, let me give this app a go, shall I?"

"Fire away," said Marco.

"First, I'll launch the application. I am relieved we receive such a good signal here. I'm rather surprised amidst all this concrete...And now I just attach these photos...and enter...And once this spinning-wait-cursor image stops, we should have our answer."

We all huddled around Walter's phone, faces leaning in toward the screen. It seemed like minutes had passed and then, "Oh my goodness, oh my goodness," said Walter. "We have a match!"

"I can't see those details," I said. "Can you read them out loud?"

"It's simply called a Statuette of a Man, from Egypt...obviously...black stone...height is 3.3 inches. It was bequeathed to the National Museum in Warsaw by the Society for the Encouragement of Fine Arts in Warsaw in 1919, and it is from the Lohojsk collection of the Princess Tyszkiewicz."

"Does it say how old it is?" I asked.

"How did it get in here?" said Camila.

Walter scrolled down a bit further. "It just reads antiquity, no specific dates. And...it was looted during the Siege of Warsaw in the invasion of Poland by the Germans and Russians in World War II."

"That blockade was early in the war, if I remember my history correctly," said Benny.

"Yes, 1939. But what is going on here?" asked Walter. "It seems like my phone has locked."

All of a sudden large text flashed on the screen reading 'Your location has been determined by local authorities. Do not move. Any attempt to do so will be regarded as an attempt to obstruct justice.' Walter started sputtering, but nothing that made any sense came out of his mouth.

"Oh my god," wailed Camila, "we're all going to prison!"

"Looks like my quiet Sunday evening watching trash reality TV has just gone up in flames," I said.

Marco whipped out his phone.

"Who are you calling?" asked Benny.

"The guys at CSIS, of course. They might be the ones who are on their way anyway."

"Nice app, Walter," I said.

"I...I...I'm dumbfounded. We would have called the authorities nonetheless." Walter's hand was trembling. "I am cancelling my cell phone contract immediately."

CHAPTER TWENTY-FIVE

On Monday morning, as I walked towards my streetcar stop for the first leg of my trek to work, there were literally more than a hundred people waiting. I drew my phone out of the side pocket of my Roots lunch bag and took a picture. I then composed a tweet to the public transit customer service Twitter address and sent it with the message, 'Crowd waiting for the 504 streetcar, you know where. What's going on?' Next, I attached the picture to a text and with the message, 'my typical Monday morning commute.' I punctuated it with an angry-face emoji and sent it off.

Within moments my phone rang with the ominous sound of the bell chimes from *The Exorcist*. "Hullo," I said.

"Huuullo, Sis. Having a rough start to the week?"

"Sometimes I just want to crawl into a hole."

A mini chime rang, and I pulled the phone from my ear to have a quick gander. A return tweet from the TTC.

"What is going on there?" said my brother.

"The King streetcars are apparently driving through a black hole and resurfacing in another part of the city, completely bypassing my stop."

"Translation?"

"The cars are being diverted somewhere along the route. Probably because of an accident."

"But that's an insane amount of people. Where the hell are they all coming from?"

"I've been telling you about the rampant development along this corridor. This neighborhood's nothing like it used to be compared to when I first moved in. Most of the area west of Bathurst was industrial. As a matter of fact, some of the first condos on this strip were old factories. But developers have been erecting huge condo towers or complexes on any parcel of available land. Seems the powers that be never turn down a developer's request because the building is perpetual.

"It's still better than a lot of cities, Sis. Trust me."

"I know, but they're not taking basic infrastructure into account, including not factoring in the amount of public transit that'd be needed to transport the tens of thousands of new residents to the nearest subway station. It's the busiest and most inadequate route in the city."

"Why don't you just grab a cab?"

"Hold on a sec. I'm going to take another picture and text it to you." I aimed my phone to the east, clicked a shot, and sent it off. "Got it yet?"

There was a brief pause. "You just took this...on King? The street looks like an abandoned ghost town."

"Exactly. The city's implemented a wacky pilot experiment on the strip of King between Bathurst and Jarvis. Cars can't drive further than one block in the same direction. In other words, every car has to turn either left or right at the end of each block or else they're zinged with a hefty fine."

"You're kidding," said my brother. "I've never seen that in any city."

"I know. Really, eh? Like you saw in the picture, there is NO traffic. On good days it means streetcars can move twice as quickly as they used to. But on days like today, when streetcars are being diverted, there're no other options.

Taxis have stopped patrolling this route because it's impossible to get anywhere. I'm starting to lose my mind living here."

Laughter echoed from the phone. "Sorry, Sis. I feel for you, really, I do. But I just came back from Naples, and you have no clue."

"Oh man, I completely forgot to ask you where you were. Naples. *Mamma mia!* Actually, I was there – years ago. You're right. I've never seen such organized pandemonium on the roads as in Naples. Are they still cramming eight lanes of traffic into four?"

"Yep. I rented a car the first day, then gave up. I was shaking all night from the stress. But what about you? Are you staying out of trouble?"

"What do you mean?"

"What do you mean what do I mean? What have you been up to lately? Anything exciting?"

"Um, no. Not really. Well, actually, yesterday I went for a tour of a water treatment plant."

"That's something you'll have to share with me sometime." My brother chuckled.

"Oh wait, I might have to hang up, I think I see a streetcar coming."

"Don't get trampled."

"Crap. False alarm."

"I have to get going anyway. I'll give Mom and Dad a call soon," said my brother.

"Oh, good. That'll make them happy."

"Byyyyyyye, Sis. By the way, time to download the Uber app."

"Ugh, no. Say it ain't so. I miss you. Bye." I disengaged and frowned. I really did miss my brother. He was my best friend, and we shared everything. Well, almost everything.

After my last art theft adventure with Marco, I had signed a non-disclosure agreement with the Museum in order to protect its reputation. But even if I had confided in my brother, he probably would have gone ballistic and joined my parents in trying to get me to move back to Hamilton.

I glanced at my watch and then at the crowd, which had now grown by about another third. Threading my way in and about the throng, I paused outside the transit shelter. Ugh. The pixel board was still not live – they hadn't activated the arrivals announcer in the relocated shelter (that was a whole other saga). I pulled out my phone again but this time to launch a public transit app to check on the approach of the next vehicle. Crap. When there were delays such as this one, the app simply advised that 'There are no current predictions.' Crap.

After yesterday's turn of events, I was still on edge and my ability to tolerate this kind of urban nonsense was currently nonexistent. And as if the universe were responding to my internal curmudgeon, it started to rain.

I metaphorically threw my arms in the air. What was the point? Once the streetcars started running again, it would be an eternity before I could even force myself onto one. And I just didn't feel like having my face jammed against the window of a streetcar door. Nope! Not today.

In the brief jaunt to my building, the front of my trousers became thoroughly soaked from the rain. What kind of sins had I committed in a previous life that left me with this karma, one that included an imponderable amount of water and rain in my life? Perhaps I had lived in a desert culture in a past existence.

Once in my suite, I opened my umbrella, flung it to the living room rug, and catapulted myself onto the couch. I lay

207

motionless, not even bothering to remove my coat. While sprawled out, I kept envisaging yesterday's events. After Walter's anti-art theft app had advised us to stay put, we had remained in silence, like cattle waiting to be slaughtered. Marco had called the CSIS team and advised them of our precise coordinates, and it seemed like just moments before a small troupe of sturdy law enforcement types of all shapes, sizes, and genders arrived.

A man who had introduced himself to us as the Plant Manager was with them. He had worn an indelible grimace the entire time and had kept ranting that security in the building had never been breached prior to this day. He had been reminded by the investigators that the person or persons we were dealing with were international criminals and highly sophisticated. I didn't for a second doubt that he believed his job was at stake – after all, if someone could make their way into the treatment plant to drop off a stolen piece of classical Egyptian art, they could just as easily have sabotaged one of the principal water supplies of the ninth largest city in North America.

The plant manager wasn't the only one who had felt they were totally cooked. Poor Walter had been on the edge of coming completely undone. But the officers had lauded him on the use of the app and on the first successful match using the technology in Canada. Immediately afterwards, it had seemed as if something had washed over Walter, and color had returned to his previously blanched complexion.

Camila had been released rather quickly. It hadn't taken long to determine she was an innocent bystander, in the wrong place at the wrong time, who had been swept up in some intrigue about which she knew nothing. But it had been Benny about whom we were all most concerned, especially since she had been so inexplicably forthright in revealing her status in Canada. Ironically, the investigators had warned her NOT to contemplate returning to Italy in the immediate future.

And, of course, Marco had had no choice but to call Malik and inform him of our latest entanglement. But seeing that this incident had occurred off Museum property, Malik had been quite content to postpone a debrief until the following day and to continue to spend a rare Sunday off with his family. That had saved us at least one level of interrogation and got me home in time to lose myself in some escapist television that evening.

I ignored the mindless reality TV fare and let my PVR record it, including back-to-back Real Housewives episodes and, instead, immersed myself in Brit crime dramas on PBS. A touch of *Grantchester*, a dash of *Endeavour*, and a dollop of *Shetland* seemed like the appropriate recipe of television entertainment to make me realize things could have been worse – like we could have been dealing with serial murders instead of serial surrenders of stolen works of art. Unfortunately, by bedtime, my head was still whirling, and sleep did not come until the wee hours of the morning.

"Huh, what?" I was suddenly aroused to full consciousness by a loud ringing. Frig. Something or someone had set off the building's fire alarm. I looked down at myself and saw I was still sporting my coat and shoes. Only half cognizant, I cast my eyes at the digital clock on the PVR. It read 10:30. What the heck? I must have conked right out after my botched attempt to go to work earlier. Tumbling over to one side, my feet landed, and I jumped to attention. I picked up my phone and checked my emails. Whew. No evidence that anyone was urgently trying to hunt me down.

But there was an email from Malik – not a surprise – and from Geoffrey – now what did he want? It would have to wait as I needed to speed off to the Museum before too many people noticed I had gone AWOL.

Announcements related to the fire alarm started to play over the loud-speakers, but the messages went in one ear and escaped just as quickly out the other. I dashed out the door and lunged towards the elevator, where my neighbor, Mex, was sitting on the carpet across from the lift. The door of one cab was wide open, revealing furniture and boxes stuffed to the brim.

"You weren't planning on getting anywhere quickly, were you?" he said, pointing at the hallway speaker. "The elevators aren't running while we're in fire alarm mode."

I closed my eyes momentarily and sighed melancholically. "Right. But what's going on with you? Are you moving already?"

"I'm doing it in stages. But depending on how long this alarm goes on for, I might be adding an extra stage."

I grinned, then pushed up the sleeve of my jacket to check the time.

"You're still of a generation that uses a watch instead of a phone for that," said Mex.

"Uh, huh. I'm so frigging late. Looks like it's the stairs for me."

"At least it's all downhill." Mex winked.

"I guess. Hey, make sure you say goodbye before you're out for good. And have plenty of fun today."

"I will."

"I have to run – really – before the Museum sends out sniffer dogs to hunt me down." With that I hopped into the stairwell and began the descent of the dozen plus floors.

Once at ground level, I popped out the back door of the building, avoiding the accumulation of residents hovering in the lobby waiting for the go-ahead from the fire-fighting crew on site to return to their units.

Out on the street I spotted a streetcar making its way to my stop. I dug in my heels and galloped towards the intersection, racing the ultra-long vehicle and crossing the street just in time to bounce into the last set of open doors.

I arrived at the Museum just 15 minutes later. It was a much lovelier experience riding public transit outside rush hour. But no sooner had I stepped foot inside the Museum when I encountered Marco, who was stationed at the Staff Entrance.

"Where've you been?" he said, almost pouncing on me from behind the security desk.

"Now what? Listen, I just can't deal. Not after yesterday and Monday morning baloney."

"Well, I hate to be the bearer of bad news, but there's kind of big surprise in your office."

"What kind of surprise?"

"You should really talk to Gaspar," said Marco.

"In Shipping and Receiving?"

"Of course, Gaspar in Shipping and Receiving. How many other Gaspars do you know? He said he called you a whole bunch of times, and he even came by to ask if I knew where you were."

"Well I do have meetings off site sometimes, you know. Why didn't he try calling my cell number?"

"How should I know?"

"Should I go to Shipping first?"

"Maybe you should head to your office first."

"And this isn't about another art delivery? There's not an army of Chinese terracotta warriors from the Shaanxi site waiting there for me?"

"What?"

"Never mind." I spun on my short heels and went through the set of doors to the hallway leading to my office. It felt like my head was going to pop off. Marco was irritating the heck out of me these days. I couldn't believe there was a time that seeing him used to bring a flutter to my heart chakra.

As I approached the door to my office, I paused. Something was different. Hmm. Well, praise the lord. The Mugwump was gone. I started to sing 'Ding-Dong! The Witch is Dead' in my head and added a bit of a skip to my saunter. Is this all Gaspar wanted to talk to me about? Did he think I was going to have withdrawal anxiety or something? Unless, unless...no they didn't, they wouldn't.

My saunter transitioned into a sprint, and I leapt into my office. "You've got to be freaking kidding me!" I screamed aloud.

Contrary to my initial conclusion, there was no Mugwump in my office. Instead, I was greeted by wall-to-wall, piled-high boxes with just the narrowest of gaps that would allow me access to my desk. I shimmied my way through, plunked myself down into my chair, and allowed the sensations of a déjà vu to filter through my body.

Not so long ago, when my department was located near the gems and minerals collections, I had walked in one morning and encountered a similar scenario. Boxes of a variety of Mexican wares intended for the Museum's gift shop had been crammed into my office. But at least that space had been more expansive. The current one had a claustrophobic

212

feel to it even without the clutter of containers. I ripped the X-ACTO™ knife out of one of my drawers and sliced through the packing tape of the nearest box. The flaps popped open to reveal the moss-green presentation boxes I had ordered to encase the commemorative medals. These weren't supposed to be delivered until the medals were pressed and I'd given the novelty ware company the go-ahead to deliver.

I picked up the phone and rang Shipping and Receiving.

"Gaspar, here," said a voice with a thick French-Canadian accent.

"Gaspar, give me a break?"

"I have been expecting your call."

"I'm sure."

"I tried to call you over and over again, but a decision had to be made. Staff are dismantling the Cronenberg exhibit and preparing items to be shipped out, and we have no room on the dock today...or for many days."

"But, c'mon. You really had nowhere else to stack these boxes? Why do you hate me so much? What have I ever done to you?"

Gaspar started to laugh. "You are so funny. You know I don't hate you. I would only do this if I had no other choice. I was trying to warn you all morning."

"Yeah, yeah." I slumped my head down. "I had some issues trying to get into work."

"Are we still friends then?" he asked.

I hesitated. "*Bons amis.*"

"Good. But I make you a promise. As soon as the exhibit is gone, I will move the boxes back."

"Thanks for the offer, but we may just as well leave them here until I am ready to ship them back out again. Not to worry. I'll survive."

"Yes. I am sure you will. *Bonne journée.*" Click. Gaspar had disengaged.

I set the receiver down for a second, scooped it back up again just as quickly, and pressed four digits.

"Dara speaking," said the voice.

"Hey, Dara. How are you?"

"Okay for a Monday, I guess."

"I know exactly how you feel," I said. "When I got to work today my office was filled with the boxes I ordered for the medals."

"You're kidding."

"Long story. But I'm kind of hoping you're going to tell me that the medal production is ahead-of-schedule, and we'll be able to pack them off to Saudi sooner than later."

Dara didn't say anything for a moment, and I thought I heard some kind of sputtering. "It's interesting you called about that as I was going to give you an update this morning...but I sort of chickened out."

My knees locked.

Dara continued. "The production facility has run into a bit of a problem. I mean, it's crazy. This kind of thing just doesn't usually happen."

I sat to attention.

"The machine they use to churn out the metal blanks kind of had a meltdown."

"What does that mean exactly?"

"Well you know that for each medal, they have to produce a round piece of metal that will take the engraved impression from the die, the part that carries the design."

"Uh, huh."

"Well, they think someone might have intentionally messed with the part of the manufacturing process that produces those flat metal rounds."

"Intentional? Like corporate sabotage?" I asked.

"Well, I don't know that it's that sinister. But I heard, very confidentially, that they had an employee who was asking for some time off, and then when it wasn't granted, coincidentally a wrench, not a real wrench, but a figurative wrench, was thrown into the equipment."

"And this can be fixed quickly, right?"

"Well, that's the thing. It's very specialized equipment, and they might have to fly in someone from Germany to do the repairs."

My eyes darted towards a cheesy desk calendar. This month's reproduction was of a painting entitled *Harvest Time* featuring an orange tractor sitting in a partially snow-covered field. "You know we have zero wiggle room in this production schedule."

"I know, I know. But this is truly beyond everyone's control. And we're just going to have to plan the next steps to a T to get the medals shipped on time."

I sat silently.

"Kalena, are you still there?"

"Yeah. Plan to a T."

"Listen. It's going to be okay."

"Yeah."

"It might involve an overnighter to box the medals once they're delivered."

"Uh, huh. Great."

"Do you want some chocolate?" asked Dara.

"I always want some chocolate. Listen, I've got to go. Lot's on the go. Talk to you later."

"Uh, okay. Bye."

I set down the receiver delicately. But I would have thrown the phone across the room if I didn't risk it ricocheting straight back at me off the boxes staring me in the face.

CHAPTER TWENTY-SIX

My initial reaction after speaking to Dara was to crawl under a massive rock, but as though a fairy had flown over me sprinkling me with some kind of turbo-powered magical energy dust, I was suddenly overcome by a strong ambition to prove to myself – to Dara, to Stewart, to Geoffrey, and, well, to the whole frigging universe – that I wasn't going to let these circumstances destroy my spirit. I could have chosen to wallow in victim mode as I had just this morning during the public transit debacle, but I decided now was the time to dig deep, to buckle up, to do a Sheryl Sandberg lean-in, and to just get it done whatever it took.

I began by using all my might to rearrange the boxes so it didn't feel quite as claustrophobic in the immediate vicinity of my desk. I then called up the factory where the medals were being stamped and told them as firmly as possible that they needed to find a more immediate resolution to their production issues or the Museum would never contract work with them again. It wasn't likely we would have another job like this one again, but they didn't need to know that.

Next, I took a huge gulp, got myself on Skype, and dialed up Stewart and Geoffrey.

"Kalena," said Stewart, "what a nice surprise."

"Yes, always good to hear from you," added Geoffrey. "And I see you've fixed that problem with your computer's camera."

"Oh, yes. Turns out it was just a loose cable connection or something."

"My goodness, what are all those boxes behind you?" asked Stewart.

I rotated around. Crap. I forgot they'd be able to see the cardboard backdrop behind me. "Well those are the presentation boxes for the medals. It's kind of a long story, but the Museum's shipping out the Cronenberg exhibit, and there was no room for storage on the loading dock. So, *voilà*. My office is now a warehouse. Anyway, I can't believe I managed to get you both on line considering your time zones." I peeked behind me, but the pixel board time keeper was now obstructed.

"Yes, fortuitous timing indeed," said Stewart. "But Geoffrey, after Kalena is through with us, perhaps we can continue speaking on our own. I need to touch base with you on a few matters."

"Of course," said Geoffrey.

"So..." I said.

"Oh, yes, apologies. Go ahead, Kalena. You did initiate this rendezvous after all."

All of a sudden, my mouth felt dry and my voice became raspy.

"Is it about your latest adventure?" asked Stewart.

"What adventure would that be?" said Geoffrey.

"Kalena and a few of her colleagues stumbled upon an Egyptian statue at a water filtration plant, of all places. It seems it's been missing since World War II."

"Like the other pieces showing up in her life?" Geoffrey shut his eyes momentarily and gave his head a shake. "But a water filtration plant? What were you even doing at such an edifice?"

"I didn't realize word had gotten out already."

"Malik is under orders to keep me in the loop of goings-on at the Museum, particularly when it comes to you. He's worried you might be at risk, that these aren't street criminals you've been dealing with in this recent spate of events."

"He's being a bit dramatic," I said.

"I doubt that is the case." Geoffrey stroked his smoothly shaven upper lip with his index and middle finger.

"Can we move on from this for now? It's actually not what I'm calling about. I have some not-so-great news."

"Go on," said Stewart.

"Well, the truth is, we've hit a production glitch with the medals. It's totally a freak thing, but totally fixable. Manufacturing just isn't moving as smoothly as I'd hoped."

"Hmm," said Stewart after an uncomfortable pause. "This is rather grave news. If we're not able to get the medals to Riyadh in a timely manner, well...I don't know if I could ever set my feet in the Middle East again."

"Not to mention the disgrace the royal family would feel," added Geoffrey.

"I KNOW. No one knows that more than I do. But I'm working with the company and even if I have to press out the medals myself, I am going to get them shipped out on time."

"You realize you need to schedule at least four days for shipping, in case we hit any trouble spots in transportation," said Geoffrey.

With elbow on the arm of my chair, I rested my cheek on my fist. "I'm quite aware," I mumbled.

"Oh, yes, yes," said Stewart, perking up. It's clear you've taken all these matters into account. We needn't worry. Kalena has yet to let me down."

I smiled half-heartedly.

"Well," continued Stewart, "except perhaps the time when you toppled over the liquid chocolate fountain at the gala opening of the Museum's last blockbuster exhibit."

My lips puckered. That again.

"But even then, you managed to pivot, and had it not been for your actions at the time, we might now be reporting to an incompetent, megalomaniac of a Director."

"The silver lining," I said.

"But DO contact us immediately if there is anything, anything, we can do from afar."

"Thanks, Stewart," I said.

"There is one thing we should consider," said Geoffrey. "It might be wise for me to be on hand in Riyadh a few days before the museum opens."

"Splendid idea. I appreciate that as we will need all hands on deck," said Stewart.

"Thanks. I, uh, I don't want to keep you folks any longer," I said, "so I'll bow out of the chat and you two can carry on."

"Kalena, can you hold on for just a moment? Stewart, may I call you right back on your mobile? There was something Brenda wanted to discuss with Kalena, just very briefly and this would solve having to coordinate another call."

"By all means. Good work, team. Geoffrey, I'll speak with you imminently." Stewart's image disappeared from the Skype window.

"Brenda? What does she want? Is she there?"

"NO, she's not here. I needed to speak to you privately. What's this about a long-lost Egyptian statue?"

"I thought we were done with this."

"No, we are not done with this." Even when Geoffrey took a harsher tone with me, his accent still weakened me.

"But I have no control over what's been turning up in my life," I said.

"Would you please describe the Egyptian statue you found?"

"Oh, lord."

"Humor me, pleeeease."

"It was just a tiny thing. I'm sure it would have almost fit into my hand."

"What else can you tell me about it?" Geoffrey asked.

"It was marbled black stone and kind of looked like a miniature sarcophagus, but a plain one. And that's about it. I didn't take a picture, but Walter did. That's how we found out its provenance. He used an app called *Looted* that identifies stolen works of art."

"Are you being serious?"

"You can't make this stuff up."

"No, I suppose not. But when you mentioned the statue, you triggered an old memory, a kind of déjà vu. But memories from childhood can be a tricky thing. Yet, when you described your latest discovery, I realized I likely wasn't imagining things."

"Like what?" I asked

"A reminiscence from when I was a lad."

"And..."

"My grandfather had a very private den in the family estate home. He kept it under constant lock and key."

"And you broke in? How scathingly brilliant."

"Not quite. Grandfather simply forgot to lock the room one day, and I entered his magic kingdom. I cannot say for certain that I saw the Roman cage cup. But this Egyptian statuette, I believe I may once have held it in my boyish little hands."

"WHAT?"

"When I slinked into the den, I was immediately drawn to a small black Egyptian figure. It was so black it seemed to have absorbed all the darkness in the universe. And when I touched it...it was so smooth, as though it had been weathered by sands for centuries. But wouldn't you know it, Grandfather walked in on me. I thought he was going to have a coronary event."

"That sounds like a scene from *All the Money in the World*, about John Paul Getty. I can just picture your grandfather looking like Christopher Plummer. Not the way he looks now, but the way he looked in *The Sound of Music*. Be still my beating heart, he was so handsome."

Muffled chortling was transmitted through the receiver. I continued. "There's a scene where John Paul Getty III picks up an Egyptian artifact in his grandfather's study. Senior tells his grandson how much it's worth and gifts it to him, but in the end, it turns out to be a fake. Woops – I should have given you a spoiler alert."

"I'm not sure what that is," said Geoffrey.

"It's an alert you give to someone when you're about to expose an important plot point in a film which might give away the remainder of the story. It's just common courtesy."

"You do have a way of lightening up any conversation."

"Are you making fun of me again?"

"Not at all."

"So, what happened?" I asked.

"I'm afraid I've lost the thread of the conversation."

"What happened when you were caught with your hands on a priceless piece of art?"

"Grandfather's expression turned from one of panic to calm in just a matter of seconds. He gently took the object from my hand and said he would forgive me for being in his sacred place, his 'refuge,' he called it, but I had to swear for a lifetime that I would never tell anyone what I had seen in the room. He looked so serious and stern, and I recall feeling as cold and dark as the stone of the statue. He actually frightened me at that instant."

"Are you implying that someone in your family has been getting rid of stolen treasures in your family's possession, and for some unknown reason they chose to involve a random woman you had a one-night stand with to serve as a conduit for returning these objects to their rightful owners?"

"Halt right there. You were not a one-night stand. Perhaps in the technical sense, but only because you have relegated me to a situation of unrequited..." Geoffrey's voice trailed off.

"Unrequited...?"

"You have spurned me."

"Oh, Geoffrey. It's not like I broke your heart."

"Gutted me."

I didn't know Geoffrey was such a drama queen. "Let's stick with the art, please. How do you explain what's been happening in my world?"

"My family has suffered great guilt from the harm my grandfather has done to so many."

I was conflicted. Geoffrey's grandfather had ruined people's lives through his gambling addiction. He was someone who fit into a criminal underbelly as easily as he did in high society, and some of his hoard of art, stolen during a catastrophic war, was now turning up on my doorstep.

Just at that moment, the door opened, and Marco burst into the room.

"Um, I've got to bounce," I said. "Someone's just

223

popped into my office."

"Bounce? That is a new one. I say ta-ra reluctantly."

I set the receiver down slowly and grinned at Marco.

"What?" he said.

"What 'what'? You're the one who steamrolled in here."

"I didn't steamroll. That's my usual way to enter a room."

"Yes, it is."

Marco subtly rotated his head from side to side. "I guess you figured out why Gaspar was trying to reach you."

I threw my arms into the air.

"Well, there's something we need to clear up."

"Like what?" I asked.

"Like you really need to kick this idea that Walter or Benny are behind all this art stuff."

"Listen, I have a major sista from anotha motha crush on Benny, but how much do you really know about her?'

"Enough to know she wouldn't be crazy enough to be involved in an international art theft ring."

"And, Walter?"

Marco tilted his head back, mouth open, and then let it drop. "Aw, c'mon. You can't be serious."

"Well, there's a couple of other options, certain people who know our every move."

"Like who?" asked Marco.

"You and I."

"Are you on drugs?"

"Well, think about it," I said. "It's more likely that it's one of us rather than some stranger who's hacking into our phones and tracking us, and getting to places we're going to just before we get there, sometimes it seems, before we even know we're going to be there."

Marco scratched his head. "Yeah, I know. But people are becoming more and more tech savvy every minute, so I don't think it's so far-fetched. I mean, look at the damage Aurelia caused us."

"Oh my god, you don't think it's Aurelia?" I asked. "Come back to haunt us?" Aurelia Alberti was a former Museum IT staff member whose obsession with Marco had wreaked havoc in our lives months before.

"And she'd get her hands onto stolen art how exactly?" said Marco.

"Okay, okay, you're right." With the information Geoffrey had just relayed to me, I decided to back down. I was not about to share Geoffrey's childhood memory of his father's den. "I don't know what I was thinking." I rotated my index fingers near my ears. "I'm a bit *pazza* these days."

"I think we're all feeling a bit crazy."

Catching me by surprise, an unintelligible message unexpectedly emanated from Marco's walkie-talkie. Marco unhooked it from its holster and brought it up to his mouth. "Roger, that."

"How the hell did you understand what they said?" I asked. "Never mind."

"Yup. Gotta bounce." Marco winked at me and exited as quickly as he had entered.

I leaned my head back and closed my eyes, pondering whether I needed to work harder at manifesting a different future for myself, like a really early retirement, to some island like Bora Bora. But they had mosquitos. Actually, I think mosquitos were everywhere these days. Maybe not in Antarctica or Iceland.

The phone rang. Another international number. It was Harry Cavanaugh's number. I hadn't heard from him in days.

Maybe the Prince was behind this. "Harry, Harry, Harry," I said after lifting the receiver. "Are you staying out of trouble?"

"I've been too busy to get into trouble, thanks for asking. How in the name of Jaysus are ya?"

"Good. And probably almost as busy as you."

"I'm sure you know why I'm calling, don't you?"

"The Prince is looking for an update on the medals, I surmise."

"I always tell Stewart he made a fine choice in hiring you."

"Ha, ha," I said, grabbing a pen and tapping it on my desk. "You can tell him everything's under control."

"And is that the case?" asked Harry.

"It's the best answer I have at the moment."

"Aw shite, Kalena, you're making this a wee bit hard for me."

I sighed. "Do you believe in miracles?"

"Actually, I do," said Harry. "Are ya suggesting that's what it's going to take to get the medals here?"

"I'm telling you to reassure the Prince. It won't serve anyone any good to panic. Listen, Harry, I really need to get going. I promise to give you an update, and it'll be good news."

"I'll let you get to it. But we're all counting on you."

"I know." I pulled the receiver away from my ear, stretched my arm to its full extension, and I could still hear Harry nattering away. I retracted my arm and blurted out, "Harry, I've got to go. Sorry. Talk soon."

No sooner had I hung up the phone when it rang again. I checked the call display, and my heart felt as though it had skipped a beat. It was an incoming call from my parents' number. What the? Within seconds my mobile started ringing. It was my brother calling. I clenched my hands into fists triggering a rigidness that spread throughout the whole of my body. I glanced at my desktop phone, then at my cell phone, then back to my desktop. I swiped the screen of my cell phone, denying the call, and scooped up the receiver of my land line.

"Hi...Mom?" My voice quavered.

"Kalena. Oh, thank god I found you," she said in Ukrainian.

"Mom, what's happening? Why are you calling me at work?"

"You need to come to Hamilton right away."

"Are you okay? Is Dad okay? Is it my brother?"

I heard a loud knocking in the background. "Just a minute," screamed my mother in English. "I have to go. I think your father has had a heart attack. The ambulance is here. Call your brother. He said he would meet us at the hospital."

"He won't know which hospital. Go let the ambulance people in and ask them right away which hospital they are taking Dad to."

There was a loud thump. My mom must have dropped the receiver to the tile floor. I imagined the coiled telephone cord stretching and retracting repeatedly. Tears formed in my eyes. SHIT. My car battery was dead. I hadn't gotten around to boosting it yet. Water was now streaming from my eyes uncontrollably, the droplets falling to my mauve silk blouse, forming a series of dark spots.

CHAPTER TWENTY-SEVEN

I stared blankly out the train's window as we passed through Toronto's closest suburbs, my stomach grumbling and feeling hunger for the first time since early morning. It had long transitioned to darkness, but the lights from an unending stream of urbanization felt blinding to my eyes. The drizzling of rain streaking the windows seemed to magnify the intensity of the incandescence even more. I squeezed my eyes closed, but the light seemed to penetrate my eyelids with an inexplicable ease.

Children spend a great deal of their lives in denial about their parents' mortality, otherwise they'd fret perpetually about losing them. But several years ago, for whatever reason, I became suddenly cognizant of my parents' increasing fragility. I grew so fearful they would die I started losing sleep. But then a very wise person told me it was imperative to stop grieving the loss of my parents while they were alive or I would physically make myself sick over it. The advice made sense to me and it stuck – until this day, that is.

Earlier in the day I had raced into Hamilton as fast as possible via public transit. I suppose I could have asked Marco to drive me – I'm sure Malik would have approved given the circumstances, but things between Marco and me seemed so strained as of late. While in transit to Steel Town I was a mess. At least it was in between rush hours, so I was able to sit in an isolated section at the end of the train car without being disturbed. My brother had reassured me he was certain my father was going to be fine, but I still went through tissue after tissue mopping up the tears. The trek involved subway, train, bus, and taxi, and it felt like hours had passed before arriving at the Hamilton General Hospital, Hamilton's primary hospital for cardiac care.

When I arrived, my father was in the Intensive Care Unit, and my mother and brother were standing outside of it, trying to make casual conversation. It was almost impossible to hold back the waterworks, but my brother gave me one of his looks that reminded me so much of my father. I knew he wanted me to keep it together so as to not further distress my mother. I supposed coming undone in front of her wasn't going to help. But truth be told, my mother had more strength in her baby finger than the rest of the family combined.

Crises such as these required considerable patience – it was one long waiting game – waiting for doctors to do tests, waiting for diagnoses, waiting to see if vitals stabilized. And by later evening, things had in fact stabilized. The sighs of relief we all breathed could not have been deeper, but the primary doctor told us my father would likely need bypass surgery to minimize the reoccurrence of future cardiac crises.

I had wanted to stay the night, though I had brought nothing with me, but my mother and brother insisted I return home and go to work the next day. I resisted. My brother ended up almost dragging me to his car and driving me to the train station.

My stomach grumbled again. My head was throbbing. I was craving chocolate, but all I had with me were memories of chocolate. I decided to distract myself by checking the emails I had consciously chosen not to open earlier. Doing so would only have added to my anxiety. When I scanned my personal mailbox and noticed a package delivery email received from my condo building's security desk, I believed it to be the yoga outfit I had purchased online the previous week. That would cheer me up – for a nanosecond, maybe.

When I finally arrived home, I nipped into the grocery store at the base of my building and picked up an organic and vegan Caesar salad, then, about to hop onto the elevator, I remembered my package. I glanced at the elevator button, but decided to make the slight detour.

When the security guard picked out my parcel, I was a little puzzled. The deliveries from that supplier usually came in a plastic bag. Hmm, I did have some organic shampoo coming from the UK. That had to be it. But once I had the box in hand, there was no shipping label. Whatever. I was too exhausted to worry about it.

Upon stepping into my doorway, I felt a sense of comfort. I had let myself trust that my father was in good hands. But then I thought of my mom on her own at home, and I swear I could feel my heart crack. I dropped the package on the counter, opened up the plastic lid on the salad, added the dressing and nut-based croutons, grabbed a fork, and dropped myself onto my couch, slinging my feet up onto my ottoman. I was feeling quite proud of myself for having fully ignored the shelf of organic chocolate bars in the store and for nourishing my body with some valuable nutrients.

It was already past 11:00 pm, so I flipped on a rerun of *Law and Order*. I'd probably seen every episode ten times, but it wasn't about the entertainment, it was about numbing the brain. After finishing the last bit of the greens, I returned to the kitchen and noted the unopened parcel. "Let's see what this is."

After pulling out a drawer and grabbing a small knife, I sliced the plastic packing tape. The cardboard flaps flipped open, revealing a layer of bubble wrap. Suddenly my heart fell to my stomach. Using the knife tip, I pulled up the bubble wrap and slipped the plastic onto the counter. With a reaction that only comes with complete exhaustion and surrender, I stared at the contents and started to laugh hysterically. It was a hideous laugh, like that of Bette Davis in *Whatever Happened to Baby Jane*. Or maybe it was Joan Crawford.

What I witnessed was not a work of art, nothing that was likely to have been hijacked in World War II as I was expecting. But I knew exactly what it was. It was a calling card I recognized immediately despite my extreme fatigue. Resting there, about 10 inches in length, with fur trimmed around extended claws, was a leopard's paw still attached to the lowest part of the leg. It was an old, desiccated, and faded one that reminded me somewhat of a larger version of a rabbit's foot lucky charm on a chain that I had as a kid. It was likely removed from an old taxidermy specimen, not overly horrific looking, but disturbing.

The owner must have been certain I would recognize the item and know to whom it belonged. And now it was clear they were definitely connected to all the art objects showing up in my world.

Why were they torturing me? Why this day of all days? Why on Earth did an international art thief like *Il Gattopardo* decide to toy with me? And why would The Leopard essentially confess to all the recent escapades by handing me the paw he had likely used to leave his signature claw marks at sites from which he had stolen art all these decades? For god's sake, WHY ME?

CHAPTER TWENTY-EIGHT

I stood, arms crossed, staring at the bizarre claw, then pulled out a pair of tongs from one of my kitchen drawers. Carefully, I replaced the bubble wrap over top of the leopard appendage and then retrieved a pair of rubber gloves from underneath the kitchen sink. After sliding them onto my hands, I closed up the box, opened up my refrigerator, cleared out a spot for the box on one of the lower shelves and placed the paw inside.

I had picked up some valuable information from staff in our former Taxidermy Department when I had volunteered at their table during some holiday programming one year. It was a given that animals yet to be preserved were stored in refrigeration units, but even after being stuffed and mounted, taxidermy specimens are susceptible to pests, lights, temperature, and humidity. So, the fridge seemed like the best home for my unique gift – at least for now.

Calling the authorities at this moment, I decided, would be unproductive and wouldn't likely lead to any big breakthroughs. The CSIS folks had not lifted any fingerprints or DNA from any of the artwork we had discovered previously, so I highly doubted *Il Gattopardo* had left traces on his 'pen.' They would surely want to grill the security guards that staffed my building's lobby, and I certainly wasn't up to a CSIS sweep of my own home and building. It would be an invasion of privacy with which I was currently unable to cope. Consequently, I changed into my nightwear and tried to fall asleep while the television played on a channel airing back-to-back episodes of *Law and Order* throughout the night.

Drifting in and out of sleep, I woke up occasionally to the show's distinct theme song. In the morning, I woke up about an hour and a half before my alarm was set to go off, and, despite being overloaded with weariness, I wasn't able to fall back asleep. I was grateful I hadn't heard from my family or the hospital overnight as no news was definitely good news. But just in case my mother and brother had better luck getting a good night's sleep, I decided not to ring them immediately.

Zombie-like, I opened up my fridge to take out ingredients for my morning smoothie and saw 'The Box.' I slammed the door shut, shook my head, and reopened the door. I'd already decided I was going to live with 'The Box' until my father was out of crisis, and I really didn't care what the damn consequences would be. They could throw me in the frigging clink if they wanted, but I was determined to not allow a big cat claw in cold storage remove my focus from my family.

Around 8 am my brother called and he was already at the hospital in hopes of catching doctors on early morning rounds, but all they had to share was that my father was stable, conscious, lucid, and resting. When I told him I'd be catching the next train to Hamilton, he replied with an 'absolutely not.' He insisted my father would be fine and that there was no point coming in. He promised to text or call with updates as the day progressed and said if I was still intent on coming in that I could come after work. I resisted of course, but at the same time, I knew staying busy would help get me through the day faster. I surrendered.

233

During the next several days I was in auto-pilot mode, and my schedule became routine. I would wake up each morning, open the refrigerator, see 'The Box' in my fridge, and feel like a serial killer keeping a human body part on ice as a souvenir. I would go into work, call the company producing the medals, listen to them say 'the part they needed would be in any time now,' carry on with other work, then at 4 pm race down to Union Station to catch a train that went all the way into Hamilton to visit my father. My mother and brother were taking day shifts, so I was usually alone for the evening shift with my dad. Then, each night after returning to Toronto, I would get home, open up the refrigerator for something, and again be reminded of the *Silence of the Lambs*-like trophy. I would sigh, then tumble into bed.

Since the arrival of the paw, nothing else unusual had happened, so I purposely avoided Marco and Walter at work. Benny had sent me a few emails, but I kept my responses brief. Lone wolf was a good descriptor of my behavior during crises, and sharing with others what was going on in my private life was not the way I operated. And now that I knew who, at least to a limited extent, was tampering with my life and that my colleagues were not involved in any way, it somehow put me more at ease. I felt that at least I wasn't being betrayed by anyone close to me.

On my numerous return trips to Hamilton, I came to realize I had not spent much time alone with my father in a very long time prior to this situation. The two of us were very similar in many ways – facial features, sense of humor, we were both very organized and meticulous – but there were a lot of awkward moments as we searched for things to talk about to each other. Other times I gained fascinating and previously unknown insights about him. He had also shed a few tears, the first I'd ever seen released from him in my entire life. He confessed to me that he had felt guilt his entire life about being 'the one' in his family who had escaped to the West during World War II and had avoided the increasingly harsh Stalinist rule and poverty in Ukraine that his family, and people in the Eastern Bloc countries in general, continued to experience after the war.

He also had me very close to tears many a moment, but particularly with his talk of legacy. My brother and I promised him we would make a donation on behalf of my parents to Toronto's Holodomor Memorial Project. He was keen to help fund the creation of a site and statue, in an area very close to where I lived in fact, that would commemorate the genocide of millions of Ukrainians who had perished as victims of a man-made famine under Stalin's regime. Up to 25,000 people had died each day at the peak of the famine in 1932 and 1933. With the donation my father requested us to handle, our parents' names would appear on a plaque at the site, and they would be indefinitely memorialized.

There were other intriguing, but tragic, tidbits I learned about my father while he was hospitalized. I knew he'd been involved in anti-Soviet espionage after the war, but this was the first time he confessed to me the guilt he harbored about the part he played in coordinating the deployment of young Ukrainian spies into the Soviet Union to conduct internal espionage but who were subsequently killed because there was a mole in their group. These burdens, I was convinced, all sat very heavily on his heart.

Miraculously, my father was scheduled to be released from hospital sooner than we anticipated. Yes, he still had pending bypass surgery, but that needed to be booked for a future date. So, on the same day I finally received news that the mechanical part had arrived and that the medals had gone into production, I made one last post-work commute to Hamilton and then returned to the Museum that same night. The security guard on duty raised his eyebrows at my late-night entry, but when I explained I needed to start prepping the boxes that would house the medals being shipped out in a few days, he gave me an authentic look of sympathy and wished me good luck.

Even with the Cronenberg exhibit and the Mugwump vacated from the Museum, it was still a spooky amble to my office. I scampered to it at a faster pace than usual. At one point, while nearing the base of the Sagaẃeen crest pole, which boasted a detached carving of a cormorant, I could have sworn I saw a shadow flicker.

The fine hair on my arms stood on end. I paused. I listened. I stuck my neck forward and slivered my eyes, then galloped the remaining short distance. With trembling hands, I unlocked my office door, switched the lights on, stepped in, and slipped on something that found me in a wide standing split. It was a brown kraft interoffice envelope that someone had slid under my door. Damn, these things were a safety hazard, I thought to myself as I picked it up and frisbeed it onto my desk.

I circled around my desk and dropped into my chair, wondering why I had tried to push myself so hard. There wasn't an ounce of spare energy left in my body. And there wasn't any room in this space to do the kind of prep I'd hoped to do to save time once the medals arrived on the shipping dock. I leaned forward and, towards me, slid the 8 ½" x 11" envelope that almost landed me in a yoga pose I wasn't actually capable of achieving. I checked out the front and back of the envelope, but there were no previous names or departments written on it. In fact, there wasn't anything written on it, not even my name. I turned the envelope over again, unwound the thin red string wrapped around the two paper buttons on the back, and flipped open the flap, allowing me to withdraw the single sheet inside. Before removing it fully, my feet became leaden.

I dropped the envelope back onto my desk and picked up the phone receiver. It was late, yes, but I thought I'd take a chance.

"Oh my god, you're there," I said once the connection was made.

"I was most tempted to not pick up the phone, but I saw it was you. What are you doing at the Museum at such a late hour?"

"I'm not really sure. I could ask you the same thing."

"Oh, you know," said Walter, "just some month-end reporting I am impelled to complete, and I am most productive when it is quiet and everyone else has vacated."

"Can you come down to my office, like pronto?"

"Well, I..."

"It's important. Something turned up in my office."

There was a pause. "Can we not pretend just for tonight that everything is quiet and status quo?"

"I've been trying, believe me. But I'm just too exhausted to do anything else, and I just, I don't know..."

"I will be down instantaneously. Please give me a moment to let Security know I'll be traversing the galleries, as I'll likely be setting off some motion detectors."

"I'll see you soon," I said. I plunked the receiver down and took the piece of paper all the way out of the envelope.

On the sheet was an image I was 99.9% sure was a reproduction of yet another part of the Museum's Rotunda ceiling, but I had no clue what it represented. It looked like it might be a South American reference, but I hadn't studied ancient cultures of the New World since I was a kid in primary school.

Just as I was about to start Googling, my office door thrust open, and I leapt to my feet...and then sat back down. "For crying out loud. I just lost ten years off my life."

"I do apologize, but you did know I would be here lickety-split," said Walter.

"Yeah, I know, sorry. I'm just on edge. I haven't been getting much sleep lately."

"Well you should go home as soon as possible then."

"Have a look at this," I said holding the image facing towards the librarian. "Someone had slipped it under my door."

"Should we not we be careful about our fingerprints and such?" said Walter.

"The cops haven't found any yet to this point; do you really think our nemesis got sloppy all of a sudden?"

"You have a point."

"It's from our ceiling, isn't it?" I asked.

Walter nodded yes. "Catequil, the Inca god of thunder and lightning," he said of the image of what appeared to be a stout person wearing a bird-like ceremonial mask and clinging onto something.

"He is holding a snake in each hand. They represent lightning bolts," added Walter.

"Oh, I thought those were sticks." I chuckled.

"Definitely thunder bolts. Catequil was also considered to be the god of weather and an oracle that predicted the future. He was worshipped from Quito to Cuzco, and the Inca often carried an idol of Catequil into battle. All in all, he was

238

a rather complex deity."

Walter's briefer-than-usual treatise was met with my silence.

"What are you thinking?" asked Walter.

"There's no sign of any South American object around here."

"Hmm, well it might not necessarily be an Inca artifact we're expecting. Augustinian priests from Europe meticulously gathered and recorded information about the Inca's ancient beliefs when they arrived in Peru in the mid-sixteenth century. Perhaps there is an antique European journal or something similar on the horizon. Speaking of which, I noticed an item outside your door, around the corner. I didn't pay much mind to it...I thought perhaps it was refuse from the recent exhibition cleanup."

"What are you talking about? I didn't see anything."

"Hmm." Walter started towards the portal. "Let me just double check. I truly hope it is not anything of consequence, but I will not be able to sleep if we do not rule this out."

Before I could take another breath, Walter popped out and returned in a matter of seconds with a package that was frighteningly familiar.

"It appears to already have been opened," remarked Walter, "but it does have your name on the mailing label."

"NO, NO, NO," I screamed at full volume. "This can't be happening."

Walter delicately put the package on my desk and cowered away. "Kalena, as Brenda is known to say, you are freaking me out."

"FREAKING YOU OUT! Earlier in the day, this package was sitting in my fridge at home."

"I am afraid I do not understand," Walter said with temerity.

"Someone has been in my condo, gone into my fridge, and delivered it here, to just outside my office. I'm not even going to look inside. I'll bet you it's a leopard's paw."

"Pardon me?"

"A frigging paw from a real leopard. Like a taxidermy specimen. Go ahead. Look inside the box."

Walter stood frozen in place.

"JUST LOOK INSIDE THE DAMN BOX!"

Walter's hands trembled as he meticulously picked up two pens from my desktop and used them to pull back the flaps. He peeked inside the package, redirected his gaze towards me, and flung the pens onto my desk as though they were coated with poison.

"I take it I'm right," I said.

"This is most alarming," said Walter. "Why would you be keeping such a repugnant object in your refrigerator?"

"It's a long story. I suspect it belonged to *Il Gattopardo*. I have no idea how it made its way from my fridge to here, but if someone has broken into my condo, I better hightail it and see if they took anything else or...ransacked my place." This was a time when having watched too many British police procedurals and *Law and Order* episodes was of no service to my peace of mind. All I was able to envision was my otherwise overly orderly place in a state of utter disarray – drawers pulled open, contents strewn everywhere, toilet lid pulled off, bed ripped apart, fridge left open.

I jumped up and reached past Walter to grab my coat. Adrenalin was flowing so fiercely through my body it felt as though my skin was on fire.

Walter reached for me and clamped onto my arm. "Hold

on there. You can't just go dashing home. The intruder might still be there."

"He dropped this thing off here, didn't he? He's long gone."

"Well, yes, I suppose. But I'm coming with you, and we should call the police. Actually, our contacts from CSIS."

"NO," I said. "I refuse to have my home turned into a crime scene."

Walter started to speak but I interrupted. "NO. And that's that."

The meek librarian took a deep breath. "At the very least I am going to call Marco and have him meet us at your residence."

"No way!"

"I swear, Ms. Boyko. I will wrestle you down and tie you up if I have to..."

I burst out laughing. Walter looked stunned for a moment. "Well that would be a bit ridiculous. Perhaps I will not wrestle you to the ground. But please, I implore you. Be reasonable. We need someone with Marco's skills and expertise in security to ensure the situation does not escalate. We just do not know what to anticipate."

I deflated. "I hate it when you're right."

* * * * *

Walter had left his car at home, so we grabbed a cab. I filled him in on the whole leopard paw situation and there were a lot of raised eyebrows, looks of horror, and guffaws. I kept peering at the cab driver to gauge if he was listening, but he had buds in his ears and was having a conversation of his own in an indecipherable language while we crossed the city to my neighborhood.

Walter expressed grave disapproval at my keeping these circumstances all to myself, especially in light of this evening's reappearance of the animal remains at work, but when I explained my family crisis and how it propelled me into denial about the whole Leopard affair, he was more sympathetic. Upon arrival at my building, the cab turned into the temporary parking bay, and I could see Marco seated in the lobby through the glass wall that faced towards the driveway. I wasn't relishing having to repeat everything I had just told Walter as I anticipated an even harsher scolding – and I really wasn't in the mood. In fact, I suddenly became aware how drained I was.

As we stepped through the first set of doors to the building, Marco leapt to his feet and opened the secondary doors from inside. "What the frig, you guys? What's the story now? I thought I was finally going to have a quiet evening at home."

"With Benny?" I asked.

"Well, that's another story."

"Oh dear," said Walter. "I hope that is no indication of trouble in paradise."

I stared at Marco. "Is that the case?"

Marco smirked. "Quit changing the subject, folks – just give me the rundown. And keep it to the point."

"Well…" said Walter.

I jerked my gaze towards Walter. "You better let me take the wheel."

"Agreed," said Walter. "But I suggest we do it here. He needs to be prepared in case there's a welcoming party."

"What?" asked Marco. I gently pushed him down into one of the lobby's sofas.

As Walter and I joined him on the couch, a young man

who had come from the direction of the elevators crossed in front of us and started to play the piano that occupied the space.

"Oh my god," I said quietly, "this is the first time in all the years I've lived here that I've seen anyone play the piano outside of a building party. It's for resident use, but nobody ever plays it."

"Until this evening," said Marco.

Walter leaned in. "And they do not even have the courtesy to play classical music. What is this cacophony?"

"Bon Jovi," I said laughing.

"Who?" asked Walter.

"You really must come out from under that rock," I answered.

Walter looked miffed, but I ignored him and began to spill my tale while being serenaded to *Wanted Dead or Alive*. The absurdity of the moment did not pass my notice. Neither did Marco's troubled expression, which became graver and graver as I continued. He was just about to speak when another resident entered the lobby and came directly towards me. It was the building's affable superintendent, who often did small jobs for me when needed, like fixing an out-of-control toilet.

"Hey, Kalena," he yelled over the music as he approached. "I think you're going to like the new addition to your place," the spectacled Latino said with some glee.

"Excuse me?" I said. The looks on Marco's and Walter's faces accurately reflected the trepidation I was feeling at the moment. "Oh, right," I said.

"Hope everything's cool. I just happened to be here when the delivery guy came and he showed me your letter of permission to set things up in your absence."

"Oh, yeah, sure," I said. Walter reached for my arm and clutched it so hard I thought he was going to draw blood. "I was just about to take my friends up there to check things out."

"Oh…are they fans too? To each his own, I guess," said the superintendent.

I shot Walter and Marco an I-have-no-effing-idea-what-he's-talking-about-but-keep-quiet look. We then rose to our feet, and I led the mad dash to the elevator. "Thanks, Ricardo. Much appreciated," I said as I pressed the up button frantically.

The wait for the elevator seemed imponderably long, and when the door finally opened, we simultaneously tried to enter it like a trio of buffoons. As the doors slowly closed, I grinned artificially at the security guard seated at the lobby's Security Desk.

At my floor I exited first with the men right behind. I heard a gasp from Walter. "I, I would have expected that you lived in a very different kind of place, something a little, a little…"

"A little less bombed-out looking?" I asked. Marco snickered.

Walter nodded. The three of us scrutinized the stripped walls with large random swatches of what looked like pale pink and blue paint. The carpet was splotched everywhere with plaster. The lighting was bright and stark from the exposed light bulbs.

"They're renovating the corridors, people. They just did the demolition and now looks like they've prepped the walls for new wall paper."

"Oh, I see," said Walter.

I rolled my eyes and shook my head, then took the several steps to my doorway. Pausing, I put my ear to the door. "I don't hear anything." Reaching into my purse, I retrieved my keys, slowly cracked open the door, and leaned in, head first. Silence.

Marco reached his arm forward and nudged me behind him.

"There's a light switch on the wall, just after the opening to the kitchen. And the switch just past that one will light up the rest of the space."

Marco turned on the lights as directed and we just stared. Before us stood a life-sized cardboard cutout of actor Chris Hemsworth decked out in a familiar superhero costume.

"What is the meaning of this? I must say I was fully prepared to find some Inca treasure here," said Walter.

"I have no words," said Marco.

"It appears to be a reference to–"

"A different god of thunder," I said. "It's frigging Thor, the Norse hammer-wielding god of thunder, lightning and storms...My superintendent must think I'm a super freak. I'll never be able to face him again!"

CHAPTER TWENTY-NINE

"This is just too goddam much. I didn't sign up for this!"

"Oh, like I did," I retorted to Marco. "I'm just trying to get through life, quietly and unobtrusively, to do my job as best I can, and to live my life from a place of love instead of fear. What the hell are you complaining about? I'm the one whose personal space has been invaded for who knows what reason. And on top of that, I've got this ridiculous cardboard actor-god thingamajig in my living room because..." I threw my arms in the air.

"Yeah, sorry. I just...Never mind," said Marco. "Listen, we should do a quick, but thorough, check of your place, just to make sure there aren't any less obvious surprises hidden somewhere."

"Exceptional idea." Walter turned to me. "I do believe that corroborates my correctness about requesting Marco's presence here."

I tilted my head with an accompanying sigh. "I'll do the bedroom, if you two want to poke your noses in here and in the kitchen cupboards, bathroom, etc. At least we don't have a lot of territory to cover."

As always, my closet and cupboards were OCD-ish neat, so I knew it'd be easy to determine if anything had been disturbed. I ruffled through all my clothes, which were ordered by color, and from light to dark hues within each color zone. I shuffled through my shoes, rifled gently through drawers, and peeked under the bed and under the mattress. There was no sign of a museum-worthy artwork tucked away anywhere that I could find.

"Nothing here in the bedroom," I yelled as I walked back into the living area.

"My goodness, I had no idea," commented Walter.

"An aberration, if you ask me," said Marco.

"What?" I asked.

"Who keeps their stuff so bloody organized? Do you actually live in this space?" said Marco.

"I happen to like keeping things tidy. Besides, when you occupy a small footprint, you need to keep things in order or you end up tripping over stuff."

"Well, I find it an admirable quality. I suspect you would have made an excellent librarian, Ms. Boyko."

"Funny you should say that. I almost did my Master's in Library Science."

"That is a shame you did not pursue it," said Walter. "But may we sit down for a moment? I have a notion about the significance of the references to these gods of thunder and storms."

"Sure. Can I get you guys something to drink?"

"You mean like that green juice you have in the fridge?" asked Marco.

"I am fine. Thank you so much for the hospitality." Walter grimaced as he stepped towards the couch.

"I do have beverages other than kale juice."

"No, no really," said Walter. Marco had a sneer on his face. The two sat down while I opted to lean against the dividing wall between the kitchen and living room spaces.

"Perhaps," said Walter, "it's not an object we are meant to find this time. I believe our perpetrator may be leading up to some larger reveal otherwise, why give himself away as *Il Gattopardo*?"

"I'm not following you," I said.

"Me either."

"What if these latest clues are in relation to an event, rather than to an object?" said Walter.

I narrowed my eyes.

"What if our thief is suggesting something is going to happen during a big storm, a thunder storm in particular?"

"I thought I had an active imagination," I said.

"I admit it is a far reach, and unorthodox, but this whole affair has been rather anarchic."

"Marco, any opinion?" I asked.

"I don't have a–. I dunno. This person's gone completely off their rocker. It's way beyond comprehension."

"Well, I guess we wait and see," I said.

"Not if I have anything to say about it." Marco's entire body tightened.

"What the heck does that mean?" I asked

"Nothing specific," said Marco. "I think we can all do with some sleep. But you're not missing any of your keys, are you?"

"Oh my god, I didn't even think of that." I did a speedy one-eighty, leapt towards the fridge, did an inventory of the keys hanging on the magnetic holder attached to the appliance, and clutched my heart. "Everything's here," I reported.

"They could have made an impression of your keys," said Marco. "Did you have an extra copy of your door key hanging there while you were at work today?"

I nodded yes. My knees felt like they were going to buckle.

"Oh dear." Walter looked like he was breaking into a

sweat. "It may not be safe for you to stay here tonight."

"Agreed," said Marco. "Why don't you grab some stuff and stay at my place. We have an extra bedroom at the house and I'm sure my father'd be fine with it."

"That's not going to happen. I sleep horribly in other beds, and I'm so sleep-deprived as it is. I'll just put the chain across the door."

"You can't be serious." Marco tugged at the brass chain.

"Even I can tell that that is a rather flimsy security measure," said Walter.

"Oh, for crying out loud. I'll sleep on your couch," said Marco.

"Uh, I don't think so." I turned to Walter.

"Please do not look at me, I could never explain it to Brenda if I were to stay overnight."

"No offense, but you're not my type."

"I can grab some toiletries downstairs in that store at the base of your building." Marco turned to me, but before I was able to utter a word said, "And that's that!"

"Should we not attempt to get a description of the person who entered today from your superintendent?" said Walter. "Or perhaps there is some security footage."

"He's never been caught on camera, at least not clearly. If Kalena wants to avoid being interrogated by the folks who run this building complex, requesting video footage is the last thing she should do. It could stir up a lot of fuss without necessarily leading to anything we can use in the end. I know it's frustrating to hang back, but—"

As Marco was finishing his sentence, my phone beeped. I snatched it up from the kitchen counter and saw I'd received an email, so I opened it up.

"I don't believe it. I DON'T BELIEVE IT!"

"Oh, my, what is it?" Walter's voice sounded shaky.

"Yeah, you're kind of making me nervous, too. What's going on?" asked Marco

"The medal production's probably going to be finished by morning!" I started to do a quirky little happy dance, with Walter and Marco staring in bewilderment. "My medals have gone into production. My medals are going to be done soon" I sang.

"Well, at least one positive thing occurred today," said Walter.

"I'm going to make my deadline. I'm going to make my deadline."

"Okay, okay," said Marco. "I think we get the message."

"Excuse me, guys. I need to shoot off a quick text to Stewart." I pulled up my phone and quickly drafted a text, but sent it to Geoffrey rather than Stewart.

Marco yawned quite obviously.

"I'm rather fatigued myself. If you do not mind, I am going to depart now." Walter put on his overcoat and drifted towards the door. "I meant to comment on this earlier. Your décor is rather interesting. I do not believe I have ever seen an aubergine and forest green color palette. It is rather rich. And I admire the mix of contemporary and antique furniture. It is done rather tastefully."

"Thank you."

"The numerous geodes are quite a whimsical addition as well. But I don't understand why you have all those small crystals suspended from that plastic grate covering the fluorescent lights in the kitchen."

"They're intended to infuse me with energy and positivity."

"You might want to add some more to the collection,"

said Walter in all seriousness.

"Good night," I said.

"Now if anything comes up, please do not hesitate to call me," said Walter.

"Everything'll be just fine," I opened the door, and Walter walked out backwards, bowing a little on the retreat. I closed and locked the door behind him and put on the safety chain.

"So, I do have some toothbrushes, still in their packaging, actually. My dentist hands them out like there's no tomorrow. And as long as you don't mind using organic products, I should have everything you need as far as toiletries go."

"Well, la di da. But I don't suppose you have an x-large T-shirt kicking around."

I raised my finger. "Give me one second, I just…" I rotated, dashed to the bedroom and started looking through a small pile of folded white shirts. "I volunteered at the Museum's March Break program," I yelled, "and the only sizes they seemed to have were extra-large and extra-extra-large." I pulled out a T-shirt, and opened it displaying the Museum's logo.

I popped back into the living room holding it up for Marco.

"Perfect. I don't suppose you have a pair of men's sweats kicking around, too," he said as he took his shirt off revealing his sculpted chest.

I shook my head.

"Well good thing I wore boxers instead of tighty-whities." Marco slipped on the T-shirt. "Just kidding. Why don't I use the facilities first? I'm sure I'll be a lot faster than you."

I darted passed Marco and from the bathroom drawers

retrieved a new toothbrush, some bed linens, a pair of towels and a face cloth. Exiting the room, I handed all but the bed linens to Marco. "You're welcome to have the bed. I barely move when I sleep, so I'm happy to take the couch."

"Totally not necessary," said Marco, who strolled into the bathroom where he put down the sundries then turned around and stood in the doorway, arms bent, resting his forearms on the door frame, leaning forward a tad with his body. The T-shirt fit more snugly than I had anticipated.

Suddenly he reminded me of the sexy, young Sylvester Stallone in the original *Rocky*, when he makes his first move on Adrian and clearly melts her from head to toe. In the movie, however, Rocky is wearing a wife-beater T-shirt, sans sleeves, and his intent is clearly to seduce the naive Adrian Pennino.

"If you take all those back cushions off the couch, that'll work. I'm not going to kick you out of your own bed."

I started to feel a little warm around the neck. I lived in an open space, so the only thing dividing the bedroom from the living room was a cream-colored fringe curtain and a stained glass window suspended from the ceiling. There would be no walls between Marco and me for the night.

Nervously, I picked the cushions off the sofa, neatly piling them in a corner, which left Marco a larger surface to lie on. "Um, okay. I'll have this made up for you in no time."

"Thanks," he said, retreating into the bathroom and closing the door behind him.

In the meantime, I pulled out some clothing from my closet as, clearly, sleeping in the buff would not be appropriate. Marco must have barely splashed his face as he was done cleaning up in no time and was back out into the living room.

"So, my alarm goes off around 6:45, if that works for you," I said meandering towards the bathroom, nightwear in hand.

Marco shrugged. "Sure, whatever."

"By the way, you mentioned something about Benny. Is everything okay?"

Reaching his hand towards his face, he started to rub his forehead. "I wasn't going to get into it tonight."

"Sorry, I didn't mean to intrude," I said, turning to enter the bathroom.

"She's going back to Italy."

"What?"

"Yeah, she got an offer she's finding hard to refuse."

"Like what?"

"Some post-doc position or something. And it's in her home town in Brescia, where there's a major movement for daylighting rivers. The drainers are a bit radical, it sounds. But it's right up her alley."

"What are you going to do?"

"I'll live." Marco looked away towards the window, as if the blinds were open.

"I'll, uh, I'll get washed up and then I'll hit the lights," I said.

"Take your time. I'm so zonked, I'm sure I'll crash in no time."

I shut the door behind me and leaned on it for a moment. Poor Marco. And Benny! I had become quite fond of her. I didn't want her to leave Canada. But she struck me as a woman who, once her mind was made up, wouldn't easily change it.

Pushing myself away from the door, I changed into

some comfy sleepwear. The top was a slinky synthetic material with a subtle animal print of black on dark chocolate brown, with straps and trim made of black stretchy lace. The bell-bottomed flood pants were made of the same clingy material, but were solid black.

While tossing the day wear into the laundry hamper, I heard a muffled repetitive noise from outside the bathroom. I inched the door open only to be pulverized by an all-too-familiar sound. It was the baritone snore of a man in deep sleep. I rotated back towards the mirror and dug through my makeup bag. There it was, I thought to myself as I withdrew a small white plastic container, just a touch larger than the size of a Canadian $2 coin. Normally, I saved the contents for my cardio classes at the gym in order to extend the longevity of my eardrums, but there was not a hope in hell of me getting any sleep without wearing the silicone ear plugs to bed this evening.

I reshaped the silicone coins into rounder, flatter forms and inserted them into my ears, further smoothing them out in such a way to block as much of the thunderous sound as possible. But not even these plugs fully muted Marco's roaring. Rolling onto my side, I wrapped a pillow around the back of my head, pressing the sides against my ears. It helped, but sustainability in this position was questionable.

* * * * *

I bolted upright at the sensation of someone shaking me from my sleep and then felt a hand cover my mouth. "Shh," said the ghostly figure. Instinctively, I grabbed a pillow and smacked the shadow with as much force as I could muster and knocked them off the edge of the bed.

"For effing sake, Kalena," whispered a voice. "What the hell?" I had just clobbered Marco.

"Well, what are you doing? I'd finally just fallen asleep." I poked my fingers into my ears and realized the ear plugs had fallen out.

"Shh. Listen."

I slid towards the end of the bed, and my toes touched the floor. I froze. There was a scraping noise at the front door. No, it wasn't scraping. It was someone trying to put a key in the keyhole...but as though having a challenge with the insertion.

I latched onto Marco's arm.

"Ooooow," he said with a controlled volume.

"Sorry." I patted around my bed until my hand landed on my phone, then put my thumb over the base for fingerprint recognition. The screen opened up to my apps. I found the flashlight app and flipped the digital switch. A bright beam illuminated, and I directed it towards the door. The grinding of metal on metal continued. Marco and I looked at each other, but my expression of horror was not mirrored in his calm face.

Suddenly, he leapt to his feet and dashed straight for the door, clipping cardboard Thor, who wobbled a few times but remained upright. Then ever so silently he slipped the chain off its track, raised his arm in the air like a weapon, and flung the door open with his free hand.

"Oh my god," squealed a woman with a short blonde bob and large, expressive eyes.

"Who are you? What do you want?" said Marco.

The woman cowered and pulled away from the door. "Who are you? What are you doing in my home?"

"Joan!" I yelled from the other side of the room.

"You know this woman?" asked Marco.

"She lives in the unit above me."

Marco pivoted to face me and discreetly rolled the fingers of one hand near his mouth, suggesting she had been drinking.

"Were you out on the town tonight?" I asked.

"How'd you guess?" Joan giggled. "I was celebrating my birthday with my daughter."

"You must have had a good time because you got off on the wrong floor and you've been trying to fit your key into my lock."

"Oh shit! I'm so, so very sorry. I...uh...you know me. I don't drink much. But I also took some cold medicine earlier in the evening."

"No worries. I've done the same thing...when I was sober even. And with these hallways ripped apart, it's even harder to tell if you're on the right floor."

"You're a good sport," she said, then paused. "Those are such cute pajamas. But I didn't know you were seeing someone."

I could feel a flush of heat coloring my face. "It's not...this is a colleague. Marco's just crashing on my couch for the night. Long story."

"Oh, okay." Suddenly, Joan tilted her head, peering most curiously into my living room area. "Is that...is that Thor?"

"Uh, yes. That's an even longer story. I don't suppose you want him?" I asked jokingly.

"My grandson's obsessed with him. I've already taken him to see that movie twice now, and he keeps asking me to take him again. I'd rather deal with lice."

"Well, he's all yours!" I skipped over to the cardboard

256

figure, picked him up and trotted him over to Joan.

"I can't believe it. You really want it?" asked Marco.

"Andrew will be over the moon."

"Can I give you a hand?" offered Marco. The figure was a good two heads taller than Joan.

"Oh, no. I'll be fine. I've kept you two up long enough." She shot me a cunning wink.

"Good night, neighbor," I said nudging her on her way. "Make sure you get off the right floor this time." I waved and shut the door.

"Oh, my freaking god. What are the chances of that happening tonight of all nights?" I said.

"Yeah, well. At least you got rid of Thor. But she was right," said Marco.

"About what?"

"Those ARE cute pajamas."

In an instant, I hopped over to the couch, grabbed a cushion Marco had been using as a pillow, whipped it at him, and then sauntered towards my bed. "I need to get some shuteye or I'll never get up in the morning."

The next thing I knew a cushion struck me on the back of my head and I zipped around. "Oh, really?"

CHAPTER THIRTY

Drowsily, I turned my head to the other side and a full body smile warmed me. Then something shifted. Please tell me that was a dream. Please, please let it have been a dream. And Benny. Crap.

Overnight I had transformed into one of those women – one of those women who didn't think about the hurt they might cause another woman. If this had happened when I was younger and naive, it might have been negligibly forgivable. But I was supposed to be older and wiser. Even more despicable was that I knew what the deep pain of betrayal felt like. Yes, Benny was leaving the country, but that was no excuse. Damn that Joan. If she hadn't have woken us up, Marco and I would have slept through the night, and everything would have been status quo this morning.

I slid my hand under the pillow, but my hand didn't land on anything other than my guilty sheets. The next thing I knew the lyrics of George Michael's "Careless Whisper" were droning in my head, but instead of 'guilty feet have no rhythm,' the words transformed into 'guilty sheets have a victim.'

I rolled over to the other side and saw that the sheets and bedding I had pulled out for Marco had been carefully folded up and stacked into the corner of the sofa. I sat further upright. "Hey, Marco, are you in the bathroom?" No answer.

Wow, he had actually sneaked out while I was sleeping.

I picked up a pillow, pressed it against my face and screamed into it, "YOU ARE SUCH AN IDIOT."

Dropping the pillow, I pushed aside a few of the blinds that shaded the window edging my bed and saw that the skies were grey, grey, and greyer. This was the autumn of 100 shades of grey.

George Michael returned to my head so I quickly turned on the television. "Storms have been pummeling parts of Canada, and they're coming our way," said the female voice. My ears perked up, and goosebumps popped up on my arms.

"It's looking like," continued the weather announcer, "conditions will be prime for some dramatically severe thunderstorms. Yes, more rain for our already water-logged city. Residents are being warned to bump up waterproofing in their basements, especially if you live in a lower-lying area. And if you're driving downtown, you will want to avoid areas of the GTA core that have been persistently flooding in recent weeks. Toronto City Council has been weighing different options to prevent new flooding, but nothing will be in place to save us from what's approaching us from the east."

Quickly, I turned off the television. If Walter's theory that our art hoarder was going to do something during the next major storm...NO! "I release what doesn't serve me. I release what doesn't serve me," I kept repeating out loud. All my attention needed to hone in on expediting the medal shipment to Saudi Arabia – and that was that.

My cell phone rang, and I dashed back to the bed. "Is he freaking psychic?"

I swiped the surface of the phone. "Well, good morning," I said. "Oh, I guess it's not morning there. "Well unless you're...I dunno, somewhere that's not London."

"Surely, I didn't wake you," said Geoffrey.

"No... Just getting ready for work...and listening to the latest depressing weather report."

"And what's on your slate for work today?" asked Geoffrey.

"Ha, ha. You know very well what I'm going to be doing, unless you missed my text."

"I saw it."

"Well, with luck, the medals will be delivered to the Museum this morning and I'll be prepping the shipment for Riyadh."

"Well, God thank the queen for that."

"I'm pretty sure she didn't have anything to do with it."

"Very amusing. But I am relieved to hear an end is in sight. And Harry will be ecstatic. He's been the one taking the brunt of the pressure the Prince has been putting on us."

"I know."

"And your anticipated shipping date?"

"You are aware that currently I'm a one-person operation."

"Understood. I honestly appreciate your circumstances. But I also cannot emphasize enough how significant this relationship–"

"I KNOW!"

"Well, then. Since that message is very clear, I best let you get to work."

"Bye, Geoffrey." I pressed the disengage call icon on my phone.

How many decades away was I from retirement? I tried to calculate the number of years and then threw my hands manically into the air. Not soon enough, obviously.

I turned the bathroom lights on and stepped in. Staring at me from the mirror mounted above the sink was a large happy face, drawn with some sort of white cream. As I leaned closer to the mirror, I recognized the scent – it was my Nourish Organic Face Lotion, with argan and rosewater. Pricey stuff.

I popped open the cupboard drawer below the basin, tore off a strip of a paper towel roll, sprayed it with some eco-friendly glass cleaner and applied it to the mirror. As I rubbed it across the surface, it made an expansive mess. Just great.

After the cleanup, I prepared for work at a turtle's pace. Another night of too little sleep was not helping my energy level. Finally, I made my way to the streetcar stop to find it, as usual, overpopulated with waiting riders. But then miracle of miracles occurred as I peered northwards up Bathurst Street. A southbound streetcar was turning eastbound onto King. It must have been rerouted. That meant only one thing – an empty streetcar, and despite a massive crowd anxiously waiting, there would be seats for all. Hallelujah! Maybe my luck was turning.

Upon arrival at the Museum, I walked timidly towards the staff entrance. Stopping, I gazed through the glass, but as there were two sets of doors, I couldn't see clearly who was sitting behind the Security Desk. I pressed forward, but as soon as I opened the second set of doors, I breathed a sigh of relief. Awkward moment avoided. No Marco.

I skipped along the corridor towards my office and noticed the lights were still dim in the arts studio. It was usually buzzing with activity when I arrived. But I continued on to my Mugwump-free office threshold and entered. I didn't have to flip on the lights to see what time it was in Riyadh, London, Toronto, and San Jose. My stomach fluttered as though there was a manic butterfly trying to escape from it. All the boxes inhabiting my office had disappeared. What the hell was going on? Had Gaspar found another spot for them?

I tossed my coat down on the chair and rang Shipping and Receiving. No answer. That was quite odd. I then called the library, not that Walter was likely to know anything about the whereabouts of the boxes. No answer. Refusing to get in contact with Marco, I called Malik. No answer. I furrowed my eyebrows. The Museum was a bloody ghost town this morning. With my positive mood quickly fading, I peeled out of my office and headed back towards the arts studio. Maybe there was an all-staff Town Hall this morning, and I'd missed the memo.

Pausing at the doorway of the studio, I thought I heard voices. But the lights were still off. I slowly opened the door. "Helloooo," I uttered.

"Shhh," I heard someone say.

"Is someone there?" My hand trembled as I fumbled for the light switch. It finally landed on it and the bright fluorescents illuminated the room. I gasped and clutched my hand to my heart. Water formed in a nanosecond and filled my eyes. I continued to gaze around the room in utter disbelief.

The studio was filled with boxes. Boxes, boxes and more boxes. Some I recognized as the boxes containing the velvet containers intended to house the commemorative medals. But there seemed to be a far greater number of boxes piled up than I remembered having been in my office. More striking was the row of people staring back at me with giant grins.

"You're medals came in early this morning," said Gaspar from one end of the room.

"I see that," I said moving my fingers towards my eyes to dab the moisture. "But what are you all doing here?" Besides Gaspar I saw Walter and Malik and Dara. And there was

Deepa, the Director's assistant, Sunny and his Programs staff, Roberto, Alana, and several other people from various curatorial departments. The list went on. And there was Marco standing in the back.

Walter stepped forward. "Brenda contacted me overnight and asked if I could rally people with whom your department has worked. And well, as you can see, when I put the calls out, people started coming out of the woodwork."

"Let's get going, Kalena," chimed in Malik. "I understand we need to get these medals in those velvet boxes and then get everything boxed up and on the shipping dock, ASAP. The sooner we get this done, the sooner we can get back to running the Museum."

"You...you people. I'm overwhelmed with gratitude." At that moment, my eyes locked with Marco's, and I thought his grin would blind me. "We need to set up a production line."

"Oh, here she goes," piped up Sunny. "That's the Kalena we all know and love to despise. A dictator all the way. Be careful everyone. She's got her whip out."

"You know I do." I mimicked cracking a whip and everyone laughed, including me, but inside I was weeping with joy. I worked in such a bubble these days, especially with Brenda currently overseas, and I often felt I was bearing the weight of the universe on my petite shoulders. I had forgotten how many relationships I had forged over the years in the Museum with so many amazing and special people. This was a much-needed reminder that I needed to reach out more often when I needed help.

We did, in fact, set up a production line for the packaging process, and my heart sang as we toiled together preparing the shipment for the long voyage to Saudi Arabia. People were assigned different tasks including opening up the boxes containing the medals and others with pulling the small velvet boxes out of their packaging. Yet others inserted the medals into the presentation boxes, which were then closed up while another person did a quality control check to make sure each green velvet box contained a medal. Still others counted and then sealed up the cartons with packing tape.

The medals looked fantastic. Despite all the production hiccups, the quality of the discs was excellent, and I had no doubt they would please the Prince, especially the gold medals for the VIP attendees. So, with my heart full, I stepped into the studio's inner office and closed the door behind me. The gradient frosted glass walls allowed me to still see what was going on in the workroom as I pulled out my phone to call Brenda and thank her for taking the initiative. She so often came across as such a hard cookie, but she never failed to have my back. And for that I was infinitely appreciative.

Once I'd finished bowing at Brenda's feet, I surveyed the room filled with busy elves. I caught Marco spying me. Immediately he dropped what he was doing and sped towards the office. No! No! No! But it was too late for me to escape. Marco opened the door, stepped in and closed the portal securely behind him. I looked out and saw Walter examine us oddly.

"Marco, this really isn't the time to chat—"

"I just wanted to explain why I left without saying goodbye. I wouldn't normally do such a schmucky thing."

"No apology is necessary. What happened last night is never going to happen EVER again."

"Because I left while you were sleeping?"

"NO! Because how am I ever supposed to look Benny in the eyes again?"

"Oh man. It's not what you think."

"Are you going to tell me you have an open relationship or something moronic like that?"

"No, of course not. It's just that...well, it's complicated, and I just can't say anything." Marco shook his head, and his previously exuberant expression turned to one of a forlorn puppy.

A tap sounded and we both jolted. Gaspar was at the door, and I let him in.

"Sorry to make an intrusion," he said, "but I wanted to let you know we're making very fast progress, and I'm going to go back to Shipping to start to fill out weigh bills and prepare the paper work. It will be a bit more complicated as the shipment will be going to the Middle East."

"And you have all the delivery info and everything you need to create the invoices, yes?"

Gaspar nodded. "I have it all in the email you sent me."

I gently took Gaspar by the elbow and walked him out of the office while giving Marco an icy look to shut him down. "Brilliant. Thank you so, so much. And you said it would take how long to get there?"

"Two days, but not counting today. Pick up won't be until later in the day, so we cannot count it."

My eyes widened. "We are going to be cutting it so close."

"We will do it," Gaspar yelled raising a fist into the air.

My helpers joined in the cheering. "Woo hoo!" "Hurray!" "We will do it."

Gaspar exited the studio with a bounce in his walk, and the rest of us returned to the tasks at hand. We labored enthusiastically and, without breaks, we wrapped things up within just a matter of hours. For those who were able to stay, I ordered in pizza and soft drinks for an early lunch. And for those who had to return to their offices or work stations, I personally delivered a slice and a drink to them.

Fortunately, Marco had to get back to his rounds, so I had been able to enjoy the feasting without awkwardness. But even with the tension between us, the morning was one of those moments in my career I would never forget. I knew such camaraderie was rare, and I tried to soak in every feeling.

After completing the pizza deliveries and inhaling a piece of vegetarian pizza myself, Walter moseyed his way over to where I was seated. "By any chance," he said somewhat nonchalantly, "did you notice the weather forecast? They're calling for severe–"

"Walter, please don't spoil this for me."

He donned a concerned look, but then cracked a smile. "I understand. I'll just say, let us be cautious."

"Roger, that!" And I took another bite of the Italian pie.

CHAPTER THIRTY-ONE

As relieved as I was to get the medals out the door, I remained constantly on tenterhooks. I regularly checked the progress of the shipment and tuned into the local news at each of its stops to ensure nothing might interrupt the next leg of the journey. But all was proceeding well, and a day and a half in, the shipment was due to land in Bahrain any time, Bahrain being one of the main gateways for deliveries to Saudi Arabia. Meanwhile in Toronto, it was impossible to ignore the escalating reports about severe weather due to hit Toronto any time. I was just thankful the system had not landed the day the medals were loaded onto the FedEx truck from the Museum's shipping dock.

Otherwise things had been unusually tranquil – no more break-ins, no more cardboard cutouts turned up in my living room, and no more stolen art inexplicably appeared at my doorstep. Perhaps my prankster was finally done. Maybe there wasn't anything left in their illegal stash to offload. I really didn't care what the reason was as long as they stayed out of my life. For all I cared, if it was *Il Gattopardo* terrorizing me, he could live happily ever after on a yacht in the South Seas.

Thankfully, in Riyadh, Geoffrey and Stewart had already joined Harry Rigger to ensure all last-minute finishing touches, of which there was an infinitely long list, were completed for the opening of the museum. Still, since the shipment left, my nights were riddled with insomnia. I seemed incapable of calming my mind. So, when I woke to the usual overly-sunshiny reportage from the female reporter on the Weather Network, I tossed and turned, moaned and groaned. It took the words, "And next up is Force of Nature," to truly awaken me.

I was morbidly obsessed with weather disasters around the globe. Reports were often horrific, but controlling the weather was one thing we humans would never accomplish. I was eternally curious about what Mother Nature was up to around the globe, and I was always amazed at how powerful she was.

"We now turn to Saudi Arabia..." I catapulted out of bed. "...where an apocalyptic storm has swept the desert and severe flooding has devastated the country, breaking a century-old record for rainfall." I dropped to my knees. "The bizarre flooding comes just two weeks after a snowstorm blasted across the United Arab Emirates."

"FUUUUUUUUUUUUUUCK!"

"More than a month and a half of rain hit the desert in less than 12 hours. Cities such as Damman, Al-Ahsa, and Riyadh were all brought to a standstill as schools, government offices, and businesses have been shut down."

"Airport, what about the airport?"

"The mayoralty in Riyadh swung into action to clear water from roads and streets, but as you can see in these images, the airport has been shut down, and all air traffic to the capital has been temporarily suspended, leaving thousands stranded..."

I plummeted onto my elbows, head hitting the carpet. "I knew it. I knew it. I fucking knew it." I lifted myself back up and sat on my heels. There was no one more responsible for this situation than me. I had totally manifested it by messing with a universal truth – the more you focus on something, the more of it you receive. Trusting in the universe should have been my tactic. But, noooooo, I had to spend all my time thinking about every possible scenario that could possibly go wrong with the delivery. It had consumed me.

"The flooding is expected to recede in the next few days, but not before a dust storm hits the region."

Dust storm? This is a nightmare? How is that even possible when the desert has been pounded down by rain?

I sprang to my feet and scurried to my phone, but when I pressed the button to wake it up, it remained black. "FUUUUUUUUUUUUCK." Dead. Dashing to the kitchen, I seized my charger, plugged in the phone, and turned it on. The device was encrypted, so startup was slow. This morning it felt like time had stood still. But when fully engaged, I was shocked. There were no messages from Geoffrey. Surely, he would have tried to call me. I dialed him immediately. Straight to voice mail. I stomped my foot on the hard tile surface of the kitchen floor. "Ow!"

I pulled up the FedEx app on my phone and selected the shortcut to my shipment's tracking. There it was. It was in Bahrain, not Riyadh. The phone rang, and it almost slipped out of my hand. With a sold grasp on it again, I swiped the screen.

"Geoffrey, I just tried calling you."

"Yes, I know. I had to pull over. There's no Bluetooth in this vehicle, and I needed to stretch my legs. I must say, I'm rather surprised I have reception here."

"Where is here?"

"I'm just outside of Um Alerrad, about half way to Bahrain."

"What, why?"

"I don't know if you have heard. There was flash flooding in Riyadh, among other places. The airport is locked down. It's a bloody mess."

"I just woke up and heard it on the news."

"I suspected you might still be asleep. The medals are being held back in Bahrain."

"I just found that out, too. You should have called me."

"There was no point alarming you in the middle of the night. There was absolutely nothing you could do about this situation."

"But it's all my fault," I said.

"Oh, really? The people here are blaming it on an angry god. Just how angry are you?"

"If I'd just hit the deadlines..."

"Now you be quiet. You are being quite silly. We gave you a near impossible target, and well, it would have been achieved had it not been for this ridiculous inundation. These random rain storms seem to be occurring more and more frequently in the Middle East."

"I've been caught in one of them myself, well not exactly in one. But I was in southern Egypt, in Aswan, trying to get to Abu Simbel. There was flash flooding in Cairo, so no planes were getting into Aswan, and no one was getting to Abu Simbel. I ended up sleeping on the airport floor. When planes starting flying again, there was almost a riot. It was sheer chaos."

"That sounds about par for the course. They've never built adequate sewage and run off systems in many of these ancient cities, so when they get these downpours, the water

270

just sits on the surface of roads–"

"And airport runways." I said.

"I was on the phone with FedEx as soon as things started getting saturated here. They ran out of vehicles they could use for land delivery, so the only option was for me to hop in a small lorry."

"Oh my god. How long before you're in Bahrain?"

"Another couple of hours. And if all goes well, it's another four-plus hours to get back."

I raised my hand to my mouth and shook my head side-to-side.

"I'm afraid it gets worse," said Geoffrey.

"How is that possible?"

"The airport situation means guests coming to the opening ceremonies from outside of Riyadh are likely to be delayed."

"Should I start humming the funeral march now?" I asked.

* * * * *

Geoffrey agreed to keep me posted as best he could about his progress, but after disengaging from the call, I just wanted to crawl back into bed and build a permanent impenetrable fortress around me. Eventually, I rallied, but I dressed in a mourning outfit – black trousers, a black ribbed sweater, short black boots, and a black hooded all-weather car-length coat. I even decided to ditch public transit and to drive into work. I'd finally had my car battery boosted, and I wanted to ensure I kept charging it more regularly. So, I flung my lunch and purse into the Smart Car and set out.

As soon as I exited the underground parking and hit the

271

road, however, I realized I had made an unwise decision. Having been so obsessed with the weather in Riyadh, I had failed to listen to the local weather report and forgot about our own system. It was blustery to say the least, and my car was not built for wind. Generally, it was only a problem during highway driving, but this morning, particularly as I turned onto King Street, I found myself gripping the wheel firmly to keep it steady. Had I not been so tardy, I would have turned around, but it was too late – I was committed to the drive.

Along the way to the central part of the city, the sky seemed to grow more ominously dark with each passing second, but I miraculously arrived intact and found a parking spot on Charles Street across from the Museum, in the middle of the University of Toronto campus. Luckily the heavens were still zipped closed, and I arrived at work dry, though a little windblown.

I scooted to my office as discreetly as possible. The last thing I wanted was to run into someone who'd assisted with the packing and have them ask if the medals had arrived safely. I didn't want anyone to know their heroic efforts were for naught. However, no sooner had I hung up my coat and sat at my desk than my land line rang, the call display indicating it was Shipping and Receiving.

"Hi, Gaspar...I know."

"But what are you going to do about the goods delayed in Bahrain?"

"Geoffrey, from our London office, is on his way there and will be picking them up in a truck and driving them to Riyadh."

"That's remarkable, but–"

"Can we just leave it at that? I'm stressed as it is."

"I understand. I understand."

"If anyone else asks, please say things are under control."

"Will do. May the force be with you." Gaspar hung up.

It wasn't the force that I needed. I needed Han Solo, Luke Skywalker, Princess Leia, a droid or two and the fastest effing starship in the whole frigging universe.

It didn't take long before Walter rang me. Naturally, he was aware of weather reports in Saudi. After all, as the head librarian, he would have been exposed to a number of daily newspapers from the moment he got into work. A short while later, Marco called me as Walter had already spoken to him. Subsequently, both of them started calling me regularly. Stewart didn't call though. He wouldn't waste his time with conversations that couldn't change circumstances. His patience was a lesson to me. I, in turn, didn't bother contacting Geoffrey every two minutes, as tempted as I was.

But I kept checking my phone for texts. Geoffrey did send them occasionally, letting me know his progress. He was, in fact, traveling through desert areas without service, so there was only so much he could do to stay in touch.

I did, however, check in with my family, and I was so elated to hear my father was going to be released. I was beyond elated and made plans to visit my family on the weekend – my mother had said my father still needed a few good days of rest.

As best as possible, I tried to keep myself busy with other work. With Stewart's long stays in California, he always had a hefty quantity of expenses for which he needed to be reimbursed, and that involved a good deal of tedious paperwork. At one point, while processing the receipts, I checked my phone and squealed with glee at a text informing me that not only was Geoffrey in Bahrain, but he had the truck loaded

273

with the medals. Authorities were initially reluctant to release the shipment, but apparently Geoffrey charmed everyone with his Arabic, and they ultimately capitulated.

I was still slugging my way through Stewart's often illegible writing when Walter unexpectedly appeared at the door, pressing his face to the glass. It was too late to duck underneath my desk. He plowed in.

"You ARE here. Have you not noticed I called you several times? Five times in the last half hour, actually."

I glanced at my phone. A small red light was flashing. "Oh, was that you? Sorry, I really had to buckle down to something. I've been letting my calls go to voice mail."

"Come with me! This instant!"

"Pardon me?" I said.

"There is something very significant going on, and you must see it."

It took a nanosecond for a whole bucket full of pits to form in my stomach. I threw my arms up in the air and rose from my chair. "Okay, whatever."

"Follow quickly, please."

"Where are you taking us?"

"We are heading to the elevator."

"Why? Why, why, why?" I must have sounded like a petulant tween.

"It would be best if you brought your outerwear. It is sure to be chilly and windy up there."

"Up where?"

"You will see soon enough."

I sighed, retrieved my coat, and locked the door behind me.

"Honestly, Kalena. Sometimes I think you live and work in a bubble."

"Me?" Was he kidding?

"Although your office is rather isolated, I find it difficult to believe you are unaware of what is happening outside these doors?" Walter led us to the Rotunda elevator.

As we waited for the lift to arrive at the B1 level, I clocked Marco racing towards us. "Hold on guys," he yelled.

The elevator arrived, and Marco herded us into it.

"Where to, Walter?" I was standing directly in front of the panel with the floor buttons.

"Fourth floor," answered Marco.

"The boardroom?" I asked.

"We will need to take the stairs from there," said Walter.

I pressed the number four button, and we ascended. This bank of elevators was the less-used set in the Museum, so we arrived at the fourth floor without any stops. We stepped off and then Marco led us towards a stairwell.

"Doesn't this go to Liza's Garden?" I asked. "I didn't think we were allowed up there."

"Technically, we're not," said Marco.

The Museum's green roof may not have been the city's best kept secret, but certainly most people weren't aware of its existence since even staff, other than those in the Biodiversity Department, weren't allowed access to it. It was a designated research site and usually only visited by groups such as students from the University of Toronto's Green Roof Innovation Testing Lab.

"I remember when they were creating the garden, we all thought they were going to haul truck-loads of dirt there," I said.

"*Au contraire*. Soil is far too heavy. Ours is a particularly fine example of a compost roof. It is rather shallow, but it holds a great deal of water and provides all the necessary nutrition required to support a variety of vegetation. But the unique roof is not just for research. It has a much more pragmatic function."

"What's that?" I asked.

"Well, it enhances the sustainability of the Museum. It retains storm water, reduces heat island effects, and helps to clean the air while offering a habitat for birds and insects."

I wasn't even going to ask what heat island effects were. There was only so much I could take of Walter on any given day. We reached a door, and Marco pulled out a large ring of keys. After sorting through them, he finally landed on what he appeared to be looking for, inserted the key, and opened the door.

Immediately, a forceful gust of wind caught the portal, and I thought for a moment it was going to pull it off its hinges. My hair was blowing in all directions and, having failed to have closed my coat earlier, I struggled to pull the two sides together to zip them shut.

"Are you sure it's safe for us to go out there in this wind? I don't want to end up in the air like Mary Poppins, but without an umbrella."

"Don't worry. We won't be here long," said Marco.

"We wanted to see this up close and a bit more personal," said Walter. "It is all over the Internet."

"What is?" We began walking, but I quickly threaded my arms with Marco's and Walter's. "Safety in numbers," I said, constantly turning my head to get the hair out of my eyes and mouth. "And if I get scooped up into the sky, you guys are coming with me."

"Thanks," said Marco.

We all lowered our heads, trying to keep the wind out

of our faces as we made our way towards what looked like a large field of yellowed chive plants. There seemed to be the odd shrub or small tree, but that's about all that was visible as I kept my gaze down.

"This way, to the east side," said Walter.

I peeked up slightly. My knees started trembling, and my stomach began somersaulting as we walked towards an edge. "Did you guys bring me up here to make a human sacrifice of me?"

"Do not be absurd. Look over there. LOOK." Walter was fully upright but was finding it difficult to stay steady on his feet.

Marco and I straightened up. I gasped as I gazed eastwards over the city. "I have no words."

"Holy mother of god, I've never seen anything like that. Like ever," said Marco.

Looming off in the distance was the most foreboding cloud of immeasurable proportions I had ever seen.

"It is, it is a shelf cloud," said Walter. "It is text book wedge-shaped."

"That's some bloody shelf."

"My god," continued Walter, "It is so low-hanging I imagine the inhabitants of Scarborough could reach up and touch it."

"Excuse me while I kiss the sky," I said.

"What was that?" asked Walter.

"Actin' funny, but I don't know why. Excuse me while I kiss the sky," said Marco at full voice. "Jimi Hendrix, *Purple Haze*."

"I do not know what you two are nattering about, but that is the leading edge of a gust front of a thunderstorm."

"THE thunderstorm?" I asked.

"Catequil, our Inca god of thunder and lightning," said Walter with the wind howling.

"Oh, c'mon, you guys. How could our tormentor possibly have known this was coming? He may be very clever, but he's not psychic."

"No, but he's patient. This is it. I know it is," said Marco.

Once again, I pushed the hair away from my face and stared at Marco intensely. "Marco, what's going on?"

"*Buon giorno*," yelled a familiar voice from behind, startling all of us.

"Benny, what on Earth are you doing here? How did you get up here?"

"Marco called me. He left the door to the roof unlocked for me."

"I...I didn't notice him do that," I said.

Benny, who had her camera with her, reached us and interlinked arms with Marco. I started to feel ill.

"The wind is so strong," said Benny.

"It's time," said Marco.

I noticed Benny's eyes widen. "Are you certain?"

"I've never been more certain about anything. Let's get inside," he said.

Benny let go of Marco and started snapping shots of the foreboding force of nature.

"BENNY!" shrieked Marco.

"But it is a very unique perspective here. It is a chance of a lifetime to get such photographs."

"That's enough. C'MON!" Marco said.

"*Sto arrivando*." Benny walked backwards taking shots while she stumbled towards the doorway.

Walter and I entered the stairwell, where Marco was waiting for us, but he stepped back out and grabbed Benny by the elbow to drag her in. "Oh, Marco," she said exaggerating the rolled 'r.' "You really are a worrywart."

The four of us descended the stairs and took the elevator back down to the B1 level. En route, I pulled out my phone to check my emails. There was one with the subject heading 'URGENT' and I clicked on it as we came off the elevator. Oddly, an image opened up immediately covering the full screen of the telephone.

"What's this?" I said.

Marco had pulled out his phone, and so had Walter and Benny, since this is what people do these days if they haven't checked their phone for two minutes.

"I just received an urgent email—" started Benny.

"Me too," added Marco.

"Me three," said Walter.

"Me four."

We all pointed the screens of our phones at each other, each screen sporting the same image.

Marco cleared this throat. "Told you so, Benny."

"Let's get to my office right away," I demanded. "There's some 'splainin' to do, and I don't want any more pussy-footing around."

The Musketeers seemed shocked at the sternness of my command and exchanged nervous glances before setting out in silence. Upon entering my office, I removed my coat and sat on the edge of my desk. "Sorry, I'm not set up for more than one visitor at a time."

"It is okay," said Benny and the other two nodded.

"Walter, you're up first," I said.

"Me? Why me?"

"It's clear that the image on our phones is another mosaic from the Rotunda ceiling."

"Correct," said Walter.

"And it's also clear our friend wanted to make sure this was not missed, otherwise why send it to all four of us?" said Benny.

"Is it Indian or Arabic?" I asked. "It kind of looks like one of those Jell-O salads sitting in a bowl resting on the backs of a bunch of dogs."

"Very close," said Walter.

"Really?" I asked.

"NO! It is a representation of the Court of Lions in the Palace of Lions in the Alhambra complex. The symbol to the left is that of the crescent moon, as one would find on top of the minaret of a mosque. It has been the symbol of Islam since the time of the Ottomans. The symbol on the right, I must admit, I am not sure of its meaning. It appears it might be a calligraphic representation of a ship, perhaps." Walter shrugged his shoulders. "I am stumped for once."

"The palace is in Spain, THAT I know," said Benny. "In Granada. My parents took me there as a child. It is a wonderful place with a very long and diverse history."

"There is evidence of Roman fortifications on the site, but then it was rebuilt in the 13th century during the Emirate of Granada. It was the last Muslim dynasty on the Iberian Peninsula in the southwest corner of Europe," continued Walter.

"So, are we looking for something of Arabic origin or Spanish or even Roman again?" I said.

"Or are we looking for something or somewhere?" said Benny, glancing at Marco.

"Why do you say that?" I said.

"The feature that makes the Alhambra Palace so magical is water. It has so many fountains, pools and water elements," said Benny.

"For example," picked up Walter, "the fountain represented here is said to represent the heavenly garden of Islam. A large bowl," Walter turned his gaze to me, "yes, a bowl sits on the back of 12 lions, not dogs, and each one has a unique face and markings."

"*Si*," interrupted Benny, "but I remember there are a number of channels running underneath the fountain, I think representing the four rivers of paradise. Many years ago, perhaps in 2010, they did considerable restoration work and they discovered many new things about the water supply for the complex."

"Like?" said Marco.

"They found that this fountain had it its own water supply while the rest of the palace was supplied by the Acequia Real, an aqueduct. We studied the complex thoroughly in one of my classes during my studies in Italy. Even today it is considered to be one of the most splendid examples of water engineering in Europe."

"Listen guys, I'm really enjoying this urban planning lesson, but I have no idea where you're going with this," said Marco.

"Well the Museum is resting on top of a water channel," said Benny.

"You mean Taddle Creek?" said Walter.

"But there are other secret tunnels under this complex, yes?" said Benny.

"I would not say secret," replied Walter. "We have a food tunnel that is used by the cafeteria and restaurant staff. And let us not forget about the relatively unknown Lower Bay subway station which allowed passengers to travel from one line to the other without changing trains. The TTC tested the system for six months but users found it too confusing. It was ultimately decommissioned in 1966 as they decided two separate subway lines worked best."

"How confusing could it have been? Have they seen what the underground systems are like in Paris and London, to name a few cities? The second Bay station's a ghost station now, right? It's used mainly for film shoots and special events," I said.

"The Lower Bay subway station," said Marco rather pensively.

"What is it, Marco?" said Benny.

"I remember Bob once talking about being involved in checking for weak security points involving the Museum when they built that subway line. He would have known the station inside and out."

"Bob, as in Bob-just-call-me-Bob Bob?" I said.

"Why do you always call him that? It's a bit weird, you know," said Marco.

"Well, so is he. Why are we even talking about him? Will you please tell me what the frig is going on?"

Benny turned to Marco. "I think it is time to share what we know. I do not think we can delay any longer, especially if things are going to end as we believe."

"End...what end?" I started flailing my arms spasmodically.

Marco stared directly into my eyes. "Bob is The Leopard. He's *Il Gattopardo*."

I dropped my head slowly into a sideways lean, and just as I was regaining my ability to speak, the door to my office flew open.

CHAPTER THIRTY-TWO

A tremor of surprise waved through all of our bodies when Malik strode in. He was clearly agitated.

"What are you people still doing here?" he asked.

"Um, we work here. Well, except for Benny. But she's an invited guest, sort of." I shrugged my shoulders as I exchanged glances with the Musketeers.

"And what's this I hear about you being on the green roof. Are you insane? In these winds. All we needed was for one of you to blow off the building Mary Poppins style."

"That's exactly what I said." I gave Marco an I-told-you-so look.

"I take accountability for being up there, sir."

"No, I insisted," said Benny.

Malik turned to Marco, "Some days you really test my patience."

"Yes, sir."

"If you people were actually working you would have heard by now that we're sending all non-essential staff home early."

"Why?" I said.

"You were on the roof. You saw what's coming. Not only are dangerously high winds about to hit, but they're expecting that shelf cloud to dump an incredible amount of water. The city's anticipating flooding everywhere. It's going to be worse than anything we've seen so far this fall. They may even have to shut down the subway. So, if you don't leave

283

now, you may not be able to get home."

"I, drove today." My shoulders were now up by my ears.

"What? In that Smart Car of yours? You might just float off into Lake Ontario," said Walter.

"You three, go home right now. This is about as close as we've been to an emergency situation yet this decade. Marco, I know it's the end of your shift, but could you stay longer to do office-to-office checks?"

"I have to respectively decline, sir," Marco said.

Malik looked puzzled "I can't force you."

"Is it your family about which you are concerned?" questioned Walter.

I'd never seen Marco look so uncomfortable. "Well, sir, I believe we may have discovered the location, at least approximately, of a large cache of stolen art. And if it's where I think it might be, it could be at risk of serious damage if there's severe flooding."

"You need to call CSIS right away then," said Malik. "This isn't something any of us can take on."

"Sir, respectively, I am CSIS."

I looked at Marco, then at Walter, then at Malik, then at Marco, then at Benny, then at Marco.

Marco reached for his wallet, and from a slot that appeared to be behind his driver's license, he pulled out a plastic card. Depicted on it was what looked like the British royal crown, and below it a red maple leaf encircled with a series of blue stripe-like shapes. Beside the logo were imprinted the words 'Canadian Security Intelligence Service' and below a picture of Marco.

I edged over to a chair and sat down, then lifted my gaze. "Benny, did you know?" I stopped in mid-thought. 'It's complicated,' Marco had said of his relationship with

Benny the other day. "Benny, you're...you're one of them, too," I said as though speaking of aliens from another galaxy.

Benny looked down at her feet.

"What in the world?" said Malik.

"You know we couldn't say anything. It was restricted information."

"Yeah, I BET!" I said.

How could I have been so naive all along? All this time, so many signs were there, but I failed to put them together. Marco seemed so savvy, and yet here he was working as a junior security guard at the Museum. I couldn't believe he'd been lying to me all this time. It was all a lie. One immense lie.

"This is more unbelievable than a Tom Cruise *Mission Impossible* movie," said Walter.

"I need to head over to the Lower Bay subway platform. Sir–"

"I think you can stop calling me 'sir' from now on," said Malik. "I may need to start calling you 'sir.'"

"I agree that we should let Kalena and Walter go home," said Marco.

The phone on my desk rang, startling us all a little. I was going to ignore the call until I saw the foreign number. I scooped up the receiver. "Geoffrey, where are you?"

"I finally have everything loaded up, and I'm on my way back to Riyadh. I just had to stop for some petrol," said Geoffrey.

His comment was met with silence from me.

"Hello. Are you still there?" said Geoffrey.

"Um, yes. I'm not alone in the office."

"I was just obeying orders, calling you that is." Geoffrey chuckled.

285

"I truly appreciate it, honestly. But things are a bit crazy here, too. The city's about to be hit with a huge storm and everything's shutting down. It'll be best, I think, if you text me, in case I'm not able to pick up a call."

"There is no rest for the wicked in these times, is there?"

"Um, yeah. Listen, I'll talk to you later. *Bon voyage* and stay safe...please."

"Cheerio then." Geoffrey terminated the call, and I put down the receiver.

Looking around at my colleagues I said, "Meanwhile, on the other side of the world...the medals should be getting into Riyadh," I looked up at my band of clocks, "by the time this storm is over."

"Well you are having a simply splendid day all around, are you not?" said Walter.

"Just dandy."

"Well, Walter, I suggest you advise your staff to go home," said Malik. "No one needs to use the library during the worst storm of the decade. Marco and Benny, you do what you need to do, but above all else, make sure Kalena goes home immediately."

I tapped my fingers to my chest in a 'huh-me' gesture.

"Get what you need and let's go, Boyko," said Marco.

"Are you parked nearby?" asked Benny.

"Just on Charles Street."

"Marco and I will be walking in that direction. We will ensure her safety," said Benny to Malik.

Malik and Walter exited and headed in the direction of the library. I grabbed my purse, and, with Marco and Benny, we shuffled towards the Staff Entrance. Benny threaded her arm through mine and nuzzled close to me. "We are so sorry. I know this must come as such a shock. It is *sempre, sempre*

286

difficile when we break cover. There are such feelings of betrayal and mistrust that result. You must believe us when we tell you that it had to be this way."

My eyes started to fill up with water, but I diverted my gaze. I didn't want them to know how wounded I was. Staring far ahead towards the glass doors that formed the outside wall of the Student Entrance area, I stopped in my tracks, jerking Benny to a standstill.

"What is it?" she said.

"Look," I said pointing ahead. "Look what we're walking into. It's as if we're stepping into Niagara Falls."

Looming in front of us, on the other side of the doors, was a wall of rain. It wasn't pouring, it wasn't cats and dogs, it was full on deluge.

"*Oddio*," cried Benny. "I thought that cloud we saw upstairs was the most incredible thing I have seen since coming to Canada. But for this, *non ho parole*."

"This is not good," said Marco.

Suddenly, a blinding flash lit up the row of high-mounted narrow windows lining the hallway, and a bang cracked so loudly I thought the roof of the Museum had been ripped open.

"That must have hit somewhere very close," said Benny.

"No, no, no," I said, letting go of Benny and running the remaining length of the hallway.

I could hear Marco's and Benny's footsteps speed up behind me. "I'm sure your car's okay," yelled Marco.

"It's not my car I'm worried about." I passed through the first set of clear glass doors and stopped inside the vestibule.

"What is it?" cried Benny.

"The tallest summit around here is that magnificent oak tree in front of Falconer Hall," I said.

The three of us pummeled through the last set of doors into the teeming rain, turned left, and soared up the small set of stairs. Already drenched in those few short seconds, I could no longer hold back tears. It felt as though I had a hidden reservoir of water in my head and the damn just broke.

"Ooooooh my god, it's toppled across Queen's Park," bellowed Marco.

The tree had cracked in half and fallen on one of the busiest north-south thoroughfares in the city. There was no evidence any cars had been caught in the plummet of the several-stories high tree, but branches were strewn everywhere, and four lanes of traffic were blocked by the oak.

Marco was racing while talking on his phone, to the police I presumed. Benny and I were close behind, and I was praying with all my human powers that the intense rain had minimized pedestrian presence on the sidewalk in front of the old Faculty of Law building.

As Benny and I drew closer, we breathed an intense sigh of relief. No human carnage in evidence. The two of us looked at each other, and for a moment forgetting Benny's betrayal, we locked in a bear hug. Upon releasing, Benny said, "I cannot believe no one was hurt."

"I know. Sometimes there are hundreds of students walking this route." I realized the tree must have fallen right when the lights bordering the two ends of Queen's Park were red, creating a gap in traffic.

Sirens were screaming in the distance, getting louder and louder. We were getting wetter and wetter, and the wind kept pushing us two lightweights around.

Soon the police had arrived, and Marco had a few words with them while Benny and I huddled. He then strode over to us. "There's nothing else we can do. It's definitely not safe to drive. With this wind, this kind of thing is happening all over the city."

I thought of tree-lined Charles Street, where my car was parked. "I know I said I didn't care about my car. But I lied. I'm not abandoning it. It's just a 15-minute drive or less to home."

"No way," said Marco.

"Way." With that I dashed down the opening of the Museum subway stop that was directly in front of us. It provided an underpass to the other side of Queen's Park over to Charles Street. When I turned back to look, Marco and Benny were at my heels.

Upon surfacing on the other side, with broken branches flying everywhere in the wind, I galloped the quarter block to my car, which was parked right in front of the University's Ned's Café. I reached into my pleather purse, but before pressing my key fob to open my car door, I turned to Benny and Marco. "I'm not going until I get at least some explanation."

"There's no time," said Marco.

"You owe me," I demanded.

"Well let's at least step inside this building to get out of this out-of-control rain," said Marco.

"I have no arguments with that," I said sweeping a collection of water away from my forehead and eyes.

The three of us shuffled into Ned's entryway. We smelled like wet dogs. I shivered. My upper body was dry enough, but my legs and feet were drenched to the bone. We all were. "Well," I said.

"Well," said Marco. "Where do you want me to start?"

"From the beginning might be a good idea."

"I told you, we need to keep this short and sweet for

now."

"How long have you known that Bob-just-call-me-Bob..." I asked with daggers in my eyes, "was *Il Gattopardo*?"

"I mean, there have been suspicions for decades, but despite appearances and mannerisms, he's a really slippery guy. No one could accumulate enough evidence to charge him with anything."

"Was he really your neighbor?"

Marco nodded yes. "That's actually how I got involved. It didn't escape the notice of the CSIS rank and file, when I was in training, that I happened to be living beside a suspected international art thief. So, they approached me to keep an eye on him. It was a tough decision for me. He knew my family for a really long time, and he never did us any harm. But..."

"But..."

"A criminal's a criminal. I couldn't give him a hall pass just because he'd been a family friend."

"So how did YOU end up at the Museum playing a security guard?" I asked.

"Bob's been tied to the place since he was young, and my superiors thought it would be a good cover for me. Even they weren't sure how this was going to play out, but they thought if Bob and I shared a Museum connection, he might really open up to me. Bob actually recommended me for the job."

"And Malik really didn't know about you?

Marco shook his head no.

My mind was spinning with the speed of a super tornado. I leaned my head down for a moment and was silent, then jerked it back up.

"You've been in on this. You've been setting up these

pranks."

"I wouldn't call them pranks," said Marco.

Benny was becoming visibly agitated. "Bob caught onto Marco's cover," she blurted out. "We needed a new strategy."

"To terrorize me?"

"It didn't start out that way. Man...it's–"

"Keep going, Zeffirelli," I said.

"Like Benny said, I don't know how, but he caught on to me. We were sharing some Canadian Club on his porch, and he just came out and said he knew I was CSIS and that he was in possession of a bunch of art stolen during World War II and he wanted to get rid of it."

"So why didn't he just turn it over?"

"Because he's twisted...I mean clearly. He was the one who came up with all these insane reveals. We had to go along because he wasn't just going to give up the art in a normal surrender."

"But surely, once the first object turned up, you could have arrested him."

"He threatened that if we didn't do it his way, in his own time, the treasure would be lost forever," Marco continued. "And he meant it."

"But Bob would still have been fairly young during the war," I puzzled.

"Yeah, he was, but in the process of becoming one of the best cat burglars of his generation, he got bored. He was doing messed up stuff like stealing art that had already been stolen before he got his hands on it."

"And the so-called owners couldn't report it as missing to the authorities." That, I knew already.

"But then he'd also leave stuff he'd previously stolen in

the homes of new victims. He was really messing with people's minds. I don't think it was ever about the money for him. It was one big game."

"And that included plaguing me."

"I don't think he saw it that way. He just thought he was being clever – all those Museum references and stuff."

"And CSIS went along with this? C'mon. That sounds just implausible," I said.

"Listen, about $6 to $8 billion dollars' worth of art is stolen a year – A YEAR. International policing agencies can only do so much. They already had me on the case, and they kind of threw up their hands and said 'just go for it.' I mean they were really embarrassed by him. He actually worked for them as a security contractor in the past."

"But why me? Why me? Why mess up my life?"

"He said he thought you'd make a good mouse to play with. He once told me he thought you had spunk."

I stomped my foot. "SPUNK. Are you kidding me?"

"We did not know it would get this much out of hand," said Benny.

"And what's your tie in this? Does CSIS really recruit university students as covers?"

Benny shot a glance at Marco, then turned to me. "This is so very confidential. As they say in the movies, if you tell aaaanyone, I may have to shoot you."

"I'm waiting."

"I truly have credentials in environmental studies, and I have worked as a drainer. Perhaps you are aware that the wave of eco terrorism is growing."

"Of course," I said. "Like in films like *The East*, with Brit Marling. And *Night Moves* with Jess Eisenberg."

"She's an expert," said Marco.

"Oh, be quiet," I said.

"Most people do not know how extensive it is. And most people do not know that Brescia, my home in Italy, is a breeding ground for radical drainers. It is another very long story, but that is where I became involved. One of the leaders of this radical group decided to come to Toronto, so I came here to keep an eye on him. Marco and I met at some CSIS training sessions in Toronto and one day he invited me to dinner at his house. Bob was there, and he grew very interested in my stories about Toronto's underground waterways."

I threw my head back for a moment. "So, you inspired Bob."

"I do not like to look at it that way. Our Leopard was going to find some *bizzarro* way to toy with all of us."

"But you're returning to Brescia?" I said.

"Our person of interest has gone back, and so shall I."

"And you and Marco were never..."

Benny wrapped her arm around Marco. "He is a fine Italian-Canadian man, but we have been colleagues all along."

Marco smiled.

"And my friendship with you was genuine. It is such a difficult position that our work puts us in, but it does not mean we do not grow fond of people. It is so difficult for us to wear two faces." There were tears forming in Benny's eyes, and I thrust my arms around her and over her shoulder I noticed Marco rubbing his eyes.

I stepped away from Benny. "So, you really think Bob has stashed away a massive trove of art, right under everyone's noses somewhere?"

"We can be damn sure of it," said Marco.

I became aware again of the wind's howling. Another bolt of lightning struck with thunder following close behind.

293

"You've really got to get out of here. And that's an or-der!" barked Marco.

Ned's was set at basement level, so just as we passed through the exterior set of doors, we paused to brace our-selves from the elements. Branches and debris continued to scatter along the ground and in the air.

"DUCK," Marco suddenly shrieked.

The three of us plunged to a squat. Marco put his index finger to his lips then pointed to the street, to an ominous spectacle looming – a vintage Lincoln Continental with black-tinted windows was slowly moving west on Charles Street to-wards University Avenue.

It paused when it reached my car, as if scoping it out. It was Bob-just-call-me-Bob's vehicle. It seemed to me as if he had recognized my car. Was that possible? Why not? He knew everything else about me.

"Do you think he saw us?" asked Benny.

"I doubt it. That railing and bushes are giving us some cover," said Marco.

The car edged forward and suddenly sped up.

We straightened up and Marco leapt up the stairs to street level at almost superhuman speed, then halted ab-ruptly. "He's not going anywhere. Looks like the police have blocked off the end of the street to keep traffic off University while they get the tree out of the way."

"He's coming back," I yelled.

The Lincoln was speeding backwards at break-neck speed, yet incredibly controlled. The brakes were hit and the car stopped dead in front of us. The window rolled down, and we saw the red glow of a lit cigarette end before Bob's face became visible.

"Well, well," he said before breaking into a sickening

cough.

"Where is it?" said Marco. "Where are you hiding the rest? Let's finish this now. You've got to be tired of all this."

The window rolled back up and the car continued to drive in reverse.

"Kalena, QUICK, give me your car keys!" ordered Marco.

I rapidly scooped my keys out of my purse and ran to the driver's side of my car.

"What are you doing?" said Marco.

"You're not driving my car."

"Oh, for crying out loud. Benny, you better get over to the Lower Bay Station *subito* and call the team. I'd start searching at track level. Maybe there's a doorway no one's paid attention to. Maybe Bob's left a trail there for us, maybe some symbols or splattered paint."

Benny raced off without a word. I hopped into my car and Marco dropped himself into the passenger seat. I turned the car on and moved the gearshift forward, and the car advanced a few feet. I then, moved it into reverse, rotated to look behind, then paused.

"What now?" said Marco.

"I don't drive well in reverse and this is a one-way."

Marco hurled the door open, raced around to the driver's side. I hopped over the gear box, plunked myself in the passenger seat, strapped myself in, and looked at Marco. "You're not getting rid of me that quickly."

"You're impossible, Boyko. And you may have just cost us losing Bob."

Marco attacked the wheel, pressed on the gas, and did an almost 360-degree turn driving over two sidewalks and some of the lawn of the University of Toronto property on the south side of the street. I held on to the dash with all my might, "I could have done that. I didn't know it was an option!" I shrieked.

"That's my point."

Marco peeled down the street in the wrong direction. In my head I kept repeating, 'I trust in the universe to protect me to everyone's greatest benefit.'

We reached Bay Street in a matter of seconds, and when I looked to the right on Bay, there was Bob's car, as if parked.

Marco made a hard right, and the Lincoln started up again, proceeding south on Bay Street. "He was waiting for us. He wanted us to catch up and follow him."

"Ya' think?" said Marco. "I told you he's crazy."

We continued to streak down Bay, but we had to keep dodging all sorts of obstacles from cardboard boxes to sidewalk sandwich boards that had collapsed and been pushed on the street by the wind.

"How do you drive this frigging car? I can barely keep control of this thing. Did you ever think of getting something more stable?"

"I can find parking spots anywhere."

"Number one on my list of must-haves in a car."

"It's easy on the environment–"

Marco slammed on the brakes and my seatbelt tightened. We skidded within inches of sliding into the black starship. Bob had actually stopped for a red light.

I clutched at my chest. Breathless I said, "Shouldn't we get out of the car and jump him?"

"He's obviously leading us somewhere. Maybe we got it wrong. Maybe the stash of art is nowhere near the Bay Station...or the Museum."

Sirens began screaming from behind us and within moments a firetruck and an ambulance passed us. We could hear more sirens, but they didn't seem to be coming our way. Every EMS vehicle in the city was probably on the streets responding to the havoc the storm was wreaking.

On the green light, Bob picked up again, and so did we, but as we approached the base of Bay Street, there were countless flashing lights. "What's going on up there?" I said, and then barricades came into view. "Oh my god, it's flooded and he's leading us right into it. We're going to drown!"

"We're not going to drown. This car is made by Mercedes. I'm sure it's watertight."

I didn't say anything.

"Right?" repeated Marco.

"Well, when I wash the car, water gets inside the door a little. You know the panel at the base of the door, I always have to wipe it down."

Marco turned to me for a moment, his eyes bulging. "But you can get a parking spot anywhere in the city. Of all the freaking cars to have on a night like tonight."

"Maybe you should take a moment and be grateful you have a car at all. Where's your car, by the way?"

Marco shook his head. Bob unexpectedly cut a right, and so did we. And then a left. "I think he's heading to the lake. HOLD TIGHT. I don't know how this car's going to handle this."

Up ahead the Lincoln was hydroplaning in about a foot of water, but its weight seemed to give it stability. And then we skidded into the water. It felt as though the wheels had lifted off the ground and we were floating. Sure enough, water started to seep in under the door, minimally, but I pressed my hands on the seat, lifted my legs and sat crossed legged, my one knee pressing on the door so hard I was sure to bruise.

The car started to slide, but it was a different feeling from that of a car skimming on ice. I was certain my heart was no longer beating. The wheels hit something and veered us sideways.

Marco turned the wheel away from the middle of the road and somehow managed to get us on a straighter track. I saw Bob's car start to come out of the deep puddle ahead of us, and it was back on unsubmerged road. In a moment I felt the Smart gain traction. My heart restarted.

"That was kind of close, huh?" I said.

"We're not friends at the moment. Would you mind not speaking right now?"

I dipped my chin towards my chest and interlaced my fingers on my belly, my legs still up on the seat in lotus position.

Bob zig-zagged a few more times, taking us further west of the city's main core. Before we knew it, we found ourselves near Toronto's Harbourfront Centre. We were still close behind when Bob took a left and we took a left, crossing the streetcar tracks and ending up near the Fleck Dance Theatre, in an area that was once a parking lot. The Lincoln pulled up just at the start of the East Pier. There was a series of small boats tied up there rising and falling madly, like toy boats in a bathtub being splashed around.

With the car still, we were feeling the full brunt of the wind. In the distance, towards Toronto Island, I could see flash after flash of lightning, but the thunder was now quieter.

Bob jumped out of his car and scrambled down the quay. Marco flew out of the Smart to chase after him. Shit. I straightened out my legs, pushed the door open against the

298

wind, and took off after them. The rain was falling horizontally now.

I battled to catch up when I saw Bob descend a ladder and climb into a motor boat. Marco was standing above him on the dock staring down at the precariously rocking vessel.

Waves were crashing all about, and the light show in the distant sky was creating a surreal scene. It was the first time I'd seen Bob without his aviator sunglasses on, but there wasn't enough light to make out the full features of his face.

I heard an engine start and Marco screamed, "Bob, what are you doing, where are you going?"

"Don't you worry about that. You've got things in hand. I'm pretty sure of that now. Where's Benny?"

"What?" said Marco.

"At the subway station, is she?" said Bob. "By the way, pretty lady; that British fella of yours – didn't have anything to do with this. His grandfather though – quite the collector he was. Maybe you know that already."

"Bob, this is insane. You can't possibly think about going out into open water in that thing." I looked out towards the lake and then back at Bob's small motor boat. "The swells must be 15 feet high."

"There's only one outcome awaiting me tonight."

"What's going on, Bob? You've never let anything get the best of you," said Marco.

"Well, the doctors might not agree with that."

"We can hardly hear you," I shouted. "This wind..."

"I'm on my last days of cancer."

"Your lungs?" asked Marco.

Bob laughed, then coughed. "You'd think that, wouldn't you? No, pancreatic. Benny almost called me out when she noticed the jaundice that night. There's no happy ending for me. And what the hell am I gonna do with all that art when I'm dead. What good did it do those Mayan rulers stockpiling it in their temples? Didn't do anything in the long run for their glory."

Bob reached into his pants' pocket and then threw something at Marco. Marco extended his reach to catch the object, but between the rain and the wind, he missed and it fell to the dock. It made the sound of keys landing on wood. Marco stooped down and picked them up.

"Those'll make things a bit easier. People've missed it for years. I kept figuring they'd find it and save me all this trouble of having you folks look for it. But they never did. I have to admit, though, the last while's been a fun ride. Gave me something to live for, you know."

"Please don't do this," Marco pleaded.

"Do you really think I want to spend my last days in jail?" Bob pulled a small object out of the inside of his drenched coat and put a cigarette in his mouth. He looked up and let the rain pelt his face, then turned to us. "We don't look up at the sky enough in this day and age."

Marco and I turned our gaze towards the heavens, the rain striking our faces with intensity.

"One of the things those Maya people got right was mapping out the stars all those centuries ago and developing that complex calendar," said Bob.

Marco and I looked at each other with puzzled expressions. "Hey, Bob," I said, "was that *Treasures of the Maya* exhibit at the Museum ever at risk before I kind of bungled things up?" I noticed Marco surreptitiously creeping towards the edge of the dock.

"Might have been. But all that crazy stuff you were doing had all eyes on it. I decided to give it a pass...I wasn't ready then to give up the ghost yet," said Bob.

With that Bob started to reverse the boat and then pulled forward. The boat was rocking so violently I felt sick just watching it. With his back now to us, he lifted one arm, his hand in a victorious fist. A bolt of lightning lit up the entire sky creating a powerful and tragic image of Bob's silhouette growing smaller and smaller as he drove further and further into the lake.

Marco and I stood there, helpless; tears were streaming down my face, but they were indistinguishable from the rain. I wrapped my arms around Marco. "He can't possibly survive for more than a few minutes out there."

Marco held me tight with desperation and eventually released me. "C'mon. Let's get to that thing you call a car, and I'll call in for some help.'

"But they won't be able to go out in these conditions," I said.

"Nope. They won't be able to do a search until things clear."

I felt as though I'd been literally gutted.

CHAPTER THIRTY-THREE

We climbed inside my car, Marco in the driver's seat, with no arguments from me. His first call was to CSIS. He gave them a brief rundown, and they confirmed that though they'd make a report and contact the Canadian Coast Guard immediately, they remarked that the CCC were over-extended trying to assist boats involuntarily stranded on the lake. They also commented that they hadn't heard from Benny. After Marco ended the call, he said he figured Benny was probably in a tunnel somewhere and wouldn't have any service. But why hadn't she called anyone before becoming unreachable?

Marco turned the car ignition keys and nothing happened. "Oh, for fuck's sake." He let his forehead fall on the top edge of the steering wheel for a second, then slowly lifted his head. "Your engine must have taken on too much water. It managed to get us here, but once we shut the car off..."

"Did we kill it for good?" I asked.

"It might start again once it gets a good drying out, but if not, I'll get it towed for you. At least it's not filled with water and mud, like some of the cars we saw."

"We've got to get to Benny," I said. "I withdrew my phone and pressed one of my contact numbers.

"Who are you calling?" said Marco.

"Walter, where are you?"

Marco jerked the phone out of my hand and disengaged

the call.

"What are you doing?" I screamed.

"Walter? Are you kidding me?"

"How are we going to get back up to Bloor? There's no cabs, there's probably a million public transit delays, and it'll take us an hour or longer to walk there in this weather…And Walter lives in one of those buildings over there," I said pointing. "I'm pretty sure he lives in the one designed by Arthur Erickson."

"Who?"

I grabbed the phone back from Marco and redialed Walter and put it on speaker phone. "Walter, sorry about that. We lost the connection. Listen, I know you're probably home safe and dry by now, but Benny's not. And we need to get from Harbourfront back to University and Bay. You don't have to do it. I know it's a lot to ask. It's pretty dangerous outside at the moment."

"What? Where are you?" he asked. "The city's likely to call a state of emergency any moment now."

"We're on the East Pier. It's a long story. But we'll walk up to Queen's Quay West, and you can pick us up right in front of the terminal."

"I can be there momentarily."

"Walter?"

"Yes."

"You need to be really careful. There's all kinds of flooding and there's crap flying everywhere. We already murdered my car driving it through an impromptu lake."

"Do not worry about that. I have been listening to the news and I know precisely where the trouble spots are. I know all the detours that will lead us to the Museum area."

"You're a champ," said Marco. "We wouldn't ask if

Benny didn't need help."

"I am disengaging now," he said. "See you in a jiffy."

Marco and I looked at each other and burst out laughing. It was the kind of laughter that came out of desperation, out of the sheer insanity of the situation, and was probably a by-product of our shock at watching someone we knew heading out to virtually kill himself.

"Are you ready to head back out there?" Marco lifted his hand and gently brushed my cheek with it.

"I couldn't possibly get any wetter, or colder." My fake suede booties were like wet rags on my feet.

"That's the spirit," said Marco. "But hey, how is that you have Walter's cell number?"

"Once he got his phone, he started giving out his number to every Tom, Dick and Harry. I'm surprised he didn't give it to you."

"Whatever," said Marco.

We hurried over to the Harbourfront's main thoroughfare. There were no cars, no public transit vehicles in sight. It was similar to times when there was a heavy snow storm in the city, but without snow, it seemed post-apocalyptic. It felt like ages had passed before Walter arrived in his classic beige Volvo, but it had probably only been minutes. We piled into the car and set out with Walter intricately weaving his way through Toronto's streets with the skill of a maze runner. We filled him in on what had transpired. He had remained silent save for a few guffaws and deep sighs.

Unlike my car, the vintage Volvo had some weight to it and was bearing the wind well. There were a few streets that were strewn with too much debris, and we had to back out and detour. But Walter skillfully maneuvered us to an underground parking lot on Cumberland Street in the heart of Chi-

Chi Yorkville, where we knew his car would be safe from the elements. Once landed, the three of us inhaled a deep breath of relief.

Marco patted Walter on shoulder. "Good work, man. I didn't think you had it in you."

"I like to surprise people." Walter turned to us and winked.

"That you do," I said.

Marco threw open the door. "C'mon folks. There's no time to waste. God only knows if we can find Benny."

My stomach tightened. "I'm sure she's okay. Don't you think?"

Marco didn't reply. Instead, he galloped to the parking garage exit, with Walter and me close behind, and we crossed Cumberland. Marco started to enter the nearest subway entrance when I hollered, "Where are you going?" I checked my watch. "I don't think those gates are staffed right now. We'll probably need to talk to someone. Let's use the entrance off Bellair."

"Well, come on."

I had a strong sense of dread.

It was a half-block sprint through more wind and rain. Another half block to get sodden again after having been on the path to drying out in Walter's warm car. We turned south on Bellair, crossed the street, and scrambled down the stairs to the Bay subway station. Marco cantered directly to the transit attendant in the booth.

"If you want to know about the delays, we're not making any predictions at the moment," said the husky attendant who looked to be in his 50s.

"That's not—" Marco started.

"It's pretty chaotic since that GO train got bogged down

near Bayview and Pottery when the water got higher than its wheels. Passengers were stuck for over half an hour, and, get this, they were dodging some kind of snake. *Snakes on a Train*, who would have thought it in Toronto, eh. They ended up sending in police and firefighters in inflatable boats to get all the passengers off. Didn't you hear about it on the news?"

"Uh, yeah sure. Um, this is the same entrance you use to get to the Lower Bay subway platform, right?"

The attendant's eyes darted from side to side. "Weird question. But, yeah. They use it for training, shifting trains, and moving work trains."

I nudged myself in front of Marco. "We've been scouting the city for locations for a film shoot. It's actually been kind of a good day to do it since the city's so deserted." Looking around there were no passengers coming or going. "And we were down here anyway, so we thought we'd make some initial inquiries."

"They do do a lot of filming here."

My eyes widened. "*Johnny Mnemonic*, *Suicide Squad*, *Pixels*, *Extreme Measures*, *The Handmaid's Tale* TV series–"

Marco prodded me from behind. "We better stop her now or she'll go on forever, heh, heh," he said.

"Well, ya know, ya hafta contact the TTC Film Coordinator."

"Goodness," said Walter from behind us. "I had no–"

I spun my head around and glared at Walter.

"Yes, we are aware of that." Blood was draining from Walter's face.

Marco chimed in again. "We just wanted to get a basic sense of the location, how the crew would get their equipment there, that kind of stuff."

"Well, ya know," the entrance is just down there, at the

base of the stairs and escalators, through the double metal doors."

Really? I must have walked past those doors a million times, I thought to myself. I had no clue they were the portals to the defunct subway station.

"Not easy for crews to get their equipment down. There's no elevator and the escalators aren't operational. But the platform's treated like a working platform every single day, whether someone's shooting or not. The lights are turned on, like right now, because we never know when we might use the line for a diversion. Air quality's crap, though. I don't think they turn on the ventilation system, to tell ya the truth. It rains brake dust there all the time."

"Brake dust?" I narrowed my eyes.

"Every time a train comes to a halt on the upper Bay platform it shakes clouds of dust to the lower station."

"Like concrete dust?" I asked.

"Naw, just regular dust."

Walter straightened his spine. "About 70 to 80% of dust is said to be made of human skin cells."

"Oh my god, Walter. I didn't need to know that."

Marco grimaced and faced the attendant. "That's helpful information. We'll contact the coordinator."

"Wait, huh?" I said.

Marco pulled me by the elbow and whispered, "Just trust me. I've got an inkling." Then more loudly, he said, "Do either of you two have a token?"

Walter looked bewildered.

"I have my pass," I said, feeling a little baffled myself at what Marco had up his sleeves.

"It's on me," piped in the attendant. All of a sudden, the gates on one of the Plexiglas entrance barriers popped open.

"I'm not even sure you're gonna catch a train in the next while with all the delays. You mighta been heading back this way sooner than later, asking for a refund."

"Thanks, thanks so much," said Marco scuttling towards the stairs. Walter hopped on the escalator.

"What are you doing?" Marco sounded exasperated.

"When given the option, I prefer to take an escalator. It's easier on the knees."

Marco tore down the short set of stairs and I followed in his wake. The next thing I knew, Walter was scrambling down the last set of escalator steps frantically grabbing onto the moving rubber railing to disembark onto the platform. All three of us halted abruptly. There it was, directly in front of us – a set of shiny double steel doors.

"What are you going to do, bust the doors down?" I asked.

Marco dug his hand into his pocket, pulled out some keys and jingled them in the air. "Remember these?"

"The keys that Bob threw to you. What are the chances of there being a key to these doors on that ring?" I said.

"Well, if there is," said Marco, "we know we're on the right track."

"You mean to say that we are going to attempt to sneak through those doors? Surely, we will be observed," said Walter.

"Like CCTV cameras," I said.

"This isn't the UK," said Marco. "Coverage here's a lot spottier. Besides, I'm sure the transit authorities have more important things to worry about with this storm raging."

"Like snakes," I said.

"But what about the possibility of rats down there?" said Walter.

"Oh my god!" I shrieked. "What if water in other parts of the tunnels have sent herds of rats this way?"

"Mischiefs," said Walter.

"Huh?" said Marco.

"A group of rats is referred to as a mischief of rats."

Marco rolled his eyes. "Come here and give me a bit of cover, just in case." He was already trying the keys out on the lock. On the third attempt, we observed the key turn. "You two still want to come with me?"

I paused for a moment and said, "Let's just go."

"Speak for yourself," said Walter.

Grabbing Walter's arm, I said, "If I'm going to get the Bubonic Plague, I'm taking you down with me."

Speedily, we zipped through the doorway and Marco quietly closed the metal door behind us. There was no turning back now.

We were descending the echoing stairs when Walter piped up. "We will not be going down to track level, will we?"

"Probably," said Marco.

We reached the well-lit platform in no time. "My god," said Walter. "It is a doppelgänger."

"That's a good way of describing it," I said. "It's an exact double of the other Bay station. Same colors and everything. But they clearly don't wash the floors here," I said while examining the platform. There appeared to be decades of ground-in dirt in certain areas. It definitely could have used a very thorough scrubbing.

"You know," said Walter, "that seeing a doppelgänger is considered a harbinger of bad luck."

"Whoever came up with that superstition was not referring to a subway station. And besides, can things get any worse than this?" I asked.

"Good point."

"BENNY!" Marco screamed, frightening Walter and me out of our skins.

As the name reverberated down the platform, we stood waiting for a reply...but nothing.

"You guys check out this side of the platform, and I'll do the other," ordered Marco. "Scour the walls from top to bottom."

"And for what are we searching?" asked Walter.

"I don't know exactly," said Marco already rambling down the tunnel.

"Did Bob say anything in that last conversation with you that might have been a clue of some sort?"

"Not that I can think of," said Marco.

I halted. "WAIT! Remember Bob started talking about the Maya. He made an odd reference to Mayan temples. And the way he looked up in the sky and went on about the Maya calendar. It's not like you could see the stars tonight, or any night for that matter in this city, but especially not tonight."

"Are you aware that there is a mosaic rendering of a Mayan temple on the Museum's Rotunda ceiling?" said Walter.

"Oookay," I said. "Well at least we know what we might be looking for now."

"We do?" said Marco. "What do they look like?"

"They're not much different from Egyptian pyramids, but they have a flat top instead of a point," I said.

Marco resumed scanning the tunnel. "So are their insides like Egyptian pyramids?"

"In what way?" Walter asked.

"Well do they have secret passageways leading to a pile of loot?"

"Nothing quite as extravagant as the cache discovered

310

in Tutankhamun's tomb, for example. But, yes, Mayan temples have been known to be filled with astounding treasures."

"So, we could very well be on the trail of a room filled with art galore." Marco was already nearing the end of the platform. We were close to catching up on our side. "Anything?" asked Marco.

"Nothing unusual," I said.

"Well, we've got no choice," said Marco. "But at least they made it easy for us. Come over here, you guys. There's actually a small set of stairs leading to the track level."

I glanced over at Walter with an expression of hesitation. He lifted his shoulders and dropped them abruptly. As we joined Marco, he began to slide along the wall that ended the public platform area and he suddenly disappeared from sight. We heard what sounded like Marco trudging on steps and he instantaneously reappeared down below.

"And what are you waiting for?" said Marco, turning his palms upwards.

After scrambling around the corner, Walter and I treaded carefully down a set of concrete stairs with a railing on one side.

"Whatever you do, DON'T touch that middle rail. That's the one that's electrified," said Marco.

"Where do you mean?" I asked.

"See how the rails are sandwiched with wood in between. It's the central one that carries the charge."

"Oh, my goodness," said Walter. "I had always assumed it was one of the tracks on the actual ground surface. This makes far more sense in terms of safety."

"Well, you won't catch me walking close to the tracks, period." A shudder fluttered through my body.

As we drifted away from the platform, we entered a considerably darker environment prompting Marco to withdraw his phone. He turned on the flashlight app, and striding forwards, began to scan the walls and ceiling with an eerie robotic precision. Walter and I followed suit with our own phones.

"Run your lights over everything," said Marco.

"What if whatever we are looking for is towards the opposite end of the platform?" asked Walter.

"This tunnel leads towards the Museum. It's got to be this way."

Walter suddenly froze and shrieked.

Marco and I shone our lights on him. His elbows were tightly tucked into the sides of his body, his hands clenched tightly into fists and pressing deeply into the hollows of his cheeks.

"I think a rat crawled over my foot."

Marco flashed a light down at Walter's feet and then panned down the track with the illuminated beam. "Is that your rat?" asked Marco. There trembling in a small niche was a mouse.

"Maybe," said Walter.

"That thing is far more scared than you are. C'mon." Marco did a 'follow-me' gesture with his arm.

Walter continued trepidatiously, taking smaller steps than previously. There were pools of water here and there, and the air itself was saturated with moisture. But there didn't appear to be any evidence of leaking…or signs of impending flooding at least. Keeping my phone turned towards the ground so as to avoid any further encounters with rodents, I probably wasn't being very helpful with my limited scope of view.

"BENNY," Marco cried out. Again, the echoing floated through the man-made cavern for what seemed like forever. But we were met with silence. We forged forward. Then Marco paused. "Did you hear that?"

"Please do not tell me it is the sound of a subway train rumbling," said Walter.

"No. Shhh." We heard nothing. "I think I'm losing it," said Marco. "I thought I heard a tap or something."

"Step by step, inch by inch, slowly I turn," I said as we continued our ambling. "Wait, I think I heard something." I sped up my pace, and, before we knew it, the three of us were trotting faster and faster deeper and deeper into the tunnel. Marco and Walter were scouring the walls and ceiling with their modern-day torches while I kept lighting the way ahead of us, keeping an eye out for mice and rats and lions and tigers and bears.

Without warning Walter stopped. "EUREKA!"

He directed his light toward the roof of the tunnel, and indeed, there it was, faded or dirty, hard to tell, but there it was – a stylized depiction of a Mayan pyramid. At first glance and at this distance, it almost looked like a bee with its wings held close to its body. But then I distinguished the steps running up the middle of a pyramid structure crowned by a temple.

"How would Bob have painted that? I mean, he would have had to have had a ladder, some kind of stencil. How would he have gone undetected?" asked Walter.

"The man is a master of stealth, remember?" I said.

We heard a tap, and we all swung our lights towards the wall. "Benny are you there?" Marco yelled. Another several taps sounded.

"It is a door," said Walter. "It appears to have a concrete

coating over it to camouflage it, but you can see the outline. It has invisible hinges. Very clever."

Marco took his hand to the edge of the mid part of the apparent frame and rubbed his finger along the surface. "There's a keyhole here," he said.

"Well a lot of good that does us," said Walter.

Marco reached into his pocket. "Bob's keys, remember?" Marco scratched the concrete and wedged a key into the previously invisible keyhole.

There was no handle with which to pull the door open so Marco raised one foot, planted it on the outside of the frame, turned the key with some difficulty then started to pull the door. "Get over here and help me, will you. If this key breaks, we won't have a second chance."

Walter and I leapt to Marco's side. I grabbed the edge of the bottom side of the door, and Walter took a section of the door above the keyhole area. With the three of us tugging, we heaved it open.

Dust on the portal became airborne and we started coughing like mad. But through the particles we observed that the door opened to a small landing and to a short set of stairs leading upwards. We moved inside where Marco slipped his arm around the door and removed the keys. He sprinted up the stairway and we were right behind him.

At the top of the landing Marco drew the keys towards yet another door that now faced us. He tried one, but it failed to insert, so he switched it out for another, and success. Marco pressed the door forward and the three of us inched in. We stared at the spectacle in front of us. I was certain Marco and Walter shared the same sense of awe I felt.

"*Per gridare forte!* What has taken you so long?"

CHAPTER THIRTY-FOUR

"Sorry, Ben," said Marco. "The breadcrumb trail this time was a little sparser."

Benny was seated on the ground, leaning against a square column, legs bent and pressing into her chest. Her knapsack was propped up against one of the other sides of the supportive structure.

Although we all had our breath taken away when we first saw the space, it wasn't because we had happened upon some *Lord of the Rings* cave full of gleaming gold and brilliant gems. It was quite the opposite, actually. We had entered a room about 200 square feet with the pillar upon which Benny was resting over to one side of the room. The walls were painted pristine white, clearly with several coats. The ceiling had a few slotted vents, and the surprising freshness of the air indicated much attention had been given to the air quality. There was further validation of unusual care in an instrument I recognized from the Museum. It measured both temperature and humidity levels. The whole room was reminiscent of a museum collections room, or a small off-site storage area, including shelving to house all the items being stored there.

Nothing was clearly identifiable, but we could hazard a guess as to the types of contents in the various containers. There appeared to be paintings wrapped up like that first painting we discovered in the Museum's warehouse. There were also countless art attaches and all-too-familiar Pelican cases.

"My god," said Walter while perusing the shelves. "Bob must have had a previous life as a collections clerk."

"Or as a librarian," I said. Walter did a little sideways nod with his head.

"He has labelled everything very meticulously," said Benny. Marco strode over to her, extended his arm, and helped her up to her feet. She seemed a little unsteady at first, but soon regained her grounding.

Walter meandered towards a short, aluminum two-door file cabinet, opened the upper drawer, and started leafing through some folders.

"How did you get in here?" said Marco. "You clearly didn't enter through the subway tunnel."

"Is that where you came from?" said Benny. "I decided first to venture down to the basement level of the Museum. I found the food tunnel you mentioned, and I decided to explore that route first."

"That's not what we agreed upon. Why didn't you call for backup or least call someone to let them know which way you were heading? What if we hadn't found you?" Marco stamped on the floor. "We just barely heard your tapping."

"Tapping? I was pounding."

"This place is almost soundproof," said Marco.

"How did you enter this room?" Walter had wandered towards the door Benny must have used and tried to turn the door knob, but it wouldn't budge. And there was no sign of a locking mechanism on this side of the portal."

"I stumbled upon this door by accident. There was a sign on the other side that said 'TTC Staff only.'"

"So, no one from the Museum would ever have tried to

trespass," I said.

"It was locked, but I had some tools and was able to open it. But I made such a big mistake. I let the door close behind me without putting something in the doorway to keep it open."

"But what about the door we came in?" asked Walter.

We all turned towards the door and suddenly noticed that it sported the same kind of door mechanism as the one found on the door Benny had used. But there was a plastic doorstop inserted in the door that had kept it from fully closing. "I saw that as soon as we came in and stuffed it in the door," said Marco. "That's the kind of thing we've been trained to look for in these kinds of circumstances."

"You pass with flying colors," said Benny sarcastically.

"Bob clearly built this as a fortress. It's amazing he was able to accomplish this without anyone from the Museum or the Toronto Transit Commission ever noticing. And then to get all of these things in here," said Walter.

"Not to mention creating this kind of environment," I said. "I wouldn't be surprised if it took him years."

"Remember, the guy had security clearances from both the Museum and the TTC at different times, maybe even during overlapping periods."

"From what I saw in that file cabinet, I wouldn't be surprised if this is all worth millions and millions," said Walter. "The international authorities are going to have a field day returning all these works to their respective owners."

"For once," I said, "I'm happy to say that's not my problem. Let's get out of here, contact your CSIS crew, and close this chapter once and for all?" I said. "I have a call I need to make to Saudi Arabia."

"We'll have to go back through the subway tunnel," said

Marco.

"Oh, joy." I tossed my head back.

"It is the only way out, thanks to me, I am afraid." Benny leaned down to pick up her knapsack. Its zipper caught my attention as it seemed to be on the edge of bursting.

"Need some help with that?" said Marco.

Benny clutched the bag closer to her, then hiked it onto her back. "No, no. I am perfectly fine."

The hairs on my neck came to attention. "It does...it does look rather loaded."

"I'll take that, Benny," said Marco.

"NO," said Benny forcefully.

"You must have had a lot of time to kill in here," said Marco, "time to sift through these documents."

I whipped my gaze towards Marco.

"Plenty of time to figure out what the smallest and yet really valuable pieces might be," said Marco.

"Do you realize what you're suggesting?" I said. Benny was looking towards the floor.

"Aw, Benny, please don't tell me you've flipped."

"What IS he talking about?" said Walter.

"She's been radicalized," said Marco.

"I can't believe it. You've fallen for the guy from Brescia you were informing on, haven't you?" I said. "Stockholm Syndrome. Well, not technically speaking. Benny hasn't been held hostage, but she may have developed an alliance with the group she was intending to uncover. But it wouldn't have been a survival strategy. A change of mind, so not really–"

"Not really anything to do with Stockholm Syndrome," said Walter.

"No," I said.

Marco walked over to Benny. "C'mon, hand it over," he

318

said. Benny drew back.

"I can't," she said. "Do you have any idea how much we might get for just a few pieces? How much good it would do for the cause?"

"Oh, Benny." Marco's tone was saturated with disdain.

"These things have been missing for more than half a century. What difference would it make to the world?"

"These people you want to help are dangerous," said Marco.

"They have not harmed anyone."

"Not yet. But you know it's inevitable."

Benny reluctantly turned over her knapsack to Marco. "My camera equipment is in there as well. I would like to keep that."

Marco unzipped the bag, reached in, and struggled to pull out a couple of small Pelican Cases. He gently placed one on the ground, and while still crouching, he popped open the closures and revealed a stunning necklace and matching earrings – diamonds, rubies, emeralds in a gold setting. Now this was the kind of thing one saw in movies like Alfred Hitchcock's *To Catch a Thief.*

Marco closed the case back up. "Please put these back where you found them," he said to Benny.

Benny stood still, looking around the room, but avoiding making eye contact with any of us. She then gruffly snatched the cases from Marco, walked to a shelf, and easily slid the cases into a couple of vacant spots. She one-eightied, picked up her bag, zipped it shut, and returned it to her back. Marco and I then proceeded towards our exit route and pulled the door open, allowing Benny and Walter to exit first.

"What are you going to do?" I whispered to Marco.

"I'm not really sure, but–"

"A criminal's a criminal," I said. "No hall pass...even for Benny?"

"Just go, please."

We descended the stairs and opened the exterior door that led us back into the ghost subway tunnel. "I'll just repeat – watch out for that middle track, folks. Nothing's changed with the electrification. Benny, you march close here beside me. One wrong move and..."

In silence we walked back towards the Lower Bay subway station. For people who had just uncovered a huge cache of art missing since World War II, there was never a more solemn group. As we neared the station area and the steps that would take us back onto the platform, I heard what sounded like my phone chime. I withdrew my cell from my purse. "I don't believe it. How is that possible?"

"What is it?" said Marco. Everyone stopped in their paths.

"A text message got through."

"We may have passed one of those Wi-Fi hotspots. It's possible the TTC installed one so its staff could connect to phone or Internet service in times of emergencies. Is it important, your text?" asked Walter.

"Is it important? Is it important? It sure is freaking important," I said while reading the text. "Geoffrey's made it back to Riyadh and he, Stewart, and Harry are literally walking around putting 1,200 medals on the visitors' chairs."

"That is no small task," said Walter.

"Especially on zero sleep. And the airport's opened up. Most of the international guests should be able to get to the opening ceremonies on time. It's a bloody miracle. Look," I said, "he sent a selfie of himself putting the green velvet boxes on the gold chairs."

"It is a stunning visual," said Walter.

"Yup, we did good," I said, then looked up and noticed Benny had sneaked away from us in the direction from which we had come. She had slipped her knapsack off and one of her hands was in a pouch on the front of the bag. "Benny, what are you doing?"

"I'm not coming with you," she said.

"Don't be insane." Marco edged towards her.

"STOP!" she warned. "Now who is the one making mistakes?"

Marco sighed. "I didn't search your whole bag."

"I'm armed, Marco. *Per favore*, do not get any crazy ideas. I'm going to leave you now and DO NOT follow me!"

With that, Benny turned her back to us and hightailed like a gazelle in the direction from which we had just come. Within a nanosecond Marco started to follow. She stopped, revolved towards us, and raised her arm. A flash went off and a deafening shot sounded.

Marco dropped. "GET DOWN, YOU GUYS!"

Instead, Walter and I grabbed hold of each other as we heard a couple of pings, bullet ricochets, I could only presume.

"Okay, okay," said Marco in a calmer tone. "You do what you need to do. But you know you won't even get out of the country."

"*Forse, ma questo è il mio problema.*" Benny spun around and vanished into the darkness. It was just seconds before she turned on her phone's flashlight, and we watched an elongated shadow disappear into the abyss of the phantom subway tunnel.

"Oh, Marco. How is she going to get back aboveground?" I asked.

He turned to me. "That's one thing I don't think we need to worry about. She's a drainer remember. And she's been hanging out with infiltrators."

"What, may I ask, is an infiltrator?" said Walter.

"It's a crazy group of people that try to get into areas off-limits to the public, like underground waterways and subway tunnels. They publish their experiences on the Dark Web. Worst thing is the information they share can compromise national security. Benny was supposed to be helping us put an end to that kind of thing. Instead, she has so many photos, so much data now. She's the one who's a huge threat now."

"Good god," said Walter to Marco. "I presume you never saw this coming, Benny's turning, that is?"

The expression on Marco's face look pained. "Never in a million years. Doesn't make me very good at my job, does it?"

My stomach grumbled. "Anyone else hungry? What do you think the chances are of finding a pizza joint that's open in this storm?"

"Ah, the storm." said Walter. "I wonder if it's still raging."

CHAPTER THIRTY-FIVE

I stroked my fingers across the smooth surface and traced the letters of the names with my finger over and over and over. But it had only taken one repetition of the ritual to conjure a well of tears so plentiful I felt they might flow indefinitely.

There were five long panels of names, but the ones I looked for at each visit were easy to locate because of their central position. To one side of the panels with donor names was a three-dimensional representation of the Ukrainian coat of arms, the Trident, or *Tryzub*, which dates back to Kievan Rus times. Flanking the names on the other side was a panel carved with an image of a tree, its branches laden with leaves, fruit, and birds. But when I sat down on the long stone bench, I turned to face the haunting bronze statue of an emaciated young woman.

My vista included the majestic Prince's Gates to the west of me. The monumental arched gateway at Exhibition Place always made me feel like I was in Rome as it reminded me of the monument to Vittorio Emanuele II, although there was really very little resemblance.

To the east and north was evidence of the city's unbridled condominium development spanning the area from the lake to King and Queen Streets. To the south, Lake Ontario bordered the other side of the constantly humming-with-traffic Lake Shore Boulevard. But these days, any glimpse of the lake triggered the painful memory of Bob departing in his shoddy little boat.

It was now late winter – perhaps the greyest one I ever remembered experiencing. The somber skies were relentless, and persistent moistness in the air had made it one of the most difficult seasons for me to endure, among other reasons. I was surprised and elated when the sun peeked out momentarily. It magically drew striated shadows on the ground due to the trellised roof covering the benches in the parkette.

As I stared at the earth a pair of legs appeared, and I tipped my gaze upwards, shielding my eyes with one hand.

"Brenda told me you were spending time here on the weekends."

"Good old Brenda. Just another reason to rejoice her return to Toronto. That and the fact that she's turned into a bridezilla ever since she and Walter got engaged."

Marco set himself down beside me and raised his hand to wipe away the traces of tears from my face. My instinct was to pull away, but I let him dry my cheeks. "Well, she told me you come here a lot, but she didn't know exactly why."

"I can't get to the cemetery as easily as I can get here, seeing as this is only a ten-minute streetcar ride from home. That statue, it's called 'Bitter Memory of Childhood,' and this whole area is the Holodomor Memorial commemorating the millions of Ukrainians that died during the famine in the 1930s."

"Whoa, pretty heavy stuff."

"Over there," I said pointing to the donor plaque, "are the names of my parents. Our family made a donation in their names when my father went in for his surgery. As you know, it wasn't long after that...I'm grateful...thanks for coming to the service. Ukrainian funerals are pretty grim."

"Italian ones aren't much cheerier, let me tell you. But do you really think this going to help you with your grieving?"

"Have you been talking to my brother? He thinks I'm totally fruit loops."

"How is he doing, and your mum?"

"You know, my mom's so incredibly resilient. She is such an inspiration to us. But my brother's moved in with her, and he's cut way back on his traveling, so that helps a lot. I don't know what I would have done without him."

"I'm glad you've got him to support you. Your dad's passing happened just way too soon after—"

"We made the biggest bust of stolen art on this side of the Atlantic. Yeah, I hadn't even started processing that yet." I looked back out towards the water and then turned again to Marco. "What are you doing here anyway? Are you stalking me?"

"Well, you've been hard to get a hold of, and there's something I wanted to tell you."

"Did they find Bob's body?"

Marco shook his head. "You know, Lake Ontario doesn't always give up its dead. I mean it's a pretty brutal body of water."

"Or he could be living incognito on Toronto Island."

"That boat was smashed up that night, I'm sure of it."

I sat up straight. "Has Benny surfaced?"

"No. No news there, either. She's definitely gone deep underground – excuse the pun."

I rolled my eyes.

"I wanted you to know I'm moving to Ottawa."

"You're going to leave your dad on his own?"

"He's got a girlfriend, if you can believe it."

I chortled. "That's great."

"They're putting me in a new training program. Career advancement stuff, you know."

"So, finding that hoard of art worked in your favor, after all."

"Didn't hurt. Besides, Ottawa will be a good change of pace for me. I can only take so much rejection from you in one lifetime."

Marco tenderly wrapped his warm hands around mine, but I slipped them free. "You were lying to me from the day I first met you. It's kind of hard to have a relationship with someone you can never trust."

The undercover agent sighed.

"But we'll always have Thor," I said. We both burst out laughing.

"Hey, how's Malik doing? Do you think he's forgiven me?"

"Probably. I think he was really impressed with you in the end."

"Listen, I should get going. Can I give you a lift home? I'm parked just inside the gates there. Or do you want some more time on your own."

I weaved my arm through Marco's and pulled him up with me to standing. "Naw. I think I've used my quota of tears for today. And now that the sun's disappeared behind the clouds, the chill is getting to my bones."

"What else is new?" said Marco.

We walked for less than a minute when Marco stopped. "Really?" I said. "Really?"

Marco waved some keys in the air.

"I can't believe you have a normal vehicle for once," I said as Marco opened the passenger door of a Jeep.

"I'm going to need something reliable in Ottawa, with all the snow they get there."

Soon we were driving eastwards on Lake Shore. "Now that Brenda's back, are you ever going to do that work term in London?"

"Not for a while yet. I don't want to be that far from my family right now."

"I'm sure Geoffrey's disappointed about that."

"You still haven't forgiven him for texting me when he did, have you? You still think Benny wouldn't have escaped if I hadn't have stopped to read the text."

"Maybe. Okay, at first, I did. But Benny's pretty resourceful. I should have been a lot more careful," said Marco.

"You know, I can't help thinking of all those pictures she took of the R.C. Harris Filtration Treatment Plant."

"The only place we went that the public can't normally visit was the filtration beds...and the control room. But she didn't get any pictures of command central. So, pretty sure the city's safe. But I was told, and this is confidential, they stepped up security there, just in case."

I sighed. "Well that's reassuring."

"By the way, I can't help thinking about what Bob meant when he mentioned Geoffrey, you know, when we were on the dock. I didn't push it because—"

"Bob was out of his mind at that point. I have no clue what he was going on about."

"If you say so," said Marco as we approached Bathurst Street and slowly took a left. "So, the King Street Pilot Project is permanent now, I hear. How do you feel about that?"

"I've decided it's the right thing. Public transit definitely moves faster. And I finally downloaded a couple of car share apps so if the streetcar disappears into a black hole, I now have some options. Don't know what took me so long to enter the modern world." I grinned.

"I heard they're gonna build a subway stop at Bathurst and King."

I burst out laughing.

"What's so funny?" said Marco. "They are, aren't they?"

"Well, that's the plan but I'll probably be retired by the time it's funded and constructed. Eventually though, I'm sure it'll efficiently transport the thousands moving into this area. But you know, much as I gripe about public transit, I really can't complain. Toronto's a spectacular city and I love living here."

"Yeah, I'm going to miss it."

We soon arrived at my building, and Marco pulled into the short-term parking layby. He popped out of the Jeep and ran to my side, opened the door, and eased my step to the ground.

Once I was on terra firma, Marco draped his arms around me, and I reciprocated. I shut my eyes for a moment and felt the coolness of precipitation on my face. With eyes now open, I held out one of my hands. "Well, it's snowing. How fitting."

"At least it's not raining," laughed Marco. "Oh, I almost forgot." Marco freed me, opened the passenger door, flipped open the cover of the glove compartment and handed me a whimsically decorated chocolate-covered candy apple. "I know you've cut way back on chocolate, and you only eat organic stuff these days, but this one's organic, I swear."

I thought back to the time Marco had first surprised me with a chocolate-covered apple, the memory warming me from the inside out. "Thanks," I said. "You know, the Museum's not going to be the same without you."

"Well my life's not going to be the same without you." Marco stared at me with a melting intensity. "But don't hesitate to call me, just to talk. I know what it's like to lose a parent. It's going to be a roller coaster for a while."

"Thanks."

Marco returned to the driver's side of the Jeep where he leapt in and shut the door. He did a perfect three-point turn in the driveway, and drove off leaving, a trail in the light snowy carpet that was already covering the city's streets.

Shivering, I walked into my building and immediately noticed an attractive man at the elevator holding a guitar case. He was a good half foot taller than me with light brown hair, shaved short in the back but longer on top, and sported a turtleneck under his coat.

When the elevator arrived, he let me advance first. A little smitten with his mature Robert-Redford-like looks, I forgot to press the button to my floor. He reached across and pressed a button – no wedding ring. "Which floor are you headed to?" he said, his blue eyes gleaming.

"Um, same floor, actually."

As we neared the floor, I casually said. "Just visiting?"

"Just moved in."

"Oh, really. Well, welcome."

The elevator stopped and Redford motioned for me to descend first.

"I'm at the end of the hall."

"Mex's old place?" I said as we paused outside the elevator. "I thought there was a young couple living there."

"There was. Apparently, they didn't work out, but it's great for me. Thought I'd rent a place here before deciding to buy. It's really convenient workwise."

I looked at his guitar.

"Oh, this," he said. "Just a passion, not a livelihood, I'm afraid."

"I'm right down here," I said, pointing to the door of my unit.

"Well, I'll be seeing you around I guess," said the man as we started walking. "I like your haircut by the way. Not everyone can pull off a short cut like that."

I patted my head with my hand. "I'm still getting used to it."

"It's cool."

I stroked my hair again.

"Looks like you're going to have an interesting dessert tonight."

Lifting up the chocolate candy apple, I said, "Oh, this. It's a gift from an old friend."

"Thoughtful friend."

I smiled.

Redford ambled past me while I withdrew my key and slipped it into the lock of my door. I stepped one foot in, then leaned back to peek at my neighbor making his way down the corridor. He unexpectedly turned around, and I sped through my doorway, quickly shutting the door behind me. An inner glow filled my body and I beamed.

The End

ACKNOWLEDGEMENTS

Inestimable thanks to:

My brother Zenon Kulchisky who taught me about unconditional love and the most valuable life lessons I ever could have imagined. And also, for so quickly learning how to bring life back to a light bulb that had been burned out for several years.

My brother Andy Kulchyckyj who calls me from places like the middle of the Colosseum in Rome, just because, and for deciding to become a photographer later in life.

Gene Wilburn and Florence Russell for giving so generously of their time and skills in reading and correcting my drafts and for making such valuable suggestions.

The Royal Ontario Museum and its current and former eccentric, loveable, brilliant, funny and dedicated staff, including Robert Barnett and Linda Pearcey.

Kim Moritsugu of The Humber College School for Writers whose invaluable mentorship has always gone above and beyond the call of duty and apparently never ends. And to The Humber College School for Writers for invaluably supporting alumni such as myself.

Fellow writers Kim Moritsugu (yes, her again), Marsali Taylor and Beth Barany, as well as former publisher Eloise Aston, for generously writing letters of support for my grant applications and for just being marvelous, talented and wonderfully creative beings in their own right.

My dear sisters, Cathy Diklich and Joan Zaba, for keeping me afloat.

To my family at RJC Engineers, in particular Mike Moffatt, for encouraging my side hustle.

To all who provided venues for me to read from my works. Gratitude is an understatement.

To everyone who purchased a copy of *Theft By Chocolate* (some of you in multiples, several times over) and relentlessly hounded me to write a sequel, especially Kathy May, and my dear friends in Toronto, Hamilton, Burlington, Collingwood, Windsor, Calgary, London, Cape Town and Costa Rica.

To the City of Toronto for being such a beguiling setting for my story. Despite its occasional growing pains, I am so proud to call it home. I would also like to thank Lost Rivers Toronto whose walks introduced me to parts of the city unknown to me.

And finally, I would like to acknowledge that I live and work on land that is the traditional territory of many nations including the Mississaugas of the Credit, the Anishinaabe, the Chippewa, the Haudenosaunee and the Wendat peoples and is now home to many diverse First Nations, Inuit and Métis peoples. I also acknowledge that Toronto is covered by Treaty 13 with the Mississaugas of the Credit.

ABOUT THE AUTHOR

Soon after finishing her graduate studies in history, Luba landed on the doorstep of Canada's largest museum, the Royal Ontario Museum in Toronto, Canada where she worked for more than 20 years. Moving from positions in the Education and Programs Departments to the Museum's consulting branch, she concluded her career at the institution in the office that managed the Renaissance ROM renovation project.

After leaving the Museum, Luba worked for several years in an administrative and research capacity for a private museum consulting firm with offices in Toronto and London (UK). She subsequently worked in the educational sphere but currently is employed in the private sector.

Theft Between the Rains is the author's second novel (and a sequel to *Theft By Chocolate)* which is inspired by her many passions, including film. When not writing, Luba can frequently be found in movie theatres and at film festivals where she found the seeds of the story for *Theft Between the Rains*, in particular, in the documentaries *Lost Rivers* and *The Rape of Europa*.

Outside of film theatres, Luba spends her time being a culture hound and gym and dance studio rat, teaching yoga, and feeding her spirit and energy at yoga retreats in wondrous locations around the planet.

Printed by Amazon Italia Logistica S.r.l.
Torrazza Piemonte (TO), Italy

16652038R00192